HOPE

Also from Metaphorosis

<u>Plant Based Press</u>
Best Vegan Science Fiction & Fantasy
annual issues, 2016-2020

from B. Morris Allen:
Chambers of the Heart: speculative stories
Susurrus
Allenthology: Volume I
Tocsin: and other stories
Start with Stones: collected stories
Metaphorosis: a collection of stories

<u>Verdage</u>
Reading 5X5 x3: Changes
Reading 5X5 x2: Duets
Score – an SFF symphony
Reading 5X5: Readers' Edition
Reading 5X5: Writers' Edition

<u>Vestige</u>
The Nocturnals, by Mariah Montoya

<u>Joyful Heave</u>
Museum Piece: an unusual collection

<u>Metaphorosis Magazine</u>
Metaphorosis: Best of 20xx
Metaphorosis 20xx: The Complete Stories
annual issues, 2016-2024
Monthly issues

HOPE

The Thing With Feathers

edited by
B. Morris Allen

ISBN: 978-1-64076-009-7 (e-book)
ISBN: 978-1-64076-010-3 (paperback)
ISBN: 978-1-64076-011-0 (hardcover)

from
Metaphorosis Publishing

Neskowin

Contents

Copyright   255
Metaphorosis Publishing   257

Epigraphs

"Hope" is the thing with feathers —
That perches in the soul —
And sings the tune without the words –
And never stops — at all —

And sweetest — in the Gale — is heard –
And sore must be the storm —
That could abash the little Bird
That kept so many warm —

I've heard it in the chillest land —
And on the strangest Sea —
Yet — never — in Extremity,
It asked a crumb — of me.

Emily Dickinson, 1861

Hope is a strange invention —
A Patent of the Heart —
In unremitting action
Yet never wearing out —

Of this electric Adjunct
Not anything is known
But its unique momentum
Embellish all we own —

Emily Dickinson, 1931

For all those who refuse to give up,
no matter how hard the road.

Strange Inventions

Hope is a strange invention, but an essential one. We talk about 'keeping hope alive'. But the reverse is just as true: hope keeps us alive, and not only in a figurative or metaphorical sense. A sense of hope that things will change for the better is sometimes all that keeps us from giving up and letting the darkness win. This anthology is dedicated to hope in dark times and to refilling your well of hope from the fresh, clear springs of these stories.

This anthology had its genesis in a far simpler idea. I saw the cover art, by Patricia Talavera, and thought, 'That would make a great book cover'. It didn't take long to move from there to an anthology of feather-related stories or (since it was 2020) to stories that were also hopeful. I put it on the back burner until 2024, when it became clear that we were going to need a hefty new dose of hope to get through the coming years.

There's a lot to be concerned about. For me personally, the foreign aid industry I've worked in for most of my life vanished in my country in just two months. Many people's experiences have been far, far worse. There are worrying developments around the world. Hope is what keeps us going despite it all.

These are stories that, dark or light, are hopeful. They see a better moment, a better future through the murk that surrounds us. They remind us that things can get better and they *will* get better. If we keep going, keep trying, keep believing in and acting for good, we'll see some. Read on and see.

Morris Allen
1 July 2025

The Letter Writers

Chloe Smith

My brother has fallen silent. He turns his face to the walls that surround us both, leaving me to fight my own despair, to imagine alone all our possible futures: unlikely escape or endless captivity. Still, he never hesitates to open a vein for me. That's how I know he still cares.

It's the evening of one of my writing days. The light is fading and the winds that blow desert sands across the city's stone streets have stilled, even if day's heat has not yet broken. My hand cramps around the pen. It's the quill of some slain bird, with dark and ragged barbs that flutter as I scribe. Although they look nothing like my brother's brilliant crest, the movement still makes me think of him as he was. I dip the pen once more into the inkwell, where today's supply is running low.

This morning, the cold-eyed man let my brother's blood fall into a bowl, mixed it with night-dark pigments to create a thick but unclotting ink. To his customers, he boasts that the secret of its mixture is his great discovery. It took him a long time to get the recipe right. Scars ladder both my arms and my brother's, permanent lines half-hidden beneath the down that covers our bodies. They match the scar along the ridge of my brother's skull, where the hunters tore away the feathers of his crest, furious when they realized our winglessness.

When he first untied the hunters' ropes, the cold-eyed man told us we were safe now, and not just from their cruelty. He said, if the hunters hadn't come, our mother would have rejected us sooner or later. Because we will never grow up to be monstrous winged creatures like her, she would have decided we were prey, devoured us in a snap of her beak.

My brother, fierce-voiced as a hawk then, rejected this claim. Now I no longer have his denials to shore up my own, and I sometimes fear the cold-eyed man is right. Perhaps our mother would have turned on us, eventually. It *is* strange that she ever recognized us as her own — tiny, flightless things, sparsely feathered, with grasping primate hands instead of protective claws.

But I remember how she did care for us. I remember her vast shadow looming over us, the great beak depositing tidbits in our upraised hands. I remember snuggling against the fluff of her breast. I wonder if my brother has buried himself within those memories, and his withdrawal is the price of their protection.

I am not sure if the cold-eyed man has even noticed my brother's silence. He speaks to us little, now that we have learned what is expected of us. The threat of his knife needs little elaboration.

Today, what is expected of me is to listen and transcribe. I sit in the corner of the dusty, clay-walled shop with its narrow windows. Customers enter. They pay the cold-eyed man, then they tell me their greetings to distant kin, their messages and their plans for future endeavors. I turn their ephemeral voices into letters, my quill scratching out the characters in bloody ink. The cold-eyed man inspects each finished letter before I fold its paper.

In my hands, it becomes a moving, winged thing. I take it to a window, the closest I ever come to the world outside, to put the paper bird into the air.

I dream of that flight for myself. I remember the great, great wideness of the sky when our mother carried me aloft.

She didn't snatch us up the day the hunters came, though. They thought they would steal themselves a fledgling they could train up and ride aloft, and so they waited until she was out of the nest, her unimaginable wingspan only a speck in the sky, before they dared to seize us. I try not to remember any more than that.

If it wasn't for my brother, mewed up in the empty room above, I might try to clamber through this window, even though what lies beyond is terrifying: this city of men, with its winding streets and suffocating walls, where I am grounded, wingless, far from home.

I wonder if my brother contemplates this window in the same way, the days that he must scribe while I sleep off the loss of blood. I wonder if he resents me, the way I sometimes resent him.

But even if we didn't have each other, there would be no escape. The cold-eyed man would have no one else to cut, and the daily bloodletting would overwhelm all independent thought or hope or memory. A single letter writer would be nothing but a shell creature, a pen in hand, ink gradually running dry.

So I only imagine escape, even as I reach across the window's wide sill and let the paper bird go.

One last customer enters. A shadow in the doorway, a billowing robe that spreads like wings. A soft voice greets the cold-eyed man, and I see the flash of gold pass between their hands. I steel myself. For that price it will be a long message, or one that must travel far. News of a child or a wedding? Travel plans? Money matters? I retake my seat and dip my pen, ready to write once more.

The stranger bends over me. A woman's face emerges from the shadow of her hood. Her eyes are black, as shiny as a crow's. She speaks, and her voice is rough, plaintive.

"Dear Mother,

"By the time this letter reaches you, another message will be on its way —

"No, that's not it," she breaks off. My hand hovers over the page. She turns back to my captor. "I am sorry; I would say it differently."

He stiffens. Alert to the possibility of lost revenue. "The paper is not free, madam. I must pay to have it shipped from ..."

She cuts him off with another coin. "For the extra cost."

"You are too kind." He opens the chest I'm not allowed to touch and lays another sheet before me. It covers the first. A sliver of hope cracks the shell around my heart. I think of the words now hidden beneath. *Another message will be on its way.*

The woman begins again.

"Dear Mother,

"Trust that a second message will follow this one. Look to the skies and remember. The journey is long, but not impossible. The searching eye discovers what has been long hidden, but only if it knows where to look.

"Keep faith,

"Your daughter"

Keep faith. My hand is trembling by the last word. The final curl of ink is jagged, uneven. The cold-eyed man frowns as he reads it over, leaning close to best the approaching night. My breath goes tight in my throat. But then he nods and hands it to me. My pulse pounds as I fold it, as I approach the window. The letter leaves my hands.

I don't try to follow its path through the topaz air. Instead I turn back quickly, telling myself not to hope, not to scheme, that our captor will have gathered up the half-marked paper from my desk —

But no — he is bowing the customer out the door, eager to close for the night, to save the expense of lighting a lamp. He doesn't see me move. He may miss the remnant of paper in the morning. He may beat me for carelessness. But by then it will be too late.

Back in our room, I wait for him to lock our door, to leave us. In the near dark beneath the window, I unball my fist and spread out the scrap of paper that it hid. I reach up and run a hand down my own crest, its feathers short and brown, dull enough that the hunters didn't even care to strip them away. It will never be what my brother's was.

One of these quills will have to do, though. I dig my fingers in close to my skull, seize the base of the shaft, and wrench it free. I gasp at the pain — I can't help it — and I hear the sound of my brother shift behind me. I scratch at my arm, seeking an unscarred vein.

My brother catches at my hand, forcing me to turn and look at him. He frowns down at me. Shakes his head.

"This is our chance," I whisper, furious. "Let me do this."

He shakes his head again, but then he fumbles at his elbow, loosening the bandage I tied there this morning.

The message, once we've finished it, looks like a child's blotchy painting. I tried my best with my plucked quill, with the blood from his reopened cut, but it has our names, the name of the city. That has to be good enough.

I fold the paper carefully. It shifts and flutters, and I can almost sense the fierce buzz of a heartbeat. I hold it up to the window, the tiny slit that is all we have; beyond, I can't even make out sky, only the close walls of this maze-like city of stone.

In a moment, the paper bird is gone. Disappeared into the night.

I don't believe that I'll ever fall asleep, but I must have. In my dream, I look up to see the silhouette of wings, growing wider and wider as they descend.

The next morning, the cold-eyed man unlocks the door. He holds his bowl in one hand, knife ready in its sheath.

Since I scribed yesterday, today he approaches me first. The cold-eyed man cuts us on alternate days, so we each have a day to heal as we labor in the shop.

He didn't want to do it that way, when we began. I'm the scrawny, half-mottled runt, after all, while my brother is more human looking, especially without his crest, more appealing to the people who come tells us their letters. The cold-eyed man would have used me up, gotten his money's worth from my blood while my brother scribed below, healthy and well-groomed. My brother resisted him, then, forced a bit of compromise from our captor, a chance for us both to live a little longer. It took almost everything he had.

Now, I expect my brother to turn his face to the wall, to wait while the man presses the knife to the soft flesh inside my elbow. Instead he struggles up from his pallet and pushes his body between us, raising his arm insistently. It is a mirror of the pose he took the first time he argued with the cold-eyed man, although his words, which had eroded to whispered pleas by then, are now gone. Still, his eyes have the old hawk-ferocity.

The man sighs and rolls his eyes, but he harvests my brother's blood again. Later, he takes me down for a day of scribing.

The next morning, the same thing happens. After the cold-eyed man leaves with the full bowl, preparing for the day, I bind up my brother's arm one more time, the old wounds and the new. I curse him for his sacrifice and for his care. He ignores my insults.

Two more mornings he stands, and our captor does not question his wordless insistence, but on the day after that, my brother staggers when he moves to put his body before mine. He rested each day, ate the sustaining foods the man provides (on wooden plates, without even a spoon for a tool), but the repeated bleedings have taken their toll. The man scoffs and shoulders him aside. "You were wiser before. Why so stubborn now?"

My brother tries to grab the knife-wielding hand. The man strikes him with fist and hilt, and my brother falls. I scream his name without words, in the harsh, squawking cries of our nest home.

As the man cuts my arm, I think I hear a distant echo of those cries. My brother lifts his head from the floor, bloodshot eyes wide.

The cold-eyed man doesn't leave us alone this morning. "Rest and accept," he tells my brother. "Remember that foolishness has earned you nothing, but it has bought this one," he shakes me by the arm, where he holds a cloth against my wound, one-handed, "a day of double duty, until you recover." He pulls me forward, out of the room.

This time, my brother doesn't turn his face away from me. I look back, pin my gaze on his, until the door closes and the man locks it between us.

I write letters in my own blood's ink, wounded arm bound and cradled in my lap. The customers ramble on. My pen leaves long, intricate scars on the surface of the paper as I wait for each one to finish speaking.

The hours pass, and the day's heat breathes its way into the shop. When I go to the window once more, sunlight bakes the street beyond. I'm about to fling the letter upward when a shadow falls over my extended arm.

The sun has faltered. The city's press of houses, as much as I can see beyond the windowsill, all darken and grow quiet. I freeze. I know this stillness, the animal fear that holds small scrabbling things frozen beneath lowering claws. It makes the blood sing in my ears.

Beyond that joyful rush, I hear another distant scream, and then one closer, louder.

I turn to run, out into the labyrinth street. The man is just behind me, ignoring the shadow outside, the uncertain cry of the customer pressed back into a corner. He has his knife, blade bare and ready.

"We're closing early today. It's time for you to retire."

I think I could jerk and dodge, slide past him as he tangles in the clutter of table and stool, stumbles over the customer. I could reach the doorway. I know already what I'll see when I turn my face to the sky, reach up my arms for rescue.

But my brother. I can't forget his gaze on mine or the blood that binds us.

I let the cold-eyed man usher me upstairs, his free hand pushing against the small of my back. We reach the upper landing, where his key rattles against the lock in his hurry. The door swings wide. My brother has risen from his pallet, although he holds onto the wall with his good arm. Outside, the cry comes one more time. Its sound pierces through walls of clay and rock.

On the threshold, I turn back towards the man. I open my own mouth and scream, straining my soft throat with the effort. I throw up my hands and fling the abandoned letter at his face. Its wings are half crumpled and would never carry it far, but they batter at his eyes, and he stumbles back.

The world explodes with sound. The man might scream, my brother might break his silence — but I can't hear them. Something immense has struck the flat roof above us. It strikes again, and my ears resound as the floor and walls shake and dust rains down around us.

The ceiling cracks as my brother lurches forward. Our hands find each other. We shoulder past the man, who reaches for us once more, his face scored and bleeding. We run in the only direction we can.

The stairs that lead down to the shop also extend up, past our door, to parts of the house the cold-eyed man never let us see. Now, though, we dash up steps that have split and twisted with the force leveled against the building. Around a corner, and the dimness of enclosing walls breaks into daylight, the panel of a trapdoor torn away. My brother pushes me through.

We emerge onto the damaged roof — and our mother is there. Great, wide wings beat around us, as if the sky itself is falling. Her claws flex wide as she swoops down.

My brother doesn't flinch. He reaches up, and her talons lock around him. I see his grimace as they bite into his shoulders and back. There is no time for anything else, no finesse in our mother's rescue.

My brother wraps his free arm around me. One more time, he has placed his body between me and painful necessity. The world begins to fall away.

Then another grip has me around the legs. The man has followed us. He has thrown his weight against the possibility of our escape. I thrash and kick, reaching down with my own stubby claws, but his strength is too much for me.

Our mother's vast wings pump, and her scream fills the air, but the weight of three people, one with heavy landsman's bones, is too much for her. The cold-eyed man will not let me go. My brother will not release me. We will drop to the broken roof or the city streets below, where there are more strangers, more armed men. I can hear their shouts, the sounds of many city people, beyond the cacophony of our struggle.

Blood slicks my brother's arm around me. Mine or his — I can't tell. I look up at his glare, determined, despairing, wordless. He will empty his heart of blood before he will choose to let me go, before he will choose his own survival.

I call again.

A shape made of ragged paper feathers flutters up from the trapdoor behind the man. Half-torn, crushed beneath the man's boots, it rises to one last, failing flight. I reach for it, renewing its strength with my bloody hands.

It swoops over the man's head, up towards my brother's face. He flinches instinctively, grip loosening on me for a moment.

I drop, tangled together with the man. My claws catch in his flesh, but his grip is overpowering. I hear a cry I recognize. It's my name, torn free of my brother's silence as he rises away, into the abyss of the sky.

About the author

Chloe Smith's short fiction has appeared in *Haven Speculative Fiction* and *Bourbon Penn*, among other places, and her novella *Virgin Land* came out from Luna Press Publishing in 2023. She is a graduate of Your Personal Odyssey program and a member of the Clarion Writers Workshop Class of 2025. When she's not writing, she works as a middle school teacher librarian and tries to catch up on her reading. She lives in the San Francisco Bay Area in California. You can find more about her work at imaginaryresearch.wordpress.com, and she is semi-active on Bluesky @chloehsmith.

About the story

This story was originally an ekphrastic piece, inspired by a painting of Remedios Varos called *The Creation of the Birds*. It's a story that had a long journey from my original inception to this final version, with many rejections and revisions along the way.

About hope

My hope is that creatives facing the pressures and demands of life in a difficult time are able to persist with the circuitous, indirect processes of bringing their art to life. The world is better when it has your stories, your voices, and your visions in it.

Pitstop at the Lunar Station

Veda Villiers

Mina stretched her legs out across the polished floor of the Earth-Moon's pitstop lounge, trying not to stare too long at the hazy blue Earth outside. A soft murmur drifted through the space as travellers waited. Some sat alone, quietly passing the time. Others chatted with companions, their voices calm and unhurried. Like Mina and her friends, they were all waiting for the next hop, some heading to Earth, others to Mars, just like them.

"Ugh, can't believe we're stuck here for another two hours. Why couldn't we just charter our own ship?" Rhea groaned beside her.

Mina half-listened as Lila launched into another rant about Earth's overloaded infrastructure, too old and strained to keep up with the traffic. Mina knew the rhythm by now — mockery, laughter, a round of drinks.

But today, something about the view tugged at her chest as she ran her fingers over the gold-banded links of her bracelet, its filigree so fine it could only have been crafted by the master artisans of Valles Marineris. In a solar system where gold was prized above all else, their work was considered legendary. And at the bracelet's center, sealed within a tiny, airtight chamber, rested a fragile white feather no larger than Mina's thumbnail. Micro-thin protective layers preserved its delicate beauty, making it glow softly like molten sunlight.

Mina always wore it. Her mother had given it to her the day she graduated Schoolings, explaining that the feather had been shed by a dove — a pet her grandmother had rescued, fed, and kept alive despite the famine. In her mother's early days on Earth, before she married Mina's father and left for Mars, the dove had been a symbol of love, peace, and hope. Foolish things, maybe. Fragile things. Extinct things.

Mina wasn't sure she believed in symbols anymore.

She caught her reflection in the window — eyes too soft, mouth too still — and forced a smirk to tilt the balance.

"You say that, but you looked like you were having the time of your life in New Lagos," she finally chimed in, tucking her legs under her and pulling out a compact to check her makeup. "Even took that tour of the old ruins, didn't you?"

Zara chuckled. "I mean, it's … charming in a way, right?" She lifted her drink to her lips. "Like, Earth has this vintage thing going on. Can't say it's not a vibe."

"Sure, if 'vintage' means 'on the brink of collapse'," Lila replied, nose wrinkled. "The air was practically crispy. How people live there — I just don't get it. Mars has, like, ten times the air quality."

Rhea tilted her head, as if this were some revelation. "Maybe that's why Earthers are so, like, grumpy all the time. Our shuttle driver — so rude! He was muttering about fuel costs and import tariffs. I just tipped him extra so he'd shut up."

"Right," Zara added, "Like, buddy, we're not your problem. Take it up with your planet's logistics or something."

They all shared a laugh, except Mina, who glanced back at the view of Earth with a hint of something — sympathy, maybe? She tucked her compact away and joined in, though her smile was a bit forced, if only someone had bothered to take note. But alas, none of her friends bothered.

Laughing, Rhea tapped at the menu on her wrist screen, scrolling through drink options from the Earth-Moon lounge's interface. "I don't even know half of these. They're named after, like, constellations or whatever. Can't they just give us the usual?"

Zara smirked. "Lunar style. It's all about the 'experience'. You know they're charging twice the price of what we'd pay back home for some lume-sweet 'Crater Punch'."

"Ridiculous," Lila agreed, with a wave of her hand. "But if they'll throw in some 'meteor dust'," she winked, "I'll pay."

Mina, fingers tracing circles on the armrest, spoke up. "I think it's pretty interesting here, actually. You can tell there's still a bit of ... Earth in the design? I mean, it's practical, sure, but they tried to make it feel cozy."

Rhea squinted out at the barren, rock-strewn landscape. "Cozy, like, with a view of a gray desert?"

"More like a concrete jungle," Zara snorted, scrolling through her screen. "Maybe you can bring that cozy feeling to Mars, Mina, if you're so inspired."

Mina smiled awkwardly, not wanting to argue. "I mean, we could take a few lessons. My parents still talk about how people on Earth had real grass lawns, real wood furniture. Not just the synthesized stuff."

Rhea waved a dismissive hand. "Ugh, but then you get mud and bugs, and who wants that? Besides, Mars feels more sophisticated. Why hold onto those old, messy ways?"

There was a pause, as if everyone was weighing her words, then a chorus of nods. The pause hung, just a beat too long, and Mina's gaze shifted to the corner of the lounge where a maintenance bot was tidying up, its back panel covered in Earth-based certifications.

Mina lowered her voice, almost to herself, "Maybe they're holding onto it because it's all they have left."

"Who?" Rhea asked, distracted as she fished out her portable charger.

"Earth," Mina said, a bit louder.

Rhea blinked at her, then laughed, brushing it off. "Oh, Mina, you're so sentimental. Earth's fine. They wouldn't let it actually collapse, right? It's where everyone's food and materials come from. Besides, they always manage to scrape by, right? It's not like it's the first time they've had a crisis. They'll get over it like they always do."

Zara chimed in, half-amused, half-dismissive. "Exactly. They need to keep it going, at least enough to churn out the basics for Mars and the Europa settlements up and running. It's just … well, someone has to do the heavy lifting." She adjusted her jewelry, fiddling with a pendant that looked like a miniature Mars globe.

A screen above them flickered with a news bulletin: "Lunar Mining Co. announces workforce reduction in Earth sectors due to automation advancements. An estimated 40,000 Earth-based jobs will be cut in the upcoming fiscal year." A low murmur swept through the lounge, with a few nearby travelers glancing at the screen and then looking away, unbothered.

"See?" Lila scoffed, "They're just being dramatic. Always protesting or complaining about jobs. Honestly, if they embraced some of the tech we have on Mars, maybe they'd keep up."

Mina's jaw tightened, but she stayed quiet, feeling the words form but stall in her mouth. Instead, she let her gaze drift around the lounge, falling on the lone family seated at the far end. They wore simple, worn clothes — earthen tones, faded and a little frayed. The mother's face was lined, tired but kind, and her young daughter was leaning on her shoulder, eyes wide as she stared at the screens and holographic maps displaying Mars, Earth, Jupiter, and the surrounding celestial bodies.

Mina watched as the little girl traced her fingers in the air, mapping invisible shapes in the glow. She looked at the way the child's gaze lingered on Mars, her eyes full of wonder and something that looked like longing.

Rhea nudged her. "What're you staring at, Mina?"

"Oh, nothing," Mina replied, turning back. She fumbled with her drink, trying to find something light to say. "Just … it's strange, isn't it? Seeing Earth people here, traveling off-world."

"Yeah," Zara said, with a slight frown. "I mean, it's nice that they get to come here and see how things could be. Maybe it'll inspire them to, you know, try harder back home."

Lila snickered. "Or maybe they'll start a blog about how great life is on Mars. Just imagine it — *An Earther's Guide to Extraterrestrial Living*."

They all laughed, though Mina's laugh was quieter, more restrained. She couldn't stop thinking about the child and her mother. Likely one of the families hit hard by the recent layoffs.

As the girls' shuttle was announced, they stood, gathering their belongings. Mina lingered a moment, eyeing the Earth family who hadn't moved from their seats, the mother gently patting her daughter's shoulder, trying to get her to rest.

On an impulse she couldn't quite explain, Mina stepped toward the child, fingers already unclasping the bracelet from her wrist. The gold links glinted in the low light, the feather suspended at its center catching like fire.

She crouched down and held it out.

"It's for you," she said softly.

The girl stared, wide-eyed and unmoving, as if uncertain whether to trust the gesture — or believe it was meant for her.

"It's a dove feather," Mina added, quieter now. "They don't exist anymore. Not on Earth. My grandmother raised one during the famine. She kept it alive when she couldn't even feed herself."

The child's fingers hovered above the artifact, eyes wide as if she knew that this was a piece most could only dream of seeing, let alone touching. This wasn't just jewelry. It was history, loss, and luxury woven into one.

Mina hesitated — just for a breath. She had worn it every day since her mother gave it to her. The feather was more than just an expensive token; it was a piece of memory, of touch, of voice. Letting it go felt like loosening her grip on the one part of her mother that still felt close. Back when she was Mama, and Mina had been her little girl, not the hardened woman standing here now.

But maybe the girl needed this piece of the past more than Mina ever would again.

"Some things are worth holding onto," Mina said. "Even if they're gone."

The girl took it carefully, like it might turn to dust in her hands, whispering a quiet thank you before her mother noticed and nodded at Mina in gratitude.

As Mina rejoined her friends and boarded the shuttle, Zara grinned. "What was that all about? Picking up a little pen pal?"

"Just … thought she'd like it," Mina said, shrugging. "Something to remember the trip by."

The shuttle door closed, and Mina found herself staring out the window as the lounge receded. She watched the Earth below, hazy and small, and felt a pang in her chest — a sudden awareness of how she'd left it behind, and of the family stranded in that gray, crumbling world.

The shuttle lifted off, hurtling them back to their polished, perfect lives on Mars. Rhea and Lila were already laughing, planning the next big party. Mina sat quietly, clutching her wrist where the bracelet had been, and she looked out at the stars, wondering if they'd ever feel quite the same.

Through the window, Earth dwindled to a smudge against the vast darkness, barely distinguishable. And as Mars' gleaming red cities came into view, she found herself wondering about that little girl with her bracelet, stranded in the lunar lounge, gazing at worlds she might only ever glimpse.

For the first time, Mars' endless glow felt more like a mirage than a beacon, and Mina's gaze softened, settling on her reflection in the glass — a ghost staring back from a world she was only just beginning to see. In the back of her mind, a single thought lingered like a trace of Earth's dust: *How much longer can we keep looking away?*

About the author

Veda Villiers (she/her), 24, is passionate about speculative fiction and poetry that probes the complexities of the human experience. Her works have appeared and are forthcoming in *Gamut*, *Radon Journal*, *Heartlines*, *Trollbreath*, and *Star*Line*. Though her day job keeps her busy, you can find her at @VedaVilliers on X (formerly known as Twitter) and Bluesky.

About hope

As a first-gen child of immigrants who fled their home country due to war and genocide, I've always been drawn to stories about resilience, memory, and the balance between holding on to the past and embracing change. In my writing, I seek to capture both the fragility and strength of the human spirit, and the way storytelling connects us across time and space. In a world where so many still face violence and displacement, I hold on to the hope that through empathy and understanding, we can build a future where peace is not just a dream, but a living reality.

When an Angel Molts

HL Fullerton

We keep the angel in the basement. It's my job to collect the feathers. Some Mother sells; others she uses in her magics; I'm not allowed to keep any. I'm not allowed to leave the house either, unless Mother takes me. I think she's afraid I'll tell someone about the angel and they'll take him away. Or maybe she's afraid I won't come back and she'll have to train a new drudge. You can never be sure with Mother.

She doesn't share her secrets. Mother says, "Secrets are like diamonds. You have to mine for them and when you find them, you keep them or sell them, but you never give them away. Especially not to ungrateful daughters who don't finish their chores." Mother is a very good miner. She can even unearth my thoughts. That's how she found me when I ran away.

After she dragged me home, Mother made my leash. She tethers me to the iron ring above my bedboard. When it's chore time, she takes the lead off and I just wear my collar. The angel has a leash, too, but his is more shackle and chain. He never gets to leave his room.

Neither of us is going anywhere. Mother binds the things she likes best.

At first sight, I thought Mother had captured the sky. Or stolen it. The angel's body was cloud-white with veins of gray; his wings, shades of blue. Then I saw his face. Cheeks like glaciers; pupil-less eyes that flash blue then gray like tiny storm clouds; a sharp, hooked nose more beak than human; and, below, two angry slashes of blood-red lip.

Mother pushed me into the cell and said, "Bring me feathers."

The angel screeched as I stumbled about the room, snatching fallen feathers from the floor. And still I found it hard to take my gaze from his. Even angry, he was the most beautiful thing I'd ever seen.

I crouched and ducked beneath flapping wings, like how I harvest priests' fingers in bat-filled catacombs — Mother always sends me into the darkness first because I am her eyes and ears.

"To your right," Mother called, and I turned in that direction. Whack! The angel's wing caught me. Bones cracked and I fell. The angel lunged, trying to tear my face, but its chain was too short. I crawled to the door and begged for Mother to let me out.

Mother said, "You dropped some feathers." She wouldn't open the door until I recollected them. She was mad because she heard my angel-thoughts. Before today, she was the most beautiful thing in my world. "Still think it pretty?" she said, taking the feathers from me. "Next time it will be your neck."

I am better at feather-collecting now.

The day the angel lets me pet him, I almost cry. His feathers are so soft, *so soft*. I brush my fingers over them, catching the loose ones and tucking them away for Mother.

I can't believe he's allowing my touch. I keep glancing at his face, but he keeps his eyes averted. My hands shake. The more I try to steady them, the more they tremble. His wing moves beneath my touch.

"Does it hurt?" I ask. Even my voice shakes.

He cocks his head and stares at me. His eyes like faceted gems, beautiful and hard.

"I'll stop if it does."

The angel turns his head and acts like I don't exist. He reminds me so much of Mother then.

I don't know if angels can talk. Ours doesn't. Sometimes I dream of growing wings and flying into the sun. I never make it. Even in dreams, Mother's leash pulls me back. And I am careful not to think too loud about leaving — Mother might be listening.

Once I asked Mother if angels eat and she slapped me. "It isn't a pet," she said and I didn't get food that night. I worry our angel will starve. He's been here three, maybe four, months. His feathers aren't as shiny; his eyes are filmy; he doesn't flap and screech as much. He no longer smells like fog and ozone. If the angel dies, I will be alone again with Mother. I will miss the silky press of feathers against my skin. The way his vanes tickle. The soft wispiness of his tightly curled down. The jerky tilt of his head and his quizzical eyes, so blue and deep.

Mother is in her stillroom, making potions. Soon it will be time to collect the feathers. I shadow my thoughts, cloaking them to hide my secrets. I stare out my window at the sky and think TIRED. (Picture the angel soaring in the clouds, disappearing into blueness. His coloration would make him near invisible.) The sun pricks my eyes and they water. I think of the heat of the sun on my (his) face.

I sit up suddenly, think of the dust on the stairs I must sweep. The clothes in the hamper that need cleaning. I wonder if there is enough soap (I bet the angel misses the sun's light) to wash them. (Spell jars.) We are low on furniture polish; I should make more. (My collar feels tight.) I head downstairs to the kitchen and begin washing dishes. I dry the plates, the cups, the spell jars and put them away. (One large jar finds its way into my pocket. I hardly notice it.) I sweep the stairs and make furniture polish. I wash the clothes. THERE IS ENOUGH SOAP. I take my clean aprons to my room. I put them away (Open my window.) I straighten the quilt on my bed (stick the uncapped jar out into the light). I hum (catch the sun in my jar) while I work. MUST GET FEATHERS SOON.

I hear Mother at the bottom of the stairs, calling me. TIME FOR THE ANGEL. I (quickly screw the cap on the jar, trapping the fresh air inside, shut the window, hurry) hurry down into the basement.

When I'm sure Mother isn't looking, I pull out the jar — it squirms in my hands like a living thing — and hold it towards the angel. He shifts away, but I shush him and step closer. "For you," I whisper and uncap the jar.

His nose twitches, he leans closer to the jar, sniffing. My magic worked. I can see the rays shining from the glass, bathing his face. He closes his eyes and basks. Too soon, it's all gone. "I'll bring more when I can."

I think, maybe, angels drink sunlight.

Yesterday Mother searched my room and smashed all the spell jars I'd hidden. She leashed me to the ring above my bed, muttering incantations and curses the whole time.

"Think I don't know about your feeding the angel? I know *everything* you think."

(Except Mother is a liar. She doesn't know about my feather.) I cried because that is what Mother wanted. "I had to feed him," I blubbered. "If he dies, we won't have any more feathers. Please, please let me go." I had to beg all night, but by morning she freed me to clean the house. And to collect the feathers.

I am lucky angels hate the smell of demons or Mother would have traded me to them again as my punishment. People sometimes come to see Mother when they think demons are tormenting them. These people are fools. Demons may be invisible, but they are foul-smelling, nattering things. If a demon is in bed with you, you know it. Good thing Mother covets feathers more than demon spunk.

I will miss the angel when I go. Since Mother is with a customer, I don't have to be as careful with my thoughts.

She's too busy making magic to worry about me, and I've been very good (ever since I found the feather) lately.

When Mother finishes with her customer (next goes to market), I will (escape) pluck three long feathers from the angel's hide to keep her happy. Mother doesn't like that the angel is shedding less and less. She stares at him and purses her mouth and shakes her head real slow like — Mother is deciding what to do with his body.

It makes me sad.

He doesn't flinch when I yank out Mother's feathers, but it must hurt. I pulled three hairs from my head and that stung. And his quills are so much thicker. He doesn't bleed, which annoys Mother. She says she can do great things with angel blood, if only he would shed some. I cut myself with Mother's athame and willed myself not to bleed, but my veins didn't listen. Mother got angry about the mess.

Well, that's what she said, but I could tell she was more mad about not knowing that's what I intended to do. Mother hasn't realized that her thought-mining is starting to work both ways.

I dream of dead angels and it heartens Mother.

My feather. I hadn't planned to steal one, but when I undressed and found a pin feather nestled between my breasts, I tamped down that spark of hope like Mother extinguishing the flame in a fire moth's eyes. I thought about the blisters on my hands (while my fingers caught the tiny, curled wisp) and how (easily it will slice through Mother's magics) tired I was.

I picked at the puffed skin on my thumb (pricked it with the tiny shaft) until it oozed (and hid the wisp in my pillow amongst the goose feathers). Then I curled up (like a feather, like a feather) and rested my head on its softness.

I felt it shift beneath my cheek, settling into the down, secreting itself, and (forget, forget) forgot about it.

"Go on," Mother says. "Say goodbye to the angel. I know you want to."

I stare at my porridge and fill my head with thoughts of sky-bright wings and cloud-colored skin. Once cumulous white, his skin is now rainy-day gray. I picture him decomposing, (flying free, sunlight caressing his face) wings spread, bald patches showing scaly skin.

Mother laughs. "You can't hide from me."

I think, *I love him more than you*, and fight not to smile when her lips tighten.

I am an ungrateful daughter — her thought or mine, I'm not sure.

As I open the angel's cell, I am smiling. Until I think of the coming goodbye. Will he understand? He never responds to my words, only rarely acknowledging my touch, but then I am his captor. I WILL MISS HIM WHEN HE'S (I'm) GONE. I open the door and shriek.

He is tearing mouthfuls of feathers from his already ravaged wings and spitting them on the floor. A pile big enough to stuff a pillow covers his feet. His eyes, more alien than usual, glow with feverish light.

I rush in and try to stop him, pull his head away. "Your wings," I say. "Your beautiful wings. Stop, stop, please."

He shakes me free, his madness giving him strength, and continues plucking.

Mother pulls me from the room, a cloud of feathers enveloping us both. She makes me strip to ensure she gets every last feather.

I laugh because she is too late, too late, and my screeching echoes the angel shredding himself to pieces.

"I suppose I will have to sell it sooner than I expected," Mother says, shooing me out of her stillroom. "I don't suppose you got any of its blood on you?"

But no, it's all my own.

Mother is going to Gackles to find someone willing to buy an angel. I think (Today is the day.) disappointing thoughts as she chains me to my wall.

"It's your fault," she says, still angry about the angel eating its feathers. They made her magics potent and now she will have to use inferior substitutes. "You spoiled it. You're lucky I don't sell you as well." An idle threat; Mother has no intention of losing me. Her thoughts are so clear now.

"No!" I say because she expects it and I don't want to raise her suspicions. Gackles is the furthest Mother ever goes from home. She took me there once — before I ran away and she brought me back. Gackles is on the cusp of decency, where dark and light mingle. Angels patrol not a block away. It takes twenty minutes to get there. That's how long I have to escape. Maybe, when I'm amongst decent folk, I'll confess about the angel and they'll come and free him. But most likely, Mother will have disposed of him by then and they'll blame me for his disappearance.

"I thought if he liked you, he would bleed for you. But now ... when I get back from Gackles, the demons can have you."

Mother smiles at me and leaves. I keep my mind blank. Then I fear that will be suspicious and picture terrifying things. Her mind tugs at mine. I feel her energy move down the street. (Twenty minutes, twenty minutes.)

I think of my pillow (the hidden feather) and worry (what if I can't get the feather to work?) about what will happen to the angel (me).

Mother is almost at Gackles. Her delight sizzles into my brain; she expects to make a good deal on the angel. My fingers — I pay them no mind — worm their way into the goose down and sort through the feathers, feeling for a particular softness. (Found it.)

I open my palm and, keeping my thoughts quiet, look at my treasure. It is smaller than I remember and I don't have to feign disappointment. I only have one chance. If I mess this up, Mother will ensure I never get another.

Maybe I shouldn't go.

Holding that thought in my head, I saw through the ring with the angel's pin feather. Both my collar and leash are spelled; breaking either will alert Mother. So will leaving the house. I must time these perfectly or she will catch me before I reach the light lands.

The feather is sharp, but the ring is thick. My fingers are bloody from pinching the tiny shaft. I make the final cut and the feather's shaft splits in two.

I slip my leash from the ring and dash down the stairs. The broken feather clutched in my hand will make messy work of the collar. Trying to get it off, I may very well slice my own throat. But if I leave the collar on, Mother will use it to track me.

I feel a tingling at the back of my neck: *Mother.* She's coming back. She knows something's wrong.

At our home's threshold, I pause. I could leave wearing the collar, cut as I run. If Mother guesses my route, it makes little difference whether I remove the collar now or before I reach the light. We both know where I'm headed. Whoever is faster wins. But Mother has magics to call upon to aid her speed that I do not. Despite my planning, I've already failed. Unless ...

I steal another feather, a stronger feather. If the angel has any left. *The angel!*

I never said goodbye. I hurry down the basement steps and fling open the cell door. He is featherless. My eyes scan the room and it, too, is clean of feathers. I sob and Angel lifts his head from his chest.

Those blue gem eyes wound me.

Dots of blood appear on his hide, like pin-pricks. He is bleeding for me.

My hands clench into fists and his last feather stabs my palm. If I leave him to Mother, I'm as bad as her. Worse, maybe — because I know what he'll suffer in my stead.

"Can you run?" I say.

Angel looks at me, head cocked.

I rush to his leg chain and begin sawing. "You have five minutes. Turn left when you leave the house."

I can't tell if he understands me. I picture my route in my head and hope he can mine my thoughts. His chain is thicker than my ring. Time is being eaten up.

"Run three blocks, then turn right." Mother is coming.

"Fly, if you can." His wings, his poor wings. They'll never work.

"Go one more block and turn left. You should be able find help there." I can't feel my fingers anymore. I'm bleeding all over him.

"You need to be fast. She's coming back and if she catches you, it'll be worse. Much worse. Do you understand?"

He jerks and the chain snaps. Something pops, black flashes streak about the room. A spell. Mother bespelled his chain. "Go!" I scream. "Go!"

I pull at him, uncertain if he can support himself after so long in captivity. He is heavy and nearly topples us. I heave him up the stairs. His legs start to work, but not soon enough, I fear. Mother is running. She is close. Six blocks away. I can hear her chanting in my head.

Angel flings open the front door and I shove him through. Gloomy sunlight coats his skin. How much worse he looks in the light of day. I hold in my mind the image from when I first saw him. He was magnificent then. Now on the patchy lawn in front of our wicked house, he looks three-quarters dead.

"Call your friends if you can."

He doesn't move.

"Run." I make shooing motions with my hands. Blood flicks over him. "She's almost here. You have to leave."

The collar at my neck starts to burn. One of us will be free, I tell myself, and what do I know of freedom, I've only ever dreamt of it. He can't live without it — and Mother won't be able to track him. If only he'd leave.

He beckons me to join him. "I can't come with you. She'll find me. She always finds me."

He spreads his wings and lifts his head to the heavens. My vision blurs; I collapse against the doorframe.

"Fly," I whisper. "Fly." But without feathers, he can't.

Then: his skin changes color. No, his feathers grow back. Shades of blue and white, patches of dove gray. More beautiful than ever. His summer eyes lock with mine and he shoots up into the sky like a reverse lightning bolt.

I follow his flight until the sun blinds me and Mother blindsides me. Her fists are so angry, she will make me pay in blood and pain, but I lock the image of my angel, wings spread, rising into heavens, in my mind and nothing can break through it. Not even Mother, no matter how hard she tries.

Through swollen lids, I imagine Angel standing, wings folded, in front of me. *I wish I told you how sorry I am.*

You just did, his image says.

For real, I wish I could apologize for real. I close my eyes one last time. I hear the rustle of feathers and feel air rushing past my skin. I pretend I am raised into the bright light of the heavens. I turn my head and welcome the night.

Mother always sends me first into the darkness — I am her eyes and ears. But this time I'll search for patches of gray and eyes of blue and clouds like a summer's day.

"When an Angel Molts" originally appeared in
Triangulation: Beneath the Surface in 2016.

About the author

HL Fullerton writes short fiction — mostly speculative, occasionally about angels, sometimes about small hopes carried defiantly into the dark — which can be found in more than 50 anthologies and magazines including *Kaleidotrope, Mysterion,* and *Underland Arcana.* On Bluesky as @HLFullerton.bsky.social.

Birdcalls of the Carpathian Mountains

Sam Ruhmkorff

So long as Michal can hear the birds singing, he will be safe. The lazy chirping of barn swallows from the spruce grove behind him, the squeaks of a pair of wagtails from the juniper ahead, the trilling of a lone yellowhammer in a white fir. *"Shy to be seen but proud to be heard," his father says as they pause by a stream. "So look with your ears."* That was many springs ago, but Michal remembers. He softens his eyes as he walks a game trail below the tree line. The wagtails flitter away from him, their muscles thrumming. They perch on a nearby spruce and resume their chattering, as if there weren't a war on.

Michal moves as fast as he can while breathing quietly so he doesn't make his own gasping call to German scouts. Sweat beads his brow as he climbs. At first faintly, then more stridently, the whistles of a wallcreeper rise from a thicket downhill. Michal pictures its long, slender beak, its plain gray back preparing the surprise: a flash of red and white on its wings. *His father holds up the feather he found. In the golden light, Michal sees a field of rich dark brown, a streak of red like a scimitar, a pale white crescent moon.* If he were with his father, they would rest and wait for the wallcreeper to emerge. But his father is no longer here, and Michal has a rifle on his back and a message that must get to Lieutenant Kopko by nightfall. He strides past the thicket, letting the wallcreeper's song fade behind him.

His father's war was a different war. "They thought they were mountain men," his father says. "But they weren't men enough for these mountains." It is summer and Michal and his father are nestled in the mossy crooks of an old beech tree, watching for roe deer. They haven't had meat in three months. His father runs his fingers absentmindedly along the vanes of the wallcreeper feather in his hat. In his other hand he holds his Mosin. The rifle's arctic birch stock is riddled with scars. Each of those scars holds a story, Michal thinks. He is fifteen and while his father's Rusyn pride is familiar, he has never before talked about the war.

His father tells of how he stalked the invaders as they approached Łupków Pass. He hadn't had enough to eat in weeks and he'd never been so cold. Surely if he got within a mile, the Habsburgs would track him down from the chattering of his bones. He was twenty trees off the main track, his Mosin slung on his back. Deep snow spilled into his boots. His body was not warm enough to melt the bands of ice around his calves.

He'd gone two miles when he saw the first body slumped along the track, coat and boots stripped. This strange man in his pointed helmet was the second corpse he'd seen in his life. The man's toes and the tip of his nose were blackened — they'd died before the rest of him. He had a dark, unkempt mustache limned with bright frost. Maybe in Vienna he would have trimmed and waxed it before a night of dancing. Michal's father pulled out a knife and cut off the regimental badges. Then he picked his way through the drifts till he was again twenty trees deep.

"That was just the first," his father says. The day is hot and the tree bark cool against Michal's back. There hasn't been a sign of anything larger than a squirrel for the last two hours. "They became like mileposts, and then thicker than that. After a while, they were still wearing their cardboard boots. You see, it was our land that killed them, more than us." He flicks his fingernail over a groove near the base of the rifle stock. "Alive, I hated them for trampling through like we weren't here. But dead, I could only imagine them alive."

His father continues his story. The track was a mire of brown slush. Deep ruts from artillery wheels, footprints going out wider in search of firm snow, stores tossed aside to lighten the load. From the hummock ahead, his father heard rooks, the harshness of their call softened by the snow. Three of them with their big beaks huddled on the branch of a pine tree. Below them was a body. But this dead man was not yet dead. He was moaning and when he saw Michal's father, he said something incomprehensible. His father shook his head. The man mimed a gun pointed at his own chest. "Boom," he said.

His father didn't move. He'd never aimed at a person before. The man was angry now, gesticulating, the acceptance of death in his eyes. His father didn't yet know if he could pull the trigger but he stepped forward and raised the rifle. The man jerked upright, lashed out. A blade shone in the twilight. The knife bit into the gun stock, then fell with a soft thump in the snow. When they heard the shot, the rooks hastened away, their wings beating the air.

Michal's father stops his story when something rustles in the forest across the clearing. He tightens his grip on the rifle. Out of the woods comes a tiny roe, not even a yearling. In the afternoon light filtered through the pine trees, his neck is speckled gold, his haunches ambered brown.

Michal's palms sweat against the rough bark. His father looks down the scope at the roe, takes that familiar deep breath, lets it out again. Michal looks away, braces himself.

But there is no shot. "Some things, Michal, are too beautiful to kill," his father says. His voice is thick. The roe is gazing up at him, eyes trusting, curious.

With a quick torrent of wing-beats, a barn swallow alights on a branch in front of his father. Her shiny blue head is iridescent. Downy white fluff lines her breast. And on her tail, a single orange feather, long and sweeping and glowing in the shadows, out of place among its dark blue neighbors. For that matter, out of place for any barn swallow Michal has ever seen.

"Look at you," his father says. "You'll stand out in a crowd."

As if to prove the point, the swallow breaks into unfamiliar song. It has a swallow's trills and chirps and clicks, but not the rushes of seemingly aimless notes. The song weaves together like a human song. A theme develops, varies, returns. Throughout the strange serenade, the swallow looks inscrutably at his father, then the feather in his hat. She doesn't spare a glance for Michal. Still singing, she hops onto his father's hat and starts pecking.

"Oh!" his father says. Again and again, she hops on and off, pecking at the wallcreeper feather each time. "Do you want this?" his father asks, holding out the feather.

She takes the feather in her beak and brings it to her back, as if grooming. And then the feather is part of her, fully attached, yet a different shape, the shape of a swallow's tail feather. The red scimitar and white crescent moon are now part of her. She arches her neck, trills a high fanfare, and flies off.

The roe is nowhere to be seen.

Tears stream down his father's cheeks. Rather than dry them off, rather than look away in embarrassment, his father holds Michal's gaze. "Did you see that, my son?"

Michal looks away. A bird borrowed a feather. His father is crying. He doesn't know which is more startling.

A long moment passes. His father slings the rifle on his back and starts climbing down the tree. "Come on. We'll find something else to eat."

It is Michal's war, now, and his father is gone. A spring mist covers the forest. The trail climbs; the pines grow shorter. There is more birdsong ahead — the staccato of waxwings, and also more barn swallows, if he's hearing right. He listens for that long-ago song, that song that sounded human. But these swallows sound like all the other swallows.

Michal hears something else, though. Clicks and pops and peculiar gulping cries that hardly sound like they're from a bird. His breathing is punctuated by the capercaillie's strange sounds: not even music, just rhythm, an orchestra with chittering clicks and drummers from the dawn of time.

Through the mist, he sees the capercaillie in a grove below him. The bird's tail fans behind him as he sails smoothly through the ferns, a tall ship in calm waters. The black feathers around his neck bristle, then smooth; his green breast shines like an emerald. *"I'm sure she'll be impressed, my friend," his father says. On his sketchpad, his pencil shapes the ridges of red feathers over the capercaillie's eyes. After the strange swallow's song, there was no more hunting, only drawing: sometimes deer; one lucky day, a lynx; always, birds. And when they got home, his father's new favorite, kasha with lentils and onions.*

Michal's stomach rumbles, but there's no time to rummage for the walnuts in his pack. The sun is falling behind the opposite ridge. Soon the light will go, and he won't be able to get to Lieutenant Kopko in time to stop the doomed attack. He quickens his pace. The capercaillie's irregular drumbeats push him forward, a strange military march, and then they're behind him, replaced by the high bursts and low chirps of a fieldfare. Fieldfares always remind him of a radio being tuned. Be loud, my friend, Michal thinks. Be loud so I can be fast. *The fieldfares perch high up the hillside as Michal and his father walk slowly down the lane. His father's right leg is paralyzed. At the end of the road, Jan Kapral has felled more trees to expand his farm. Smoke billows from a brush fire in the middle of the field. His father stops, unable to go further, his eyes watering from the smoke. Smiling, he points with trembling hand up the hill. "Listen to them," he says. "Listen."*

The fieldfare's song stops abruptly. Michal freezes, willing his breath to quiet. A branch snaps on the trail ahead. Michal slinks downslope to hide in a juniper thicket. His lungs spasm, begging to gulp in air, but Michal won't let them.

Through the gaps in the juniper, Michal sees a young man coming down the game trail, burrowing through the mist, tripping over branches, crunching leaves underfoot. His hair is brown, messy, unwashed. He doesn't look German but he has a German rifle on his back. Perhaps he is harmless; what follows him is not. As quietly as he can, Michal unstraps the Mosin.

The young man passes the juniper, heading the way Michal came from. He's looking upslope at the firs, stunted and twisted by the wind. They've settled into the shapes they need to be to survive.

So have I, Michal thinks. He points the rifle between the young man's shoulder blades. Goose pimples cover his arms. His breath is so loud in his ears, it seems impossible he won't be heard.

In a flurry of wingbeats, a bird alights on a twisted branch in the juniper thicket and gives Michal a familiar inscrutable look with tilted head. It's a barn swallow, trilling a song Michal has heard only once before. A song like a human song. In the shadow of the juniper, her single orange tail feather glows in the soft light as if it were the source of all the light on the mountainside. The red and white of the wallcreeper feather are still there. And there are many more colors among the swallow's feathers: emerald green from a capercaillie's breast, brownish yellow from a yellowhammer's belly, bright blue and black stripes from a jay's wing.

You again, Michal thinks, though he does not see how this can be. Swallows do not live so long. Then again, swallows do not borrow feathers from other birds.

Me again, the swallow sings. Which is also not a possible thing, Michal knows, but her eyes spark brilliantly in the shadows and he feels the mountainside under him. He feels the roots curling through the soil, the bugs and worms in the ground, and under that, rock, with the memories of all that creeped and crawled and walked and flew before him. He feels how some of what is now alive will join that rock, and a million years hence the mountain will still be there, with new birds and new songs, and his father's voice a fragile weave among them. And he sees it's the mountain that's alive, and he is just a bundle of thoughts flitting around, and the young man is more thoughts walking away from him, and the birds are thoughts in the sky. And they are all the same.

This is why my father cried, Michal thinks. Why he stopped hunting, why he ate only what he grew.

The young man's back is in the rifle sights. Above the sound of clumsy footsteps, the rainbow-feathered swallow trills louder, more insistent, still human. A group of swallows high above sing their familiar swallow songs, as if in accompaniment. They squeak, they chortle, they click. *"It's hard to believe," his father says by the creek, smiling at his son, "one bird can do all that." Michal is twelve, restless, looking for stones, but he hears.*

Michal's throat tightens. The young man is thirty yards away, thirty-five. The mist is parting. The swallows keep singing.

About the author

Sam Ruhmkorff was a philosophy professor for two decades at Bard College at Simon's Rock, Smith College, and the University of Missouri, and has numerous scholarly publications in the philosophy of science and the philosophy of religion. His fiction has appeared in *Crepuscular Magazine* ("The Long Crossing") and *Deep Wild Journal: Writing from the Backcountry* ("That Is Enough For Me"). More info can be found at samruhmkorff.com.

About the story

I started this piece during the early days of the pandemic in 2020. Walking around my neighborhood, it seemed to me that the birds were louder and more plentiful than usual, and this made me feel safe.

The Lay-by-rinth

Anna Orridge

"We need to think what to do with the layby."

Avi shaded their eyes with a hand and squinted at the tapering stretch of asphalt marked out by a broken white line. "Oh. That's what you guys call this?"

"Yes. It's where drivers used to stop for a rest or to fetch something from the boot."

Avi nodded. "We'd call that a turnout in the States. I think I prefer layby, though. Laaaay-byyyy. Sounds like lullaby." They let their hands waft, eyes closed and lids quivering.

It had been three hours since sunrise and the light was now pretty blinding. We'd have to stop work pretty soon.

A cyclist whizzed along past us, with a cheeky ring of her bell. Avi shouted and waved. "Ahoy there."

I rolled my eyes. Avi had been on a tall boat from America for six months, and as a consequence felt entitled to use jovial nautical slang.

"Right," I said. "I reckon this is the right place for the orchard. It's got shelter from the wind, because of the slope behind it."

Avi grimaced. "That's a hell of a lot of work, digging up that asphalt."

"It's mostly broken up. I mean, just look over there — the dandelions and forget-me-nots poking through the cracks. The soil must have a fair bit of life in it already."

"But how will the young trees get watered?"

"By pilgrims, of course."

Avi rolled their eyes. "The old gas station is an hour's walk, Matt. You really think they're going to carry water all that way? Assuming there's even enough in the tank."

I dropped my arms. "You surely agree we've got to have some kind of food source here. We can't have a ten mile stretch without at least one?"

They crossed their arms. "The thing is, 'layby' got me thinking. I have an idea for a Waypoint."

I breathed out, long and hard. "Avi, we've already done *loads* of Waypoints."

Along with everyone else on the Pathway team, our task here was to make what had once been the M25 not just a new road for bikes and buses, but also a pilgrimage route for those on foot. We were to maintain and enhance the thin ribbon of woodland and wild grassland that had been able to thrive on the verges even during Peak Car. We also needed to ensure there were sources of food, shade and water for the pilgrims: orchards, sprawling forest gardens, edible hedges.

The Waypoints were works of art, created to make people reflect on what we had lost. Each had to incorporate a redundant technology of some kind. We, along with all the other shovel bums, had been given a sack of gadgets and digital detritus to repurpose. Often, we used the old infrastructure of the motorway as part of the design, too. A lot of the Waypoints would be transient, and we hoped pilgrims would add their own touches.

There was a rainbow mosaic mural on one of the embankments made up of old circuit boards. We had also turned a triangle of peeling, faded chevrons into the sort of snow-topped mountain you once could have found even in Britain at the right time of the year, but was now a rarity outside of picture books. We'd built a border round it with planks of wood and fashioned a dozen miniature plywood models of skiers, all perched on little clockwork cars. Passing pilgrims could wind them up and watch them go. I liked to imagine them lying on their bellies, like kids observing insects scuttle about from ground level.

We really wanted to do something with the bridges, but a lot of them were off-limits because of feather-vein fungus infestation.

Feather-vein fungus was a hybrid life form, a mycological chimera. It had originally been developed to make deep-sea mining a less destructive activity, as it was able to burrow its way through rock.

Under a hot sun, though, the veins would grow at an incredible speed. They were able to pierce through anything, although they thrived especially on the minerals in particular types of rock and cement.

It was called feather-vein fungus because when night fell, the delicate filigree of fibres on those veins would sprout like hair. And at their fullest extent, they looked very much like leaves ... or feathers. During the day, the fungus would release its spores — clouds of pink dust.

Most of the motorway bridges were now ruins, great arches festooned with purple feathers like a bridal train, surrounded by a halo of pink in the daytime.

We had found one intact bridge, though, and hung it with real vines. They were pinned back on either side, like a schoolgirl's fringe. We'd suspended two massive discs of eyes between, each a glittering mosaic of broken plastic bits. The centre of each eye had a light bulb powered by a little solar panel above the disc. At night, they were programmed to light up — little swaying dots like lit homemade joints when seen from a distance — a lighthouse of sorts, I suppose.

Then there had been that blue motorway sign we took down. We laid it on a table and turned it into a pinball-type game with lots of little chutes made out of the circuit boards we had left over after the mosaic. Avi insisted it would make people think about the nature of speed and competition. To be honest, I thought it was just great fun — the closest you could get nowadays to those old fruit machines in pubs, which were now nothing more than black and broken gravestones in gutted buildings.

Avi loved those sorts of projects. "We should make a labyrinth. A *lay-by-rinth,* even."

I laughed and whacked them in the stomach with the back of my hand. "Pretentious git. You mean a maze!"

"Nope." Avi shook their head. They also rubbed their stomach where I'd swiped with a smile. "A labyrinth."

"A labyrinth is something you go into when you're a Greek hero, and you get chased by a bull monster until you can trip it up with thread. Or something."

Avi smiled wryly. "A labyrinth only has one path you can take, whereas a maze has branches. It's like a puzzle, and the exit and entrance are always different. In a labyrinth, they're always the same."

"What's the point in that then?"

"What's the point in any journey, Matt?"

"Oh, please feel free to do a running jump."

"That's an idea — we could turn this into a long jump runway!"

"Oh God, Avi. Enough, please stop."

I acted like Avi's flights of fancy maddened me. But, in honesty, they'd made the last six months of heat and labour bearable. And I think Avi enjoyed my performative grouchiness too.

They smiled, closed their eyes. "Nobody has made me laugh quite like you do, Matt."

I wasn't quite sure how to respond to that. "I guess I'm glad I double up as court jester as well as dogsbody."

Avi breathed out through their nostrils, rather noisily. I couldn't really tell whether it was frustration or tiredness after so much work in the heat.

They opened their eyes again. "You're a fine dogsbody, too. Think about it, though. A labyrinth is ideal for this pilgrimage route too. I mean, the M25 was famously circular, with no obvious endpoint, right? And yet everybody was so utterly fixated on going straight, getting ahead."

"I think you'll find that most of the cyclists here are still pretty keen on going in a forwards direction."

"True enough. But for the pilgrims, it's more like a prayer in motion. You remember how Gina at the Assembly described it — a rosary for the feet rather than the fingers?" Avi got up and scraped the infinity sign on the dirt with their long, narrow feet.

On anyone else, those feet would look clownish. But Avi carried them off well, with their rangy limbs. They had the longest toes I'd ever seen — I'd often watched them wriggle above me in the morning, when they slung their legs over the top of the bunk.

I've always been a bit of solid, square type myself, physically. Short but strong, not lacking bulk round the belly, low centre of gravity and all that. We were a good combination as a labouring team, because Avi could reach high, and I could normally wrench, squat and pull anything loose.

And on a relational level, we'd had an easy rapport right from the beginning, when we were paired up.

"Oh, all right," I relented, brushing the crumbs off my lap. "I'll get on with planting some whips on the top of that embankment. The old hedge up there has been almost completely destroyed, so we need something to take its place. You can start painting this lay-by-rinth of yours while I'm up there. If you can get it all planned out in the next couple of hours, we'll have a look for some materials to build it. And if there's some way to integrate food into the arrangement, we'll have a go at doing it."

I felt angry at myself for being such a pushover, but that pretty much melted away in the face of Avi's huge, unguarded smile. They didn't do joy by halves. They didn't do anything by halves. Avi was a Whole Numbers sort of human.

By midday, I'd dug up the soil at the top of the embankment and planted a line of whips. It was touch-and-go whether they'd survive or not, but if they did, they'd reduce the chances of a landslide or flooding. Although the summers were now achingly hot and dry, it wasn't unusual to have rainbombs in the autumn and winter. There had already been several that had made the motorway unusable for weeks.

Avi, meanwhile, had used white paint to plan out their lay-by-rinth. It was a roughly circular iris in the eye of the lay-by, teeming with swirls and loops.

"It kind of reminds me of a fingerprint," I said, after I'd slid my way down the slope towards them. "What do you reckon we should use to build it?"

"Stone, I think. I've seen moss and lichen grow on natural stone walls — when they fill in the little dips and crevices, they almost look like labyrinths in miniature themselves."

"Hmm. There aren't any sources of natural stone nearby, though. I think rubble would be best."

"Well, it's past midday now. Way too hot to work. Let's see what's available back at camp."

Camp was a converted petrol station. The pumps were long gone. The underground tanks where the oil was once stored had been excavated too, save for one used for water. (Only for washing, mind. It was not in any way suitable for drinking).

The rest of the underground space was reserved for bunkers for roadside shovel bums like us.

Behind the station was a pile of stuff extracted from the old landfills — old trolleys, broken wooden pallets, sometimes flatpack furniture still in its decayed packaging. Luckily, there was also quite a lot of rubble from some ancient demolition. I started picking bits up, examining them and putting the promising ones to one side.

"How do you know which are best for the task?" Avi asked.

"I've built dry stone walls before, when I was doing some volunteering at farms in Yorkshire. It's all about the surfaces — what will lie flat and fit well."

"A principle that applies to so much in life."

I gave them a light slap to the back of the head, but Avi was not laughing any longer. A deep frown creased their wide forehead as they held up one of the pieces of rubble. "Holy shit. Matty — you do realise what that is, right?"

They traced a finger across the crumbling surface. After squinting for a moment, I saw it too. Violet and blue threads, crawling across the surface.

I gasped. "Oh Jesus. Fucking feather-vein fungus. What are people thinking, just leaving that stuff lying around?"

"It's not dangerous in and of itself, though, is it? Certainly not to touch. And it's supposed to be really tasty."

Indeed. The 'feathers' were dark purple and could be picked and eaten. They were highly nutritious. No wonder the fungus had been treated as a miracle of biotechnology when it first came out. People were too desperate for food to think far ahead.

"Avi, we cannot have this conversation. You know how dangerous it is."

Avi shrugged. "It was only dangerous because people persisted in living in those huge buildings when they'd clearly become unviable."

"Yeah, because the fungus had undermined their structural integrity. Christ, Avi."

They should have been more aware of this than most people, because I'd once had to pull them out of the way of a crumbling embankment they'd been admiring. Avi had wanted to paint one of the longer fungus veins blue, turn it into a river and make the whole surface a verdant landscape. A lovely idea, but one rather undermined by the landslide that could have crushed us both if I hadn't insisted on us moving well out of the way.

My irritation was rising. Why were they sometimes so provokingly naïve?

This probably would have turned into an argument between us if someone from the catering team hadn't turned up on his bike at that precise moment with dinner. We decided to go underground to eat.

Dinner was dahl, with some nettles mixed in. We also had some berries we'd foraged earlier for dessert.

"Avi, what made you come over here from America?" I asked.

They gave me a playful look. "We've been a team for six months, Matt. And now you want to do the Getting To Know You questions?"

They were right, of course. I suppose I was trying to make up for my snappiness earlier. "I'm still allowed to be curious about you. I just never got the sense you were unhappy over there. What would make you go so far?"

They sighed and wriggled their long toes. "Itchy feet, friend, and itchy heat."

"All right, fair, it's not quite as hot over here. But a two-month voyage in a tall boat is not the cure I'd take for itchy feet."

Avi shrugged. "Clearly your feet aren't itchy enough. Shall I tickle them for you with the vein fungus feathers?"

"Oh sod off."

Suddenly, they rolled over in their bunk to look down at me, their expression that combination of mischief and determination I'd come to know so well. "Seriously, though, sailing's the *best* cure for itchy feet. I was part of the crew, so I had to work — keep the rigging in good order, clean the decks, help with the cooking. We were servants to the boat and the sea wind. It was perfect."

"But why Europe? What were you hoping to get out of this journey?"

Avi smiled, eyes still closed. "Our elders told me I needed to keep walking and working until I knew my destination."

"So do you know now? The place you're going?"

They threw a pillow at me with a laugh. "God, you're so literal-minded. It doesn't have to be a physical place. It could be an occupation, a passion ... a person."

Was that a hint? Probably not.

This had always been the way of it. People liked me, for the most part; they enjoyed my company. But it so rarely went beyond that. It was a low, throbbing ache never quite drowned out by all the larger disasters I'd experienced in my thirty-five years of life.

And Avi was always so mischievious, one of those people who pretty much flirted with everyone, just as a way of conveying warmth. If I had misjudged this, we wouldn't be able to continue the easy friendship the way it had been. I didn't want to risk losing that, damn it.

"Well, what is it then?" I asked quietly. "For you?"

They did not answer me. The old clock on the wall ticked on, but I was pretty sure they had not fallen asleep. Their breath did not have that shuddering rhythm I was so familiar with.

If our conversation was a labyrinth, then the walls or hedges surrounding us would be jokes and jibes. The jokes provided us with support and structure for our friendship, of course ... but I also had to wonder what they were blocking.

Avi persuaded me to use the feather-vein-fungus-infested rubble for the lay-by-rinth. Of course they did. We were going to be in a lot of trouble if any of our supervisors found out.

Late afternoon the next day, once it was cool enough, we came back to the layby with two wheelbarrows of rubble. The painted outline had dried out nicely in our absence.

We chipped away at the asphalt to make a small dip, then laid a base of rubble. We could only build three layers, though, as the base was so narrow.

Once I'd finished a row, I sat down and wiped the sweat from my brow. "Seriously, though, Avi. Who's ever going to use this?"

"Let's make sure at least one person benefits from it."

"Who?"

"You, you insufferable grouch. You know that silly game of trust we played when we were paired as volunteers? Where we had to fall back into one another's arms? Well, I've got a better idea. Give me that damp cloth you were using to cool your forehead earlier ..."

They tied the cloth around my eyes, took one of my hands, and led me to the lay-by-rinth. I stumbled a bit at first.

"Relax," Avi said gently. "Imagine it's a dance."

So I let Avi guide me. Their hands were so cool, pleasantly callused. I focused on the feel of my thumb against the meat of their palm.

"We were talking about the Minotaur in the labyrinth," they said softly. "Do you know who built it?"

"Seems I'm going to find out."

"It was Daedalus, as in Daedalus and Icarus. You know, wax and feathers, sun, falling into the ocean ..."

"He wouldn't need to go too near the sun to have his wings melt these days."

"True. I mean, the story's all about the dangers of human knowledge and of technological overreach, right?"

They paused. "You do realise what the real point of the Waypoints is?"

"They're to ensure that we do not lose ..."

"... our memories of the old tech, the old ways of living? Yeah, I think that's probably what the Assembly believe. But let's be honest, the Waypoints will be more like standing stones, shrouded in a miasma of spiritual mystery. Perhaps it will become sacrilegious to investigate them, tinker or take them apart. I think there's something beautiful in that. I think I'd rather create ritual fodder than art."

They stopped to untie the cloth at the back of my head. When it fell away, I gasped.

We were at the mouth of the lay-by-rinth. The fungus had already started to fruit, those little purple threads pouring out like a waterfall in slow motion. I knelt down to break off a piece and taste it. The veins were rather like deep-fried tofu, once it had cooled. The fibres brushed my tongue before they melted.

"So?" Avi asked.

"Quite pleasant."

I held it out to Avi. They took it and munched thoughtfully. "What's special about *this* Waypoint is that people won't be able to keep their distance from the technology. They'll have to walk through it, touch it, even *taste* it."

I nodded. I had decided Avi was right about the feather-vein fungus. It had been a scapegoat, really, not anywhere near as bad as people made out.

There had, of course, been catastrophes. I remembered my parents telling me about the hotel that collapsed in San Francisco, killing hundreds. It was one of the last news stories they saw on the TV before they lost all signals for good.

But, for the most part, infested buildings gently and slowly crumbled. I and other children used to wander through the ruins of those houses, creating makeshift playgrounds out of the piles of rubble, the scaffolding poles. We'd even have picnics when we could muster enough appetizing food.

Like everything at that time, it was tragic. At least, though, it was a more tender sort of collapse than the wars and riots — one of flowers and coolness, of morsels shared and fingers licked clean amid the ruins.

I'd never really managed to regain that community, or sense of playful, tender connectedness.

Not until I'd met Avi, at any rate.

Everything around the motorway was bathed in warm light, the birds just starting to sing in the woodland on the side opposite the lay-by-rinth. The feather-vein fungus released their spores. Soon, we were surrounded by soft pink plumes.

"Avi, I want to thank you for this."

Avi suddenly took both my hands. I nearly pulled away. But their grip was surprisingly firm.

"Unrequited love is a feather-vein fungus of the mind, Matt. It might never grow or spore in daylight. I can come to terms with that, but I at least need to know."

I opened my mouth. There were more words caught in my throat than there were spores in the air right now. But somehow, none of them would come out.

Yet shock wasn't the right word for how I was feeling.

Avi's eyes dropped to my palm, and they started to trace one of the lines.

"If the answer is 'No', that's absolutely fine. And I'm quite happy to go away, let you find someone else to do the work with because I wouldn't want you to be uncomfortable. I know I'm hardly the easiest person even just to be friends with and ..."

The end of their sentences floated away along with the pink spores. I realised they were every bit as nervous as me.

I removed my hand from Avi's and laid a forefinger on their lips.

For the first time since we'd started to work together, I held their gaze properly. Their eyes were as bright blue as any slash of sky spied between grey granite slabs, their breath on my face a balm, even before the feather touch of their lips on mine.

About the author

Anna is a charity worker who lives in London with her family. In 2022, her piece "Fire Body" won a climate change poetry competition hosted by Hot Poets. She was also one of the winners of the XR Wordsmiths 2023 solarpunk showcase with her story "The Moon Doth Shine As Bright As Day". Her novella "Phengaris" was published in 2025 by Nefarious Bat Press. You can find out more at annaorridge.com or follow her on @anna-orridge.bsky.social.

About the story

I create climate action plans for schools, and it's impossible to miss the huge carbon impact of private car transport. This story is partly about how we could still travel, both spiritually and physically, without doing so much harm. I didn't mean to make this a love story, but somehow it became one, which is a good reminder of how transformation can be unexpected, but so welcome.

The City That Listened

Jade Scardham

The city of Halora drifts high above the planet. Its towers glitter like beacons of glass and every rooftop bristles with wind-catching sails. It is suspended by the soft roar of air currents channelled through vast feather arrays. They are mechanical turbines crafted in imitation of plumage, inspired by the aerodynamics of vanished birds. Walking along the causeways of Halora is like walking in a hymn. The arrays are sacred, because it was feathertech that lifted humanity from the ash when the world was ravaged by collapse.

The wind is faltering, though, and the plumes dimming. The arrays were once vibrant with shifting colour and low harmonic song, but are now growing dull. Halora's engineers speak of 'feather fatigue', but nobody dares speak their full fear aloud. The risk of extinction, again.

Kael is the youngest apprentice in Halora's Aerologic Guild, and his sleeves are always feather-flecked from coaxing moulted vanes back into place. Raised in the shadow of the turbines, Kael services the arrays and listens to them. He believes that they are more than machines. To Kael, the feather arrays breathe, dream, remember. And if they are failing, it is not a mechanical flaw, but a cry for balance that has been lost.

During a solo maintenance round in the Lower Drift, deep beneath the city's core array where the wind doesn't reach, Kael hears something. It has a rhythm that is soft, regular, and alive. He follows it past a corroded vent and through a tunnel nobody's mapped in decades, and finds a hidden chamber sealed by a thin feather lattice.

Inside is a creature. Its wings shimmer with a thousand colours, twitching in time with its breath. It cocks its head and mimics the sound of Kael's heartbeat. It steps towards him. It has nested here, making a weave of wind-bent metal shavings and fragments of discarded chimes, suspended like a cradle in the chamber's highest curve. Kael freezes, awe washing over his initial fear. He doesn't understand what it is, but something in him already responds to it.

Kael returns at dusk, when the winds lull and the supervisors are too tired to track the apprentices. He slips past the lower sensors with a pulse-scrambler hidden in his toolkit just in case. He brings offerings, wind-captured pollen, bits of ribbon, moulted down from a retired array. The hidden chamber is the same as when he left it, a sealed hush of velvet air. The creature waits. It doesn't flee when he enters. It observes him.

As the days pass, Kael documents its feather patterns. They respond to thermal shifts and microvibrations in the air. Its plumes mirror the function of the city's feather-inspired mechanisms, but they are richer, alive and more adaptive. It emits low pulses that ripple through its feathers like soundless music, activating filaments and resonance nodes woven into the walls, forgotten prototypes of early feathertech that were designed to test environmental harmonics. This chamber was once an acoustic lab, abandoned after the city standardized its designs. Kael begins to understand that this creature is a visitor, drawn here by the resonance of the arrays. A sentience from beyond Halora, answering a call the city never meant to make.

One evening, Kael hums an old featherkeeper's lullaby as he checks the lattice weave of the chamber, testing for tension fractures in the strands by listening to the way certain notes echo. The creature hums back with a ripple of harmonics through its chest-quills, in perfect resonance.

Later, it mimics his gestures with delicate preening motions. When he returns to it with a wind-chime made of discarded array fragments, it unfurls its wings and makes a breeze, watching the chimes sway. It seems to prefer his presence when he doesn't speak, but when he sings, its feathers shimmer faintly and change colour, like sun shifting through cloud. Kael begins to suspect that the creature lingers out of curiosity, or perhaps concern. Sometimes it listens to the wind stir the hollow arrays above and a tremor runs through its feathers, a shiver of recognition and confusion as if glimpsing a distorted echo of itself that it cannot understand.

They fall into a rhythm. He brings touch and song. It answers with pulse and pattern. Neither speaks, but there is understanding.

The central wind rotors flicker with a bloom of unexplainable lift. Bursts of clean, sustained energy ripple through the lower feather arrays. The engineers trace the source to the understructure. Kael's mentor, Architect Virel, declares it a breakthrough, a spontaneous evolution, a solution. They plan to send in a diagnostics team with containment gear.

Kael's protests are shot down. The city is dying, they say. If Halora falls, thousands will die. These regenerative principles must be studied, replicated, distributed across the city's failing wings. The feather arrays are tools, after all, and they must be fixed.

Kael makes it to the chamber ahead of them. The creature meets him in the dark, feathers dim. It can feel something is wrong. When he reaches out, it retreats. A soft, strange, heartbreakingly familiar sound rises from its throat. A thrush's call. Then a nightjar. Then a mourning dove. Extinct voices echoing in a place no bird could sing.

Kael knows that if he steps aside, they will take it. They might confine it in a containment dome, take pieces of its feathers for analysis, map its biology until there's nothing left but data and echoes. They will study it until it stops singing. If he defies them, he risks exile, or worse. But

Kael has seen its featherwork pulse when he sings, the way its energy harmonises in response to him, as a partner. Its feathers regenerate through connection and resonance. The city's arrays are failing because they were made to replicate life without understanding it. This creature could renew the arrays with its living song, but not if it's caged.

When the engineers arrive, Kael stands between them and the chamber. They carry heavy tools, cutters, pulse-measurers, containment rigs. Harmless in theory, but more than enough to pacify Kael if he resists. He steps towards them anyway, his voice raw. "You don't understand what it is," he says. They dismiss him. Orders are orders, and whatever's down here has triggered a surge that they can't ignore. They care about the data, the spike in energy, the signs of something powerful. He tries to explain, but their eyes are on the chamber, not on him. An engineer tries to push past him. He shouts, "It's not yours!"

The creature hums a warning from the shadows, sharp with fear. Only then do they pause, unsettled by the unknown sound. Kael seizes the moment. "Let me show you," he says, stepping back but not aside. The engineers continue to hesitate, glancing between their instruments and the shadowed room. One of them mutters about risk. Another tightens his grip on a plasma cutter.

Kael sings a fragment of the first song he shared with the creature, softly and steadily, inviting it forward. It steps into the light, its feathers shimmering and casting motes of colour across the men spread out in front of it. It stands beside Kael, its wings slightly open and plumage gleaming in ripples of soft wind and radiant promise. The engineers say nothing, and nobody moves any closer to it. The creature hums a deeper, rounder note, and the mood in the room starts to shift. Kael looks each of them in the eye. "You're right that this is an opportunity for change, more radical than any we can remember. But we need to answer it honestly, not with fear or greed. It's an invitation to redesign our machines and our thinking. We can become a city that lives in dialogue with a newly discovered form of life, not in exploitation of them. A city that floats because it listens."

The arrays begin to fail. There's a drift in the outer ring, then a slow, sickening tilt in the city's spine. Alarms flare across Halora's heights as wind-catchers stall and the light dims as the feathers shudder to stillness. The council convenes in panic. Evacuation is impossible.

Kael is summoned before them. His file is already open, his insubordination recorded. But desperation softens their arrogance. The creature, they say, must be used, whatever the cost. Kael has one chance. One hour, one final attempt to prove that cooperation can hold the city aloft.

As Halora lists in the air, Kael returns to the chamber. He carries no tools or gear, just his old featherkeeper's cloak, threadbare with age, and a voice hoarse with fear.

He kneels and places his palm on the chamber floor. He sings a lullaby, the same one he first hummed in curiosity, now rendered in devotion. The creature steps forward, wings trembling. It lowers its head to Kael's and exhales a tone into his bones. A resonance builds. Breath to breath, feather to skin.

In a single moment of stillness, the creature unfurls its wings. They are huge, iridescent, impossibly wide. With a motion as gentle as a sigh, it releases a halo of feathers into the air. They don't fall.

They rise, threading themselves into Halora's failing turbines, waking them with pulses of luminous energy. Across the city, dormant feathers stir, shimmer and stretch. The arrays bloom anew, no longer just tech, but extensions of a living covenant. The creature, no longer alone, finds companionship woven in breath and song. Halora lifts, smooth, steady and silent. Flight without cruelty.

In the years that follow, the old protocols are dismantled. The arrays are tended like gardens and new feather-creatures guide their growth in concert with the city's caretakers. Feather-care becomes a sacred practice, part ceremony and part communion. Songs replace schematics. Trust replaces fear. The air itself seems lighter.

Kael refuses promotion. He walks the city's spans and understructures, guiding apprentices in learning to listen. He teaches them to breathe with the wind and hear the language of the creatures who, no longer hidden, begin to choose their companions, pairing with those who respect their rhythms. Kael, once an outlier, becomes a bridge, living proof that coexistence is possible and powerful.

Halora glides through the sky like a feather on the wind. Its towers hum with quiet life. Perches have been built into the highest spires, where feather-creatures nest in radiant clutches. They soar in spirals above the city. When they return, they bring feathers to be shared.

About the author

Jade Scardham is an artist and writer focusing on fantasy, horror and sci-fi. She particularly enjoys writing creepy stories and designing creatures and characters. You can find her on Bluesky: @arcanepixels744.bsky.social.

Echo of the Desert in the Sky

Erin Darrow

Rolling dunes of coral sand stretch on and on, tumbling and swelling in ceaseless cadence. With her face pressed into their surface, coarse sand grains bite into the softness of Sora's cheeks and palms, scratching her skin raw. Her cowl has fallen aside, leaving half her face exposed to the sun's harsh, blistering rays. The pain of the scorched blush will come later, sapping her strength if she survives long enough.

Something tickles her chest, an electric prickle upon her faltering heartbeat. She instinctively reaches beneath her robes to swat it away before she thinks better, that maybe a scorpion's sting or a tarantula's venom would bring swift relief, saving her from this prolonged suffering. Instead, her fingertips brush a feather, scarlet as the sun in a smoke-hazed sky.

One delicate touch and she remembers: the canyons, the climb, the mountain, home. And the reason she must survive —

Her daughter.

Small footprints trailed away from the oasis, past the first towering rock pillar, and into the shadowed canyons where rose-gold sandstone warred with crumbling white chalk for dominance. Sora followed the tracks into the winding maze, soft coral sand yielding to crunching gravel underfoot. Dust lingered in the close air and the blue ribbon twisting above was barely visible in the depths between rock faces so close they nearly kissed. Between these ancient rock walls, the world she knew could have existed eons ago. Time paused, suspended in still life.

Around the next bend, Sora found the little wanderer crouched on her haunches in a rare sunbeam, posed as still as a statue. Even from behind, Sora could imagine the enchanted look on the little girl's face. Wonder drew her here, again and again, in search of sunspots only she could find like a flower bud ready to bloom. Sora waited a few breaths, mirroring the girl's quietude, allowing the serenity to wrap around them, tucking them into its gentle folds.

"Veery," she broke the silence. The whisper brushed into the girl, who followed the sound with her gaze, honey-speckled brown eyes aglow. Her cowl draped forgotten around her neck and delicate curls framed her face, flushed cheeks round with youth.

Shoulders rounded, Veery's lips arced down, and she traced her fingers across the rock, wistfully seeking the lizard's scuttling trail and finding only absence. "He's gone now, Mama! He doesn't like it when we move, you have to stay still as stone or they run away and hide!"

Sora knelt beside her daughter, raised the cowl over her head, and tucked a curl behind her ear. "I know, dearest, but the afternoon is late and the sun is harsh, even here, and you are a human, not a lizard." Heat radiated from Veery. Her forehead blazed like sunbaked rock as Sora kissed her brow. "It's time to go home."

With one last glance at the bare rocks, the girl unfolded herself, took her mother's hand, and followed along through the winding canyon. "I wish I was a lizard," Veery declared fervently, her eyes winking like the tiny jade scales dotting her favorite critter's spine. "Then I could stay in the sun all day and regrow a broken tail like magic!"

"You know magic doesn't work like that. It's only an illusion, it's not real," Sora reasoned. Magic could not fix broken things, a regrettable truth; it wove only lies and tricks, never truly touching reality.

"But the sunbird who lives on the mountaintop" — Veery insisted — "one feather could sprout a forest! Have you ever seen a forest, Mama? Who knows what else it could do!"

Despite the afternoon heat, a shiver prickled Sora's skin and clenched its cold fist around her heart. Who knew what else it could do? Sora knew what her daughter wanted more than to be a lizard, or to watch them scurry and scuttle over rocks all afternoon, more than anything else — to be with her first family again.

But it would never be.

The small child had arrived at the oasis alone, claiming the unbelievable. She had followed snakes across the desert from wherever her home had been. She never said what happened. She did not have to say they had come, what they had done. She did not have to say her family was dead, her home destroyed. Sora knew; they came for everyone eventually. She had wrapped the small, frail child in her arms, nursed her to health with cactus water, passionflower essence, and patience, opening home and heart to her.

"That's just a story, Veery, nothing more."

A seed of false hope would only sow disappointment and despair. Everyone knew the story of the sunbird and the feather that could rejuvenate a land. Many had perished trying to climb the mountain to attain the untouchable myth and the magical feather.

Before her daughter could argue in a storm of indignation and stubborn will, a dust cloud swelled across the horizon, darkening the sky, and billowing toward the palm trees fringing their oasis home.

Sora stiffened at the sight, knowing what came next. They were coming and they would leave none alive.

Grasping Veery tight and shielding her face with her robe, Sora gathered the sweltering heat around the two of them and bent the light a fraction. Enough to make the pair appear as a knotted, withered tree on the edge of sandflats and serpentine canyons. Unworthy of anyone's notice, safe from harm.

The effort tipped the balance of her power and cracked the illusion she had crafted to shield her oasis home. Sora's carefully painted mirage — of an impenetrable sandstone cliff, imposing as a vast canyon, red as the first pulse of blood in the dawn sky — splintered. One fragmentary moment, one tiny flicker, one reaction to save her daughter's life exposed and doomed their home.

They saw the oasis. And they came, with masks shrouding their faces and shielding their lungs from the poison they expelled. They killed all, leaving no trace behind but the bodies. As the last breath escaped the last pair of desperate lungs, they cast their nets over the land and absorbed each water droplet in filigree to take away and spend as they pleased.

Sora watched every death until she collapsed to the ground, her heart fractured shale, blackened dust and decay. Veery clung to her, trembling, head buried in her chest, broken whimpers muffled by her mother's robes.

Palm fronds dangled over the eaves of their huts, waving like a friend greeting her home, and yet, home was no longer. Friends would never wave again. Home was uninhabitable. Uninhabited. Every person who was a thread in a weave knit tight as one, was gone, sucked as dry and dead as the vanished water stolen in the massacre.

It was the way of things ... and it was Sora's fault.

Sprawled on the dunes, dehydration cracks her lips and grit crunches between her teeth. She is a shed snakeskin, life hollowed out, a paper-thin version of herself. Unlike a snake's crisp husk, her pulse flows from heart to limbs and back again.

For now.

If she does not move, she will wither and weather into a million grains of ivory sand, consumed by the dunes. A death only the desert can bring.

Move, she commands herself.

Her fingers tremble, calloused and raw, digging into the yielding surface of the dune, and she slowly crawls to her knees. Coral sand and blue sky bleed together around her in a dizzying pastel swirl. She forces herself to stand, raises her cowl over her head, and slides down the slope.

Climbing the next incline, two steps forward bring her one step back. Clutching the feather dangling from a cord around her neck, she wades onward. A pair of honey-speckled brown eyes sparkle and blink in her memory. They draw her onward, sentinel stars leading her home.

As long as she breathes, she will not surrender. On and on, she trudges, weaving up and down, across the imposing dunes and rippling sand that battles her every step of the way. Sora fights back with everything she has left. For herself, for her daughter, and for whatever scrap of redemption she can find.

At last, the scrubland opens before her, mercifully flat except the stippling of spindly cactus and pale green splotches of woody sagebrush dotting the landscape. In the unblemished cerulean sky above, dark shadows circle on rigid wings. Vultures. They signal death long before she smells the rancid decay. Sora narrows her eyes, searching for signs of life, of them, of any hidden threat to hide from.

On approach, there are no living souls here to challenge or harm her, only corpses. They litter the ground at her feet, their pale linen robes whipping in the wind, flagging surrender. Their eyes are vacant or lidded to the scene, blind to the scavengers who will devour them. One vulture already buries his beak in flesh.

It is the inevitable cycle, the way of things, so she does not disturb the bird, but merely looks away.

In death, there is rebirth, and these dead give her salvation.

Sora's robes flap like wind-billowed wings as she descends on the dead. Her stomach burns and roils up her throat, trying to empty itself, but there is nothing left to lose. As she searches the bodies, she shrouds their faces with colorless cloth. There is not enough time for proper rites and nothing she does now will change their fate. But perhaps she can still change other fates.

She pries a canteen from stiff fingers and swallows the dredges, hot and unsatisfying on her parched lips, but better than nothing. Besides a few delicate dandelions and purple-edged goosefoot sprigs, there is little to eat. Hairy, scaly leaves lodge in her teeth and throat. Gnawing them makes her stomach-ache deepen, eager to fill the growling hollow.

Just beyond the last body, she follows a shallow, dry gulch with feeble steps. A stark rift through crinkled, yellowed rushes and weeds marks where water once foamed and flowed. Beyond the vegetation, mud-cracks crease the ground in a wide circle, ringed by a white band crusting the basin's edge.

Yet another graveyard.

She has seen it before; this devastation mirrors her own home. Sora pays it little heed as she crosses the desiccated pool, the hem of her robe collecting a band of fine dust kicked up by her feet.

She does not dare imagine the relief cool water would give her blistered toes, burnt face, or sandpapered throat. There is no use imagining lost things that cannot be. She could dig in the ground and tear at the roots for the last beads of sweet moisture, but there will be none. Every drop is gone, siphoned and stolen, even from the clustered prickly-pear cacti, shriveled thorns probing against an enemy they cannot fight. Few can, even those who gave their lives trying to protect this place from rampant destruction and from the greed of those who take all and give nothing as they turn a blind eye to the consequences in ignorance or denial.

Reality is harder to swallow than her dry, swelling tongue or a cactus spine piercing her throat. She crawls beneath the shelter of a sprawling sagebrush to rest where cool shade and the woody plant's bittersweet aroma embrace her.

The scent wakes memories of a time long gone when this land was still beautiful: a living, breathing thing, from stems to stars. Before it was sapped of all that made it whole.

Spring grasslands sprouted green and growing into variegated bouquets of cloud-white lily, lilac larkspur, sunshine buttercup, and molten prairie fire dancing in the breeze. Deer and pronghorn waded through waves of flower-studded grass screening their fawns from sight, providing shelter and sustenance. Sheep careened over impossible bluffs and rocky cliffs, defying gravity. Sage sparrows heralded changing seasons, erupting in a trilling choir from spring shrub-tops and flocking together for the frosted fall.

The memories are so real, she can almost hear the gathered male grouse hooting and popping on ancestral leks, their air sacs round and yellow as the rising sun reflected in the hens' discerning eyes. It was a raucous symphony of life, of love, of the land itself.

Now, there are no seasons.

There is only blazing sun-drenched heat and bitter cold nights.

Flowers wilt if they dare to bloom.

Now, all is silent.

The sparrows took their songs on migration never to return.

The last grouse hooted and popped and died long ago.

Lingering without life, the desert corroded into wasteland, stretching ever outward, turning the magnificent, vibrant canvas into a bleached palette, starched and starved.

But life sustains in pockets where people care and cater to the land, tending her with reverence and respect. She rewards them with oases like Sora's home and the graveyard before they were destroyed.

Lying beneath the sagebrush, Sora feels the desolation in her slow pulse and weak limbs, and deeper, an insatiable hunger. As she closes her eyes to rest, her fingers graze the scarlet feather. An impossible last chance to make amends, gifted from sunbird to earth-dweller at the mountaintop, earned through her journey's trials, her persistence, her paltry hope born from a child's belief in a story.

Before sleeping, the last sight she sees is the landscape awash with gold in the dying light, the same shade as the flecks in her daughter's eyes, and the heavens steepled coral and rose, an echo of the desert in the sky.

Starving and thirsty beyond measure, upon waking, she thinks she is hallucinating. Sora knows mirages, how to weave illusions, bending water and heat and spinning light into showing something Else. Something that is not there.

On the cusp of consciousness, she peels open her eyes, peers through dark edges and blurry patterns, and focuses on the strangest thing of all.

In this desolate, barren land, a flock of birds dance and twirl in the branches above her, on the ground beside her. Their tiny feet barely leave impressions in the sand. Feathers tickle her cheek, her hair, her outstretched hand. Their trilling chatter roots her in reality; mirage-magic cannot sew song, only sights. She remains still so they do not spook and squints at the nearest one.

A black-and-white mustache lines his beak so orange it is almost red and a rufous patch bronzes his cheeks. These itinerant finches meander in search of food, rarely staying in one place for long. Inexplicably, they are here now. What is edible in this harrowed place?

Their fluttering feathers uproot something in her heart. Hope. A thin, bare wisp that lifts her up on invisible wings. Not into the sky but back into the world and onto her feet.

The finches soar as one, a fluid flight, feathers in unison, before diving down and swooping above her head. Again and again, they repeat the dance, herding her until she follows, mesmerized.

They arc gracefully overhead while she stumbles and slides over boulders on clumsy, weary feet. They lead her to a shaded ravine and suddenly hush. Too busy feeding to chatter, they pluck ripe blue juniper berries from the branches.

Sora collapses on the roots carving cracks into the sandstone and presses her forehead and palms against the ridged tree bark. Once her hands stop shaking, she crawls forward, following roots over rock like a path guiding her home.

Where the roots disappear underground, blades of grass pierce the sand and tickle her fingers. She digs and digs into the soft grains, and at last, a trickle of dark liquid seeps up. As she digs desperately, a drop becomes a puddle. Dipping down to the water like a bird or a beast, she laps at the liquid, moistening her tongue and easing a fraction of her thirst.

After filling herself with spicy juniper berries and groundwater, she leans her chest against the tree, closes her eyes and whispers, "Thank you." Her raw lips catch on the splintered bark and she welcomes the pain. Where there is pain, there is life. There is still a chance.

Throwing her head back, whorled leaves in a green veil slice the sky above her, and she repeats her thanks to the flock, uttered like a sacred prayer sent to the heavens and the sunbird on high.

The sky is awash with dusty desert rose and buttercup yellow as she takes the final steps of her journey. She returns home with blistered feet and a burnt face, the skin sloughing off. A tent flaps lazily in the wind where the pool once glimmered and whispered secrets to her in its ripples.

Crowned by the finch flock circling overhead, Sora crosses the dusty mud-cracked basin. When she slips beneath the canvas, all she sees are her daughter's honey-speckled brown eyes staring at her in wonder, in joy, in pure love. Her heart bursts and breaks, fierce and full, as she clutches Veery, holding on like she will never let go.

She buries her nose in Veery's curls, inhaling her scent, kissing her cheeks and memorizing her heart's rhythm. Veery squirms under the attention but freezes when she sees the scarlet feather around her mother's neck.

"You did it!" Glory and admiration resound. "I knew you could. We're going to grow a forest!"

"Yes." Her breath catches around the word, all she wants and all she isn't ready to give.

A graying woman stirs beside them and her keen eyes, creased at the corners, detect what Veery does not. A silent question passes from Sora to her own mother, and the woman bows her head in understanding, hiding her moistened eyes from the child.

"Thank you for crossing the dunes to look after Veery," Sora whispers. "I know it wasn't easy."

Her mother gently brushes Sora's unburnt cheek. "I would have climbed the mountain for you if I could. I wish I had been here to stop them." Her words are sheer will and devotion. They permeate Sora like lightning static, enlivening and tenacious, laced with pain.

Unable to trust her voice not to break and split apart at the seams, Sora closes her eyes and leans into her mother's comfort for one breath to gather her courage. One breath is not enough, but she cradles Veery in her arms and murmurs, "Come."

Darkness eclipses the sunset sky. At the center of the dry basin, the lost heart of the oasis, all three kneel. Untying the cord from her neck, Sora holds the scarlet feather aloft. Wrinkled hands produce a spark that bursts to flame and ignites the feather. Flaring red, Sora clutches it until the tongues of heat lick her fingertips and she relinquishes her hold.

The fiery feather floats up into midnight, flickering faint amber until it blinks out of sight.

Three generations link hands, staring after it, hope sent on high.

In response, a pinprick of light flares far beyond. It shimmers across the silver-speckled heavens and burns a fiery scarlet streak like a shooting star blazing bright as the sun. A keening screech reverberates in their bones.

The sunbird's flight.

In its wake, ashes flutter toward the earth like raindrops. The fire-dust mottles the pastel earth, blanketing the coral sand, and the night-black sky seems to deepen above the bleached land.

The sunbird's ashes are not the smoky debris of a far-flung forest set aflame come to choke creatures and plants, casting the land in an eerie, sickly hue, dousing it in permanent twilight at midday. It is not the putrid, heavy smog that clings to deep valleys and stubbornly refuses to surrender, even to the most persistent rain. It is not the sharp, sudden storm of the earth's inner body belching and spewing a destructive tide of lava, the outburst of a normally quiet thing.

It is replenishing ash-fall that will nourish brittle earth and nurture new growth, one of life and light and hope. Suffused with the sunbird's magic, this land will grow green, wild, and bountiful once more.

A soft, misty rainfall follows. Droplets gather on Sora's eyelashes like glistening dew on leaves and mingle with her tears, dampening and soothing her sun-scorched face.

"Why are you crying?" Veery touches her mother's salt-streaked cheeks.

"I did not save this place for myself. I did it for you and all those who come after you." She presses their foreheads together as a splinter pierces her heart and tears fall, unrestrained. "Listen to your grandmother, learn the mirage magic. Tend the land and keep this place safe as I tried to do. And remember, Veery, I love you more than anything."

She traded a village for her daughter's life, crossed the desert and climbed the mountain, met the sunbird, and nearly died for Veery and her future. She would give everything, and more, for the child she holds tight in her arms, and there is a price to pay. She must let go.

A wondrous lightness overcomes her as though she is a feather drifting away on a breeze.

And she is, or will be soon …

Radiant, born of solar flares, the sunbird has a single fireflight before they burn out. A new sunbird must fly where the mountain meets the sky. It is the way of things.

A ripple runs across her shoulders and twinges down her spine like a thousand beaks pecking her skin. Sora flinches and stretches her arms out to ease the pain. A fresh breeze flutters her robes and the fringes of pale linen blush like the sunrise sky deepening to crimson. She collapses upon the dusty earth and rises anew, flame-feathered and light-limbed.

At dawn, a new sunbird takes her fledgling flight on wings of coral-stippled scarlet, an echo of the desert in the sky.

"Echo of the Desert in the Sky" originally appeared in *All Worlds Wayfarer* in March 2023.

About the author

Erin Darrow writes fantasy and science fiction inspired by nature, ecology, myths, and fairy tales. When not writing, reading or getting lost in imagination, she wanders the woods, watches birds, cuddles cats, and takes too many nature photos. After many migrations across continents and oceans, she has found a nest to call home in Aotearoa New Zealand. Find Erin online at www.erindarrow.com.

About the story

The story was inspired by a future fantastical Oregon high desert and sagebrush steppe. It delves into my fears of future water wars and my grief over ecological loss and the extinction of beautiful living things. In it, I explore a question: what if older generations were willing to sacrifice for a better, more beautiful future for youth and those yet to come?

About hope

There are no magic sunbird feathers to heal the many harms we've done to the planet or ourselves, but there are so many bright spots of hope: in rewilding and restoration efforts, in conservation scientists and wildlife rehabilitators, in backyard native gardens and the species who have been brought back from the brink against all odds. At the heart of each of these bright spots is a human (or humans) full of hope, who care, who cultivate, who create change for the better.

What We Had Left

Gabrielle Contelmo

I took the stairs. I didn't want to risk the elevator in case the grid failed.

I jumped down the last three steps to the fifth-floor landing, braids slapping sharply against my upper back, and used my momentum to shove open the heavy fire door. It was probably stupid to stop on every floor. I should have been fleeing like the rest of the city. My fist stung from pounding on so many apartment doors.

"Anyone here?" I shouted again.

Maybe it was a waste of precious time. But no one had bothered to check for me, which was why I was still here, hours too late.

The fifth floor was empty, just like the three above.

The fourth floor had the same dingy carpet as the others, brown with unspeakable stains and years of street grime. The same flimsy doors with their tarnished brass numbers, all locked up tight behind inhabitants who would never come back.

Except.

The door at the end opened before I could knock. I stood, fist raised, face to face with a woman about my height, whose reddened eyelids turned her blue irises electric.

"What are you still doing here?" I demanded.

"Have you seen the sky?" she asked. Her voice was hoarse. "That's all they're playing on the news, the live feed of the fucking sky, like we can't just look out the window. They even have a helpful countdown." She tipped her head back and laughed, a high-pitched ululation that made the hair on my arms stand up.

She began to take gasping breaths between each keening laugh, and when she faced me again, she was crying.

"Let's go," I said.

"Can't." Her face twisted as she gestured to the cast on her left foot. "No chance of me outrunning it."

I bared my teeth in what I hoped was a grin. "Who said anything about running? There's a gorgeous little Suzuki scooter in the basement with my name on it."

She stepped out of the apartment, hand already clutching the straps of a sunflower-yellow backpack that bulged at the seams, same as the overstuffed denim bag digging into my shoulders.

"It won't be there. Someone will have taken it by now," she said, following me down the hall.

"Not my baby."

We took the stairs slower, on account of her foot.

"My friend was supposed to come get me," she said, leaning on the handrail. "He has a car. I guess he couldn't make it because of the traffic." At the landing, she glanced out the window. Outside, horns brayed ineffectively against the gridlock.

"Keep going," I said. I pushed through the third-floor fire door. I didn't know what I'd do if I found someone else. My scooter could only hold two.

"What about you?" she asked, when we met up on the second-floor landing. She could do one flight in about the same amount of time it took me to run down the hall and bang on all the doors.

"Night shift," I said. "Ear plugs and blackout curtains. Everyone else learned about it on the news. I figured it out when I called into work. Listened to the end of the world on the Waffle House voicemail message." I laughed at the absurdity.

The corner of her mouth twitched up a millimeter and I darted down the second-floor hallway.

"What's the deal with the foot?" I asked when we converged again.

"My ankle. The cast comes off in two weeks. Maybe less. I can still be useful!" she said, turning those electric eyes on me.

I frowned. "I'm taking you regardless. I meant how'd it happen?"

"Oh. I tripped down the stairs at work. Some luck, huh?" she called after me as I ran to check the first floor.

The old sodium lights turned the basement into a monochrome of sickly oranges limned in stark black shadows.

"It won't still be here," she whispered.

The air, thick with the khaki smell of dust, muffled the scrape of our feet on damp concrete.

"She'll be here." Even as I said it, a nugget of unease grew in my belly. While I slept the day away, people had raced towards their cars, their motorcycles, children's bicycles. We all knew the truth: we didn't stand a chance once the carbon dioxide reached critical levels. Not unless we escaped the city and got away from the coast. Maybe not even then.

My heart sat heavy on my tongue when I pulled back the corrugated metal door tucked behind the old boiler.

A frisson across my skin at the sight. A gust of relief. I stood back and gestured grandly. "This," I said, "is Suzy."

Black as an oil slick, except for a few scuffs that told stories of tussles with bike couriers and the ill-timed openings of car doors.

A hiccup behind me. She was crying again, with relief or grief, I couldn't tell.

I tried a joke. "Let's blow this popsicle stand."

She let out a wet chuckle and wiped her knuckles under her eyes. Mascara smeared on her cheeks.

I unlocked the garage doors and poked my head into the alley. If we'd been in a movie, old newspapers would have blown by in an ominous wind. But this was reality and a dank mugginess hung over the city, an unseasonable warmth that clung to the skin. With every breath, a sour, acidic taste collected at the back of my tongue, signaling what was to come.

From the street, the honking seemed more subdued, like the people stuck in the cars knew they'd lost their chance. It was too late for them to make it on foot.

I wheeled the bike out. No point in locking the garage doors. I barely squeezed my bulging backpack into the storage compartment beneath the seat. I had to sit on it to get it to latch. The sharp click, like a mousetrap snapping shut, reminded me of everything I couldn't take. My grandparents' photo albums, generations of history distilled into two or four photographs torn from a random page. My round-bellied cardinal stuffie, still propped against my pillow upstairs, a reminder of a time when birds were as common as stars. But we'd accidentally killed most of the real birds. And the stars had long since disappeared behind the ever-thickening atmosphere.

I blinked back tears. For two decades, I'd been able to bury my face in Rusty's faded cloth feathers after a bad day. He'd comforted me through disappointing report cards, my parents' divorce, bad breakups. Things that had seemed like the end of the world at the time.

I sniffled. I should have found a way to bring him.

When my companion swung her leg over the seat behind me, her cast thunked against the side of the bike. I felt her wince. Her fingers fit neatly between my ribs, tightening as though we were already going sixty. The pinch of her grip grounded me.

Suzy turned on with a guttural rumble. The tank was three-quarters full. It would get us far enough from the coast, for now.

"Hold on," I said. My hands were clammy around the rubber grips.

We roared out of the alley. Drivers shouted as we blew past their stationary cars. I bumped up over the curb to avoid the hands reaching from rolled-down windows. I was the last bike left in the city. I couldn't take them all.

The new rail trail, the city council's eleventh-hour attempt at a greener future, was empty of power walkers, cyclists, overeager dogs. It would get us out faster than the congested highway. Beneath a sparse green canopy, I opened the throttle. Our speed turned the stagnant air into a wind that felt almost cool against my skin.

"I'm Audrey!" I shouted backwards.

Her hands tightened around my waist as she leaned forward, nudging her mouth against my ear. "Tara! Nice to meet you!"

We escaped the city by following the rail trail. At first, it was empty; most people were in their cars or sardined on public buses bristling with unlucky souls that clung to bumpers and windows. We caught up to the first cyclists within the hour. They pedaled sloppily, already depleted, with miles to go.

Suzy could go where cars couldn't. When we had to return to the roads, we snaked through gaps between bumpers. Some people bashed their dashboards and hurled curses across the shimmering pavement, as though it mattered that I was breaking the law. Children pointed at us from behind window-cling rainbows and dancing bears and I wondered why their parents didn't take them out and run, run, as fast as their little legs could go, towards the hills. Then I remembered that they'd never make it in time. About half the cars were empty, doors open, motors running, radio stations all tuned to the same broadcast: the countdown that ticked ever lower, and the repeated message that there might be pockets of safety inland.

I left the highway as soon as I could, taking back roads west, always west, with Tara shouting directions from her phone, which still had service. We only stopped once, at a rural gas station, for as long as it took Tara to fill Suzy's tiny tank. I used the time to do a supermarket sweep of the dingy store, stuffing two plastic bags full of whatever food and supplies looked the most useful. I hung the bags from Suzy's handlebars.

As we wound higher into the mountains, we caught glimpses of the highway below, gridlocked with Matchbox cars. I tried not to think of the hundreds of thousands of people who lived in the city. How many down there had sat on the sticky vinyl barstools in my Waffle House and listened to the sizzle and clatter of the kitchen, the scraping of forks on ceramic plates, the chatter of the waitresses? How many had I fed with piles of hash browns and off-brand Bac'n and country grits?

I tried not to think of my mom and stepdad visiting my aunt in Florida, one of the first places hit, where the roads bottlenecked and there was nothing west but the Gulf of Mexico. I tried not to think of the endless *Not in Service* message when I tried to call.

Tears threatened, turning the vacant mountain road into a blur of green trees, a smear of blue between their leaves. I eased Suzy over the edge of the pavement and onto the grass. The tiny drop made my stomach jolt, as though expecting a long fall. As I put my feet down on earth tangled with roots and rocks, Tara made a questioning noise over the thrum of the engine, or maybe I imagined it.

"Need a sec," I called.

I cut the engine and the sudden silence left my ears ringing, seeking noise where there was none. I still wasn't used to the absence of birdsong, though it had been years since the population dropped to 'critically endangered'. Even the trees were quiet, no wind to stir their leaves.

Compared to the mayhem of the city we'd escaped, this eerie calm made my heart race.

Tara's hands left my waist. The glowing heat of her disappeared from behind me.

My palms hummed with the memory of Suzy's rumble. So did my legs when I dismounted and walked the bike into the cover of the trees. Only the humming, the shaking, didn't get better. I leaned Suzy against a shaggy trunk, managed two more steps, and sank to my knees. My heart battered against my breastbone. Inside, I was a melee of starlings whose internal compass had been ripped away.

We still had to get farther inland, but I couldn't catch my breath.

Florida would have been hit early this morning. Had my mom been drinking her coffee on Aunt Gretchen's patio, enjoying the peaceful dawn when the carbon dioxide rose from the oceans? Or would she have checked the news first? Had she and Gretchen and my stepdad spent their last hours trapped on a gridlocked highway like the one we'd just left behind?

I wished all over that I'd brought Rusty. When I was really little, Mom would make him stroke those fleecy feathers over my forehead and whisper that it was all going to be okay. A razor-edged *hah!* wrenched itself from my throat. Nothing was going to be okay anymore.

Twigs dug into my bare knees, tiny, sharp hurts that barely registered beneath the frenzy inside. I gasped and gasped. There wasn't enough oxygen in the air. Was it already happening? Had I killed us both by stopping too soon?

A bar of warmth across my clavicle; Tara's arms wrapped around me, keeping the pieces of me from shattering in the dappled sunlight.

"It's okay," she murmured, even though we both knew it wasn't.

She rocked me as I wept, her cheek against the crown of my head like we'd known each other for ages. When I was through, she helped me up, her skin pale against the deep brown of mine. She gave me a smile without any mirth, but full of understanding and I knew she'd experienced the same shattering back in her apartment with no one to hold her through it.

"I think there's an overlook through here," she said.

We left Suzy and pushed through the bushes. A stray branch scraped my arm, just beneath the sleeve of the Waffle House T-shirt I'd slept in. I hissed and pinched the flesh of my triceps, dragging it forward until I could see the bright red line beading with blood.

When Tara cried out, my heart stuttered. I darted through the brush and stopped short. Speckled gray stones jutted from the hilltop like a row of ragged teeth. Beyond that, the hill dropped away into a cliff. Beyond *that*, the horizon was a wall of viscous, shimmering air reaching up into the towering clouds. Like a desert mirage, but horribly real. Mirrorlike glints reflected back at us, obscuring the coastline.

The city I'd grown up in was beyond help. So was anyone who hadn't made it out.

My hand fumbled for Tara's, sweaty fingers linking, clinging.

"Is this how the dinosaurs felt?" I said, half-dazed and still hollow from my cry. "Seeing that asteroid in the sky, unable to do anything but watch it come?"

"No," Tara said.

I looked at her, surprised at the conviction in her voice.

Her hair shone copper in the sun. Her left eye, pierced by the light, was a clear, bottomless pool of cerulean. Her right eye, in the shadow of her face, held flecks of midnight blue.

"One second, life was ... normal," she said. "Blue sky. Nice June day, lilies in bloom. Half a second later, it was already over. Artists paint pictures of what it might have looked like, the specter of the asteroid like an extra moon on the horizon. Sometimes they make it a comet. Ghostly and romantic and so bright you could see it during the day. Maybe it's supposed to make us feel better. If you see it coming, there's a chance of escape.

"Most people, average people, they don't understand the magnitude of the impact. It's hard to wrap your mind around an object so large that when the near end hits the ground, the far end is still above the clouds. How do you comprehend a force that releases more power than ten billion atomic bombs? Something that triggers earthquakes so powerful they make the Richter scale look like a joke? Tsunami waves over a mile high? The asteroid turned rock into liquid. It punched a hole into the atmosphere, bringing the vacuum of space to the surface of the earth. Not that the dinosaurs noticed." She shook her head. "Anything in the vicinity was incinerated instantly."

I was frozen, pinned beneath her penetrating gaze. My breath was caught in the vise of my throat.

She turned, studying the roiling atmosphere in the distance. "No, the dinosaurs never saw it coming. But us? We watched this creep closer for generations."

I'd known it, too. They were already talking about species loss when I was in elementary school. I saw my last bird on my sixteenth birthday. By the time I was in my early twenties, politicians on all sides were talking about the measures we'd need to take if we wanted to survive.

They took measures, all right. Whatever they'd done to the atmosphere hadn't worked. And what they'd done to the oceans ... Well, I was looking at the result. Earlier today, Earth's largest carbon sink had suddenly started releasing all the carbon dioxide stored for millennia in the abyssal deep. The millions of people who had lived, as of this morning, along the equator had been our canaries in the not-so-proverbial coalmine.

I couldn't stomach the sight of the shimmering, mirrored air anymore. It would have engulfed both coasts by then. It seemed closer already.

When we were back on Suzy, cruising westward, I called to Tara, "How do you know that? About the dinosaurs?" It was easier to talk to her without those eyes skewering me.

"I'm a paleoecologist post-doc at the university," Tara shouted back. "Or ... I was."

I picked at the scab on my arm, a relic of that first day. It wouldn't scar or anything, though I felt like it should. As a memento.

Rain pattered into the springy, russet pine needles of the clearing. The ground humped a little in the center, allowing the water to drain, one of the better campsites we'd found. Tara set up the tent in the ongoing drizzle while I foraged for dinner in the cardboard boxes we'd lashed to the rusting trailer.

The trailer was a relic of the second day, found behind a gas station and jury-rigged to the back of Suzy. We had a routine now. And supplies, thanks to the trailer.

I lifted one of our scavenged gas jugs, testing. It came up quick, light and hollow, the textured plastic rough against my fingertips. The next one was just as weightless, as though it hadn't gotten the memo about gravity. The other two were reassuringly heavy. We could travel farther now, but the gas stations would run out soon. Tomorrow?

The next day? No way to tell. We'd have to leave Suzy behind eventually.

I glanced at Tara. She limped around the tent in a billowing, highlighter-pink raincoat. Her cast couldn't come off for another week. She still couldn't walk very far or very fast.

It was a delicate balance, our route. Inland and northward in a series of steps, keeping away from the highways where the other survivors clustered. The gas stations there must have been empty days ago. Back roads had more reliable supplies, but they ate up our gas and our time and we still had a long way to go to reach the middle of the continent. I didn't know where we'd end up, but I always knew our direction: as far from the oceans as we could get.

The heels of my palms fit neatly within the caverns of my eye sockets. I could smell myself, the film of sweat and body oils not even the rain could wash off.

"Everything okay?" Tara called.

I dropped my hands. She stood holding the edge of the rain fly, pale skin washed in shades of blue in the early twilight, a furrow between delicate eyebrows.

"Yeah!" I said, too loud. "A little tired is all."

Tara finished tying down the rain fly and limped to one of the camping chairs beneath the awning. As she lowered herself to the canvas chair, she turned her face away, trying to hide her wince. I rummaged through the saturated boxes one more time.

"For your fine dining experience tonight, may I present: chickpea puffs, stale trail mix, and one very brown banana." I tossed the banana to her.

She bobbled it and caught it with both hands. She pointed it at me like a gun. "We need to find a grocery store tomorrow."

"Yeah, yeah."

I'd trade a whole tank of gas for one homecooked meal, made with real ingredients, but I didn't like to stop in towns for too long. Apocalypse movies had made me afraid of meeting other people. I didn't want to think that the same people who'd groaned around mouthfuls of my hash browns, who had shouted coffee-scented compliments through the service window, had become my enemy while I wasn't looking.

Wordlessly, I pressed an Advil into Tara's clammy palm. Her fingers closed around mine.

After dinner, she said, "Come here."

I sat on a dryish patch between her feet.

"Give me your hand."

I twisted and laid my left hand on her thigh. From somewhere inside that ridiculous pink raincoat, she unearthed a red Sharpie. She flipped my hand over and cupped it gently in her own. The felt tip of the Sharpie tickled over my skin.

"The End-Cretaceous extinction event wasn't even the worst," she said, like it was a normal bedtime story. It was, for us.

"No?" My shoulder brushed the inside of her bony knee.

"No. The worst was the End-Permian Mass Extinction." Tara hunched over her drawing. "That was the era before the dinosaurs became dominant. Also known as 'the Great Dying'. It killed roughly ninety percent of all species."

"Why don't we learn about that one?" I asked, eyes closed. Her hand was warm and damp with humidity.

The Sharpie paused. "Dinosaurs are sexy. So is death by asteroid. It's an exotic fantasy for kids to reenact with their plastic dinosaur figures. People don't care as much about mollusks and sea sponges and natural disasters that might someday kill them too."

I let my head fall to her thigh and breathed in. She always smelled of pine, like the forests that surrounded us. "So, what happened?"

"Our best guess is that massive volcanic eruptions released sulfur dioxide and carbon dioxide into the air. The oceans became anoxic — lost their oxygen — and acidic. The carbon dioxide in the atmosphere rose from four hundred parts per million to over twenty-five hundred. Can you imagine that?"

I didn't want to imagine, but I could. Our carbon dioxide levels had already been well over five hundred. As of five days ago, they would have skyrocketed. The atmosphere was a dank exhale on my skin. Heavy rainclouds hung above the treetops.

Tara released my hand and capped the Sharpie with a snap. "There. A bit of Rusty to carry with you."

I looked down. A wispy feather in red curved along my lifeline, the same color as Rusty's feathers. A lump rose in my throat. The ink on my palm was already smudged and faded in the sodden, breathless air, a sad facsimile of the real thing.

I gave Tara a watery smile anyway and curled my fingers around it, protecting the last bit of color before it disappeared.

At our feet, the body of a giant, leggy bird. Head thrown back, wings spread, it lay splayed on sand the color of French toast crumbs scattered on a Formica counter. Clear water lapped at the tip of one wing. Rain pocked the sand around it, a million tiny impact craters.

The stream rushed over a tumble of boulders, edges shaped and smoothed by ancient glaciers. The steady, relentless rain filled the forest with the sound of static, like the white noise of the TV turned to the input channel.

A Great Blue Heron; I finally remembered the name. I stared down at the heron's thin, water-logged body. My heart kept somersaulting in my chest. The heron was the first bird I'd seen in a decade. It was half a miracle it had survived this long.

Flies buzzed around its milky eye, aimed blindly at the churning clouds above. Had it died of natural causes? Or was the atmosphere already toxic here?

In the last few weeks, Tara had disabused me of the notion that extinctions were sudden. With the exception of the dinosaurs and their sexy asteroid, mass extinctions crept along, like grains of sand falling through an hourglass, barely noticeable until it was too late. Ours had started over sixty thousand years ago when we first wandered out of Africa.

Tara crouched, soles crunching on the rough shore, and reached for a long gray feather that had come loose.

The heron reminded me of the picture of the archaeopteryx fossil she'd shown me — long, graceful neck in an unnatural position, wings outstretched as though to escape the end. Not quite a dinosaur, not quite a bird. The past and the future.

Same as us. Were we primates or were we gods?

Neither?

Both?

With its tearing teeth and long, killing claw, I'd pictured the archaeopteryx like a feathered version of the terrifying raptors in *Jurassic Park* — intrepid, inviolable — but it was surprisingly small. The size of a magpie. Those fragile bones trapped beneath layers of stone were as fine as toothpicks.

Tara held up the feather for me to see. It was as long as her forearm. She twirled it between her fingers. The tendons on the back of her hand moved beneath the thinnest layer of skin. The knob of her wrist a mirror of her delicate ankle bones. They stuck out beneath the soaked hem of her jeans, one still paler than the other, although I had excavated her from the plaster cast weeks ago.

"Beautiful," I told her.

Her electric eyes creased at the corners.

Above the rain's static, the faintest slurp of wet leaves. On the opposite bank, a figure froze. The stranger was a man, middle-aged, brown-skinned, the hood of his navy rain slicker pulled low over his forehead.

I immediately hated him in a way I'd never hated anyone before. In the remote woods, looking as startled as we were to find someone else by the stream, he shattered the fragile illusion of our solitary safety.

My heart thrummed in the hollow of my throat. I took a step towards Tara, who was still crouched, holding the long pinion. I'd fight to protect her, if I had to.

Awkwardly, the stranger raised his hand and waved. Our arms rose in unison and we waved back, a cultural response woven into our reflexes.

Like that, he became human. His rain slicker hung too loose on his frame. Beneath the hood, his glasses were spattered with water. If he'd come to my counter for a warm meal, I'd have snuck an extra helping of home fries onto his plate. A tiny stuffed bear peered out from his pocket, maybe belonging to a child who would order the Chik'n tenders and dip them into a sea of ketchup. The glint of a wedding band on his upright hand and suddenly he had a spouse who'd arrive late, stooping to kiss him before sliding onto the stool on the other side of their kid.

"We, uh. There's a group of us back there." He gestured towards the trees over his shoulder. "If you need help. Or company."

Tara and I looked at each other and held a silent conversation.

She stood up, tucking the feather into her pink coat. "We'd like that."

I washed my hands in the bucket outside, trying to rub the smell of wild garlic from my skin. At my side, Brittany complained good-naturedly about the aches in her back as she scrubbed at the dirt under her fingernails.

She dried her hands as best she could on the damp towel that hung on the hook above the bucket and nudged my shoulder. "See you in there."

I wiped my hands more slowly, nodding to the hooded figures heading towards the community building.

"Smells good, Audrey!" someone called.

Today's potato-garlic pancakes weren't so different from the hash browns I used to make. A week after we finished construction on the community building, someone had hung a roughly carved wooden sign that said 'Waffle House' above my kitchen area. It had made me laugh, then cry.

Robert waved awkwardly as he approached, the same way he had those months ago on the banks of an unnamed stream in the Canadian wilderness. "You coming to dinner?"

Linnet, his daughter, galloped up in a flower print rain suit and hugged me around the knees.

I pressed a kiss to her damp, curly head. "I'll be right there. There's something I have to do first."

Robert waved again and made his way into the community building, whose windows glowed with firelight and laughter.

I went to the rock tumble at the edge of our little village and looked up. Rain misted my skin. Scraps of ghostly clouds that seemed close enough to touch scudded above the treetops. Far beyond, way up in the atmosphere, a blanket of gray enshrouded the earth.

The air was humid and warm as a breath on my cheek. We would not have a winter this year, or any other year for a long time.

I felt her approach more than heard her. In front of my face, thumb and forefinger appeared, pinched around the shaft of a pale red cardinal feather. Rusty's memory made real. When I accepted it, my fingers brushed lightly against hers.

Tara's hand fit into mine, two strands of DNA entwining. She tipped her head back and looked up into the mist. Our nightly ritual, first begun when we were still strangers.

I leaned into the warmth of her, smelled the sweat in her hair and the resinous scent of pine shavings that lingered around her, and stared into the nubilous sky.

There have been five major mass extinctions in Earth's history. Each event cleared the board for other species to rise and try their hand at dominance. The Great Dying led to the dinosaurs we're so fond of. And the unmaking of the dinosaurs led to the ascendance of the mammals. Us.

We're living through the age of the sixth mass extinction. It won't be the last.

Over the next few thousand years, the atmosphere will thicken with carbon dioxide. The oceans will rise and go anoxic again, like they have countless times before. I don't know how long it will take. Most likely, Tara, me, our growing tribe, will live out our natural lifespans before the air turns too toxic to breathe. Maybe future generations will survive, somehow.

It's happened before. The dinosaurs lived on as birds.

I don't know what will happen, only that after this, Tara and I will go to the community house, where it will be warm and dry. With our family, we'll share a meal and stories of what life was once like and what it could be. Later, in our tent, I will add the feather to the vase next to my pillow. And then Tara and I will zip ourselves into our joined sleeping bags and I'll press my nose to the nape of her neck and inhale the pine scent that perfumes her.

Above, a glint between the clouds, a point of light so faint I might be imagining it.

Somewhere in the forest, an owl hoots.

About the author

Gabrielle Contelmo spends her time writing short stories, which often feature monsters with a twist, and character-driven romance novels, which always feature kissing. Her work has appeared or is forthcoming in *What Lurks: A Cryptid Anthology, 3Elements Literary Review, NECKSNAP,* and *Grim & Gilded,* among others. She has been nominated for a Pushcart Prize. Learn more about her work at gabriellecontelmo.com.

About hope

I hope you allow yourself to be open to small moments of joy — a found feather, a stranger's smile, the sound of rain in the leaves — even on the darkest or most mundane of days.

Blood Feathers

S. J. Fry

So, in the end they only found her jacket. No trace anywhere, except there down in the ravine, washed downstream just beyond the overpass at Monk Street. It was this oversized canvas field coat, the sleeves covered in weird, faded doodles, random shapes and optical illusions. It was all pockets and zippers and one or two sizes too big for a girl — for a young woman, I should say — but anyone who knew her even in passing recognized it, knew it belonged to her. To Angelica 'The Ten' Paloma.

Everyone at school, freshmen to faculty, knew her by the jacket. She was your standard-issue high-school senior — brown hair, brown eyes, no charisma — but she lived in that jacket. I mean, it was high school, so everybody was hiding their true selves behind clothes, status, versions of the people they thought they wanted to be. But it was nakedly obvious with The Ten that she was using this thing to protect herself, hide herself, sometimes literally, scrunching herself down into a blob of folds and pockets, drawing on the sleeves in the back row of class, at lunch, at work, at church, inside, outside. Allegedly she slept and showered in it. She wore it like armor, like a force field. Or maybe it was a kind of camouflage. Like if she put it on and held really still, the rest of the world would walk by, oblivious. Of course they didn't, because again, it was high school, and the only way people knew how to be was cruel.

There was lots of name-calling, sure — bag lady, trog, wrist cutter, Jacket Onassis — the chaff we all toss out when it seems like there's somebody else we can look down our noses on. But that was mostly transient, casual, bearable. That was the purpose of the jacket, right? To prevent the metaphorical barbs from causing physical pain. But of course something eventually made it through, managed to cut its way to her core and to hook itself onto her identity. Her nickname: The Ten. It started at the beginning of that last year. It might have even been the first day of school. She was walking through the cafeteria, stooping down into her jacket to guard against the echoing din, the crush of bodies, and had the bad luck to walk past a group of guys — boys — who were overtly discussing the physical fitness of every girl who passed their table, and loudly assigning them numerical values. She passed by and one of them, doesn't matter who, said, "Well, I'd have to assume ten out of ten."

And it wasn't that the joke itself was funny or particularly hurtful, because it wasn't, or even that it made a lot of sense, which it didn't. It wasn't that the rest of the group snorted water out their noses. It wasn't the chorus of agreement that, yes, what could you do but assume so. It wasn't the way people started calling her 'The Ten' to her face. It wasn't the way people called her 'The Ten' in conversation when they didn't realize she could hear them. It wasn't the way it became her name to people who didn't know the original joke, to people who didn't know her actual name.

It was the way it wouldn't have mattered even a little bit, a stupid comment from a stupid asshole, if she had been in other circumstances. It was that it pointed a spotlight at her and got everybody to speculate about what was underneath the jacket. It was that it made her afraid. Because of course there was something underneath the jacket, wasn't there? Something she was hiding.

There wasn't anybody who might have cared to pay attention, but if there had been, it would have been obvious that The Ten had a secret. The way her hands would disappear into her coat sleeves, and she would fiddle with something inside while keeping her face stony calm. The way she was uncomfortable leaning back in chairs or gave up carrying her backpack over her shoulder. The notes she forged from her mother that excused her from gym or drama or anything that might require her to enter a changing room. The little grimy, gray tufts that sometimes drifted out of her pockets.

It started out with these little points on her arms that came in almost like eczema, pushing up through her skin in angry red welts on her forearms, running in a wrist-to-wrist pattern across her back. Skin-care routines didn't help, creams and wraps and such, and then shaving them off didn't help either. They just grew back. The stems came in fine and sharp and painful as they rubbed against her clothes and ruptured her skin, marbling her undershirts with bloodstains. Eventually, The Ten was to a point where she was digging them out with her fingertips as soon as they broke the skin, or I guess as soon as she clawed her skin open enough to get at them. Her move, sitting in the back row of whatever classroom, was that she would sketch on her jacket with one hand, her nonsense loops and spiral patterns, thrusting the other hand into the opposite sleeve to dig at an emerging point, or twisting herself around inside the depths of the jacket so she could pluck at the ones on her back. The grinding of pencil lead on a canvas sleeve masked the sounds of fingernails scratching at skin, the sound of keratin pins popping free from flesh. Every now and then, she'd miss one, usually on her shoulder blades where she couldn't reach until it was too late, and the shaft would emerge far enough that barbules would develop and unfurl. It wasn't necessarily worse; it might have actually been easier, less painful, but it was unquestionably mortifying — in a cold-shiver kind of way — to pluck a fully formed feather from her own body.

Worse, though, worse than the raw skin, and the sharp pains, and her revolting body, was the prospect of discovery. Every new pinpoint was a razor-fine reminder of what she was. She had resigned herself to a life as the freak in a jacket, but the thought of the life as the freak with the feathers ... well, it kept her scratching and plucking and hiding and hiding and hiding.

Your average person might, finding themselves in dire and wild circumstances, turn to their family for help. But The Ten knew better, and if you'd met her mom, you'd know she was right. Mrs. Paloma — 'Mrs.' though she'd never been married — had a convert's zeal for the church, a problem's zeal for clear liquors, and a fierce standard against which she judged all other people. She was like if somebody had stretched The Ten out, cleaned her up, and sharpened her to a stiletto point. She was the kind of woman who was honor-bound to let a body know the second they turned from righteousness to deviance. She drove the other church ladies crazy, because she always had a Bible verse or something to back her up when she talked about, like, how pride is a sin so actually don't show off pictures of your daughter's enormous engagement ring, Nancy. The kind of person who when she spoke up, she was never quite wrong, but she was never quite kind either. Unless she was too deep in the bottle, and then she chucked decorum in the gutter. Like, she was the one who threw rocks at Mike McElroy that time he dyed his hair purple.

So of course, you're wondering now what kind of pressure a person like that brings down on The Ten. You're questioning what unpleasant secrets lurked in their home life, and, like the rest of us, not liking any of the possible answers.

The Ten was Mrs. Paloma's beautiful golden child. She could do no wrong, you couldn't even suggest something was off with her, how dare you speak that way about her, etc. And like I said, she, Mrs. Paloma, was on the wrong side of some church ladies, so you know if there was true gossip to be had it would've been had everywhere. But The Ten never acted out like a spoiled kid, instead always stayed buttoned-up, and even keeled, and hidden away, and picking her secrets out of her arm. The way you do when you don't feel entirely safe at home. Because would you want to be the person who told a wild animal that her perfect child was a freak of nature? And so imagine: the rigid, savage shape of her mother looming at home, and the rest of the world openly speculating about what she might be hiding. The Ten must have been in a deeply desperate corner, because she reached out for help. To, of all people, Darren Cobb.

If you haven't heard the full story, or at least the prevailing version, the long and short of it is: Darren grew up here, hated it here, left, and came back. He struck out to work with animals, roam the world and be a wild animal vet or something, and then got caught selling horse tranquilizers or something out the back door of a prestigious veterinary school, and now he's back here because, where else would he be? He's far and away the surliest person I've ever met, angry at the world for ending up back where he started. Too angry to be able to do anything about it. Instead living his cranky little hermit life out in his trailer on the edge of the woods, scraping by doing cheap, off-book veterinary services for farmers and by being good at poker. A forest druid who listens to screamo and smokes a pack a day.

I figure it was his overt unapproachableness that drew The Ten to him. She recognized in him the life she thought she was destined for: far removed from society, trying not to fall off the edge of the world. She recognized the use of the same high-powered social defenses and decided that meant he was safe. She recognized herself in the stories that got told about him — such a shame, can you believe what happened, don't go near him — and decided that if she was going to gamble on anybody, he was somehow the safest bet. She showed up at Darren's trailer one late February Saturday with a fat, grubby wad of cash, everything she'd saved from Christmas and her part-time job at the library. He answered her knock at his thin, plastic front door and said, "Fuck off. I've never actually sold horse tranquilizers."

And she said, "No, you gotta help me. You know about animals and birds and stuff, right?"

Darren's only known soft spot is for strays. He's never met an abandoned kitten or three-legged dog that he couldn't make time for. I guess that, at least on that day, the definition of stray expanded to include desperate teenagers who should know better than to show up alone to a strange man's house with a fist of cash. He let her in, if for no other reason than to tell her off and kick her back out. The trailer was its usual mess: clothes and take-out cartons everywhere, smoke and liquor smells masking any worse odors that threatened to assert themselves. A portly, one-eyed tabby cat took up the only available chair. Darren leaned on the counter in the little kitchenette and gave The Ten a little 'speak your piece' gesture.

She said again, "I need help."

He said, "What kind of help?"

"Veterinary attention."

"There's a legit vet in town if your cockatoo is dying or whatever. They do decent work."

"No, I need to be plucked and clipped and chemically burned and whatever needs to happen to make them go away."

He said, "What the hell are you talking about?"

And though it was clear she didn't want to, had been hoping it somehow wouldn't come to this, she rolled up her sleeve.

Darren kind of forgot she was a person for a minute, subsumed instead by professional curiosity. He grasped and pinched at her arm, stubbed out his cigarette because his face was so right-up-against her arm he almost burned her. He ran his fingers back and forth across the little needle heads along The Ten's skin, worrying at one with a thumbnail until a tiny, gooey down feather worked its way out. He stared at it for a long time, then at The Ten's bare arm, then at her other arm.

"Take the jacket off," he said.

"Can you help?" she said.

"I don't know what I don't know, I need to see more," he said. "Take the jacket off."

So, for the first time in what must have been over a year, The Ten let somebody else actually see her. Darren was clinical, if not entirely respectful in his examination. He muttered his way through it, stopping halfway to dig a thick and tattered reference book out from a storage cupboard beneath his unmade bed. He would consult the book, then place a calloused finger on a section of arm or torso and verbally label it with words that meant nothing to The Ten. "Tertial. Greater covert. Filoplume."

After lifting the tail of her shirt and looking up underneath it for some minutes, Darren told The Ten to take off her pants.

"Excuse me?" she said, an unprecedented edge in her voice, suddenly her mother's daughter.

Darren came back to himself, remembered that human patients had things like opinions and rights, and backed away from her. Deferential but still focused.

"Do you have them on your legs?"

"No."

"Are you sure?"

"I don't want to take my pants off. "

"I think you're sick."

"For not wanting to —"

"No, the feathers."

"Yeah, no shit."

"No, I mean they're coming in wrong. Poorly. The way they would on a malnourished bird. I suspect your diet sucks. Processed carbs mostly?"

"I guess. Pasta, mainly. Fries. So?"

"You need to eat more eggs, dairy, and seafood."

"I don't eat meat."

"Peanut butter and hummus, then. Natural fats and vitamins. Almonds, lentils, fruits and vegetables. Type of thing."

"And that will stop them growing? The feathers?"

"No, it's much better for them."

"I don't want it to be much better for them. I want them to go away."

"Why?"

"What do you mean, why?"

He didn't say anything, seemed legitimately to not understand.

"Because I'm a freak, is why. A mutant, a monster. Because somebody's going to find out and tell everybody. Tell my mom. Because ... because what the fuck am I? How can you even ask me that?"

Darren held up a placating hand and she stopped yelling.

Eventually, he said "When you want to find out what's wrong with a patient, what's really wrong, you have to make sure that you've got as many other things right as you can. When you have a picture of the correct form, of how things are supposed to look, then you can start to figure out where it might be wrong."

"The 'correct form' is to have no feathers at all."

"Almost all of what's growing along your arms and back are called blood feathers. Feathers that are early in their development, and still have blood supply in their shafts. Picking them damages the skin and can cause heavy bleeding. Like if you've ever dug too far under a fingernail and drew blood, like that. Violently arresting something in its development like that is no way to find out what it's supposed to be. The best plumage management," he said, "is done with healthy, mature feathers. So, eat better. And stop plucking them, obviously."

"Plumage management," she said, as if the words tasted bad.

"Technical term," he said.

The Ten wrapped herself back in her jacket, whatever she'd been expecting from this visit, she was clearly disappointed with what she'd gotten. "So," she said, "I guess I'll come back?"

"Two weeks. Maybe ten days. Schedule something with my assistant on your way out," Darren said. She didn't laugh.

"You can help me, though?" she said. "Help me get rid of them?"

He thought about it, finally said, "Yes." All confidence.

"I don't get paid again for another month," she said. "I don't know if I can ..."

Darren wadded up the bills she'd dropped on the kitchenette half-table and shoved them into one of the open pockets of the jacket. "Pay me when we're done," he said. "Actually, wait," he said quickly, and deftly picked a single bill back out of her pocket. "I'm short for the rest of the week. Pay me the rest when we're done."

"And what do we do in ten days?" she said.

"We'll see."

On her way out, The Ten stopped in the door. She said, "You won't tell anyone I was here."

He didn't say anything.

She said, "You can't."

He said, "Then I guess I won't."

She bunched the jacket up around her, took a few steps back. "This was a mistake," she said.

"It wasn't," he said. "See you in ten days."

So, she gave him ten days. She made the effort to eat better and discovered that the only place in town you can get hummus is the gas-station quick mart over at Skyline and Church. It's about as good as you'd expect. She made the effort to break that habit of picking at her blood feathers. Not extremely successful, but nonetheless. There were fewer blood spots to launder out of her T-shirts in the middle of the night, fewer wads of down to collect in her pockets and then flush down the toilet.

Darren didn't do much of anything. Just waited.

She came back on a Tuesday evening after work. Darren was out on the trailer's tow hitch, smoking to stay warm, tossing dog kibble to a raccoon that ran off into the forest when The Ten got close. He had possibly made an effort to tidy the inside of the trailer.

He asked her to take off her jacket and her shirt. She thought about objecting, but he was being clinical, professional even, so she did. He pointed some adjustable lamps at her back, told her to hold still. He started making notes and sketches in an old composition notebook, the kind they make you journal in at school.

He asked about her diet, how she was feeling.

She asked if the feathers were ready to come off.

He noted that she was still picking at the ones growing on her wrists and forearms.

She asked if they were ready to come off.

He asked if she had ever done any research herself into different kinds of plumage, especially exotic birds, macaws, pheasants, quetzals, etc.

She asked if the fucking feathers were ready to come off.

He said he needed ten more days.

"You're jerking me around," she spun around and jabbed a finger at him. Angry enough that she surprised herself even.

"I'm not. Ten more days."

"And then what? More drawings of me in my underwear?"

"Please."

I have never heard Darren ask politely for anything. Like, if he needs you to hand him something, he just tells you to do it. Hand me that deck of cards. Get me another beer. Gimme a light. It took me a while to realize that he does this, but I think The Ten could tell right away. Could tell that his 'please' had weight. He was literally pleading. So, she said yes. Well, what she said was, "Christ. Fine. But no more."

And she gave him ten more days of an increasingly ill-fitting jacket, of an increasingly ill-fitting existence. Struggling to hide the feathers that now started to peek out of her sleeves and collar, picking at her nails and acne instead of her arms. Skipping showers, skipping work, skipping class, hiding herself even more intensely. Fuming the whole time, silently rehearsing things to shout in Darren's smug, know-it-all face when he failed to deliver again. Terrified that he would.

A Friday. Darren again smoking on the tow hitch, watching The Ten make her way down the dirt path to his front door. No raccoon this time. She stood in front of him, hands thrust deep into her pockets, glaring at him while he took a final drag and geysered smoke into the air. Downwind of her, considerately. He hopped down from the hitch and held the flimsy door open. He said, "We have two options."

They stepped inside. He had redecorated, shoved anything that could be shoved off the floor to make room for three tall things that had been covered by bed sheets. Whatever they were, they left barely any room to stand, except at one spot roughly in the middle of the floor, which had been marked with masking tape like in a TV studio. Darren perched himself on the kitchenette counter because there was nowhere else and pointed The Ten to the mark on the floor.

"The first option is a bad idea, and I don't want to do it, but it will work." He mimed that she should take her jacket and shirt off. "I know a guy who's an electrolysis technician at a hair removal clinic about thirty minutes from here who owes me a ton of money and several favors. The technique should work just as well for feathers as it does for hair, and I think he'll be quiet about it."

"What's electrolysis?" The Ten asked.

"Removing hair with an electric needle so it doesn't grow back."

"Sounds painful."

"It is."

"Why does he owe you so much money?"

"I cheat at cards."

"And what makes this a bad idea?"

"It's slow, it's painful, and you'll have to tell somebody your secret."

"Well, I told you."

"Yeah, you got lucky with me, though. Hold out your arms like a T."

"I don't care if it hurts, I think it sounds perfect. You said the second option is better?"

"I hope so." Darren reached down and yanked a bungee cord that was threaded through the bed sheets, and they all fell to the ground at once. The one-eyed cat and The Ten both jumped, surprised by the movement. The cat ran and hid under the bed, but The Ten stared. The three mystery things were all mirrors. Big, full-length mirrors, mostly clean, sourced from some thrift shop or estate sale and propped awkwardly on two-by-fours. They were arranged cleverly so that, from her spot in the middle, The Ten had a perfect three-hundred sixty-degree view of herself, front and back. Feathers and all.

Over twenty days the feathers had all come in. Fully mature, healthy feathers. She had obviously never seen them all out and exposed before, never all at once like this. They shimmered in the harsh LED light of the trailer's overhead lamps, the rusty gold of late afternoon sunlight, except for a band of deep, brilliant blue that traced along her arms and rolled gently across her shoulder blades. The feathers were lush and thick, some of them over a foot long, maybe two. The longest ones swayed gently along with her when she moved, like an elegant gown. She flexed her arms and rolled her shoulders, watching the way the feathers all flowed cohesively, spreading out, pulling in, all together like molten metal. She tucked her arms in tight and got the feathers to puff out all at once, letting fresh air waft through to the skin beneath.

Eventually, she caught a half-glimpse of Darren's face in one of the mirrors and turned to look at him. He was smiling.

"This is the second option?" she asked.

"The second option," he said, "is to beg you not to go with the first."

"What do you mean?"

"So, to be clear, I'm not backing out. I told you I'd help you, so I will. But I want you to know that I don't want to."

"Why not?"

"This," he gestured broadly to the mirrors, to her, "Your feathers, your whole ... you. You're the most amazing thing I've ever seen." Darren is not an effusive person, and when he offers praise, it hits different. The Ten was quiet, chewing on what he was telling her.

"You used the word 'freak' before. To talk about yourself. I think a better word is 'miracle'." Darren was not used to saying this many earnest words in a row and was struggling to keep eye contact. "I know it's not my bag to hold, and I won't tell you that it'll be easy to keep going. Like I said, I'll help you because I said I would, but I feel I would be remiss if I didn't say what I think, and what I think is that to get rid of the feathers would be a great loss. You're trying to drag yourself back down to where the rest of us are living, and I don't think you have to. I don't think you should. Is how I feel."

They stared at each other for what felt like too long. Finally, The Ten came over to where he was sitting, jammed up against the kitchen cabinets, laid her head against his chest, and wrapped her arms around him tight. He rested his chin on the top of her head and held her too.

This seems like the point where it would be perfect for something more to happen between them. Something physical. But it wasn't like that. So says Darren, anyway. I think he's full of shit, and there was plenty of room for some kind of fairytale-level nonsense, smooching or love or one or another kind of happy ending, if they'd had more time together. But, instead, that's when her mom showed up.

Headlights played through the trailer windows as Mrs. Paloma's car juddered to a stop in Darren's front yard. She was screaming "Angelica!" at the top of her voice before she was even out of the driver's seat. Darren ran to try to stop her at the door, but he had to pick his way across the clutter, The Ten, the mirrors. He and Mrs. Paloma reached the door at the same time, so when she kicked it open it hit him square in the face and he fell back, half into the tiny chemical toilet room. The trailer was too small to hide or escape, so The Ten was caught out, deer-in-headlights in the kitchenette. She had only had time to pull her jacket back on, pure instinct, and was clutching it around herself, looking for all the world like somebody interrupted in the middle of doing something she shouldn't have been.

Mrs. Paloma stood in what passed for an entryway, looking all around the trailer and coming to the worst conclusions.

"Hi, sure, come on in," said Darren, finding his feet and dabbing a sleeve at his freshly split lip. "Sit down. Can I get you some coffee?"

Mrs. Paloma ignored him, pointed herself squarely at The Ten. "Angelica, is this where you've been all week?"

"No, ma'am."

"What, exactly, are you doing here?"

"Nothing."

"Don't you lie to me!"

"I'm not!"

"She's not," Darren tried to help.

"You shut the hell up or I will burn this place to the ground." Mrs. Paloma stabbed a red-nailed finger at Darren, but kept her eyes on her daughter. "Missy Carlson has seen you coming out here, and she told Kathy Cliffe, who told everybody. People are talking. Everyone is talking. Do you understand what I mean?"

"Yes, ma'am," said The Ten.

Darren plainly did not understand, but a desperate look from The Ten kept him quiet.

"Is that your shirt? There on the ground?" Mrs. Paloma was beet red, bad vibes radiating off her like heat off blacktop.

"No, ma'am."

"Get in the car, we'll discuss this further."

Mrs. Paloma turned to leave, with the clear expectation that The Ten would follow. The Ten started to pick her way across the room to the door, cowed and defeated. When she was close enough, Darren put a soft hand on her shoulder. "You don't have to go with her," he said.

The crash of glass. Mrs. Paloma snatched a whiskey bottle off the floor and smashed it against the door frame. She brandished the jagged neck in Darren's face, a talon of glass just under his left eye. "She's not staying here, you pervert."

"Okay, but I imagine she has more than just the two options."

"If you try to stop us, I will blind you. Angelica, get in the car."

The Ten shuffled out of the trailer, her eyes on her feet, hunched awkwardly into the jacket, trying to disappear, trying to blot out the world, trying to be not-here and not-now. Mrs. Paloma kept her eyes on Darren as she backed out of the trailer, the broken bottle still leveled at him.

"You're not a freak," Darren called after The Ten as the door swung shut, bouncing against the newly crooked frame. He watched the car carve deep tire treads through the mud and grass as it pulled out and away.

And after that, we only really know what they had to say on the news or in the police reports. The Ten and Mrs. Paloma drove away from Darren's, presumably towards their house, presumably sitting in the thickest air of tension it's possible for two people to share in a car. Mrs. Paloma white-hot with righteous rage, The Ten watching the actualization of her worst nightmare rolling closer and closer. What exactly they were feeling or saying on the car ride you're free to speculate as you see fit, but whatever it was, it came to a head on the bridge on Cielo Boulevard, maybe a ten-minute drive away from Darren's. Mrs. Paloma stopped at the light, and, as reported by Jim Goode and his son Danny who pulled up in the car behind her, The Ten jumped out of the passenger seat, throwing the door open before the car had even really stopped moving, and ran away from the car, her mother shouting something after her, inaudible over the radio in the Goodes' car. As you know, there's no shoulder or sidewalk on the Cielo bridge, so when The Ten jumped out, she ran around the back of the car, passing through the Goodes' headlights. They reported that it was definitely The Ten, and she did have her trademark jacket on, but notably only over one arm — as if she were halfway through taking it off or putting it back on — and seemed to otherwise be wrapped in what they described as a gold-colored silk shawl. She crossed in front of their car and was suddenly silhouetted in the headlights of Ellis Proctor's lifted truck, which was speeding through a turn into the oncoming lane. Ellis says that he didn't get a good look at whoever was in the road, just that he saw somebody square in the middle of the lane and stood on the brakes. He thinks whoever it was jumped towards the ledge of the bridge. Ellis and the Goodes got out of their vehicles and looked around, but couldn't find anybody, or even any trace of anybody, and by then it was too dark to see down into the ravine below the bridge if anything was down there. Mrs. Paloma drove off before the fire department arrived to do a proper search, though of course they didn't find anything either. Not until the next day, when they found the jacket, almost a mile away. Nothing else remarkable about it except that there was what appeared to be an eagle's feather in one of the sleeves.

She's still officially a missing person, but nobody is really expecting to find her anywhere. Angelica — everybody suddenly remembered her name — got a candlelight vigil and there was a touching tribute to her at graduation that year, and then everyone sort of forgot about her. The facts of the story got twisted and editorialized and are now mostly used as a cautionary tale about what happens when kids don't listen to their parents. Mrs. Paloma refuses to talk about it. When she's in public, she'll blank you if you try to ask questions, or offer condolences, or otherwise act like she ever had a daughter. The church ladies give her a wide berth, but they still let her participate in things, councils and bake sales and stuff, tolerating her and her garbage personality out of what I think they think is charity. But if they didn't put up with her, the only other place people would see her is the liquor store, so maybe it is a kindness.

Darren is on the record as having nothing to do with it. He told the sheriff that he couldn't say what Missy

Carlson saw or thought she saw, but she must have been mistaken because he'd never met that girl, so sorry he couldn't be of more help. He'll say as much to you, too, if he doesn't know you well, and I'll deny telling you any of this, too, if you try to confront him or something.

But. If you do know him, and if he's had a few beers and winning poker hands to get him comfortable, and if the topic of The Ten comes up more-or-less organically, he'll volunteer that he's sure that wherever it is she ended up, she's doing just fine. And you'll ask him what makes him think that? What makes him think she's even alive after all this time? And he'll ask you, "Do you know what happens when birds are pushed from their nests?"

And because he phrases it like a joke or a riddle, you'll say, "No, what happens?"

And he'll say, "They fly."

About the author

S. J. Fry grew up in Maryland and has lived all over the world, which is very out of character for him. He is most recently based in Nova Scotia. He has long aspired to write at a professional level, and is very proud to have achieved that dream with this, his first published work of fiction.

@sjfry.bsky.social

About hope

I hope that children, mine and others', will grow up loving books and stories as much as I did, and that future generations will continue to make room in their lives for art to matter.

Queen of Crows

Rachel Ayers

A Queen of Crows

Mag loved the witches' kitchen, though it did not love her back.

There were shelves of cookbooks and spellbooks as well as histories and tales, herbs hung from the rafters, spices in their jars on the shelf. The stone hearth with its tremendous mantel was her favorite place to sit and flip through the pages or sort through the apples or peel the potatoes. The kitchen garden, walled and hidden, was a tidy riot of scents and flavors, and Mag knew them all.

The witches left her alone, often enough, though not idle. Then the sparrows and robins would come and tell her stories of far-off places, good witches and dancing princesses, glass slippers, wolves in red capes, and maidens trapped in towers rescued by woodcutters.

She had no sense of her own age, though the witches often called her 'pretty young one', and she did not know how old she was when she realized that, however unlikely it was, a prince or a woodcutter coming to her rescue would be a great adventure. She was far too timid to imagine undertaking a quest alone, but a brave companion or a true love made her daydreams safer.

Mostly she was too busy to think of such things. The three witches kept her cooking, cleaning, grinding herbs for their spells, and whatever other little task they brought her. She mended for them, read to them from ancient grimoires, and brushed their long, sleek hair.

Nobody followed the road to the witches' cottage. No princes, no woodcutters, nor even big bad wolves, by coincidence or design, wandered by and invited her to be whisked away from the witches and their work.

Mag's entire life might have consisted of nothing more than fairy stories and her little bit of kitchen herbology, except that one summer morning a murder of crows flew in through the window and settled around her, on the counters and the sink and the unlit stove. One particularly fine specimen sat on the rim of the basin where she was doing the washing.

"Shoo," she said.

The crow looked at her, unthreatened.

"If the witches find you in here, you'll be baked into a pie."

The crow cawed. It sounded like laughter.

She answered the crow with a caw of her own. The bird went silent, cocked her head at Mag, formed her opinion of the young woman.

The bird shook her feathers and sent the others back out the window. One, two, three, four. Five crows for riches, Mag had heard the rhyme, so this last one must be their queen.

She got a handful of oats from the barrel and held it out. The crow gave her that doubtful, cocked-head expression again. "Go on, then, your highness," said Mag, and the crow dipped her beak into the heap of seed, tossing her head back to swallow.

"Hardly appetizing, child," the crow told her with great dignity.

"Hmm." Mag thought for a moment, then offered her a dried plum. The Queen Crow took this as well, and seemed to prefer it. She preened for a moment, ignoring Mag, who shrugged and went back to her scrubbing. "Don't want to talk, then? You aren't much company," Mag scolded, but the Queen did not deign to answer. When she splashed the crow with a bit of sudsy water, the crow squawked in indignation, ruffled her feathers, and flew out the window.

Mag laughed and thought no more about it.

A Dance for Two

The Queen of Crows flew back the same evening, as the sun turned the sky the color of ripe plums. Mag was hauling water from the well to the garden. Summer had been hot and hard. Persistent watering had kept the garden flourishing.

The crow flapped noisily from beyond the roof and landed in the cherry tree, greeting Mag with her rough voice.

"Welcome back," Mag said. The crow's eyes followed her to the herb patch beside the kitchen door. She dumped the water out, and when her bucket was empty, the crow flew to the windowsill and appealed to Mag with shining black eyes.

"I haven't any more treats for you," Mag said. "You'll have to earn your supper, just as I do."

"How shall I do that?" the crow asked.

The Queen could not haul water, or peel potatoes, or pull the boiling cauldron from the fire. "Sing for your supper, like they say."

The Queen cawed, crowed, laughed at that idea. Her throaty, cackling voice was by no means pleasant. Yet Mag found she was pleased by the effort, and went about preparing dinner for the witches, and herself, and the crow.

The Queen flew away when the witches returned, tittering and boasting more than any crow ever had. They had their supper in a swirl of merriment which did not reach out to Mag.

When they had gone back to their business, she went into the moonlit garden. A rustle from the cherry tree alerted her: there was the crow, a shadow in the darkness, studying her.

"I've sung for you," the Queen cawed. "Will you dance for me?"

"You sang for your supper," Mag countered. "What shall I dance for?"

The Queen cocked her head one way and then the other. "For my curiosity," she ventured, which Mag liked, but:

"I don't know how."

"If my singing pleased you, I assure you your dancing will please me."

So she swayed, and turned, and raised her arms to the moon. Witches' chants played in her head, and she moved to their rhythm, shuffling and then spinning with growing grace.

The crow's head bobbed to her movements. She flew to join Mag, becoming impossibly large; touched her wingtips to Mag's outspread hands. Black feathers fell away to reveal black skin, and they danced.

All night they twirled and spun in the garden, laughing and cawing at each other in equal measure.

As the sun peeked over the horizon, the crow caught up the feather cloak she'd cast aside for the dance, changed again in a burst of wings and feathers, and flew away.

Three Witches

The witches called themselves Rozhanitsy, Parca, and Norn. Their business was concocting spells of youth, beauty, and fortune. The vast majority of the works Mag read to them over dinner were treatises or spells on the subject of immortality; her own interests ranged more widely but she had less time for them. The witches were generally merry, more prone to laughter than grumbling. They teased each other mercilessly, and were carelessly cruel to Mag when it amused them.

"What's got you moping, Mag dear?" asked Rozhanitsy, who chattered more than magpies.

Mag had not realized she was acting differently, but she missed the Crow Queen, who had not returned.

"My friend has gone away," she told them.

Rozhanitsy, Parca, and Norn clucked with glee. "What friend? What friend have you got? Where has your friend gone, pretty young Mag?"

"She is a queen," she told them, holding dignity close as a cloak. "She came and sat in the garden. I gave her some food, and we danced in the moonlight. She left, though, and hasn't returned."

At this, they grew quiet, thoughtful. They consulted amongst themselves, muttering low so that Mag only caught a few words. "If she should return ... royalty ... by what path could anyone ... lest we lose her ..."

They turned back to her, three sets of eyes glaring suspicion. Rozhanitsy asked, voice sugary, "Mag, sweet Mag, how did this lady — err, queen — arrive? By the path? Through the woods?"

"She flew in the window with four of her court. Then they flew away again, but she came back alone later."

Norn, eldest of the three and sharpest, narrowed her eyes. "What did this queen of yours look like, Mag?"

"Black as my hair, with bright eyes and a sharp nose."

More murmuring and glances exchanged.

"And how tall was your queen, young Mag?" asked Rozhanitsy.

Mag spanned her hands in front of her.

Their concern turned into a fit of sniggering.

"And how wide her wingspan, your flying queen?" Parca peeked at the others for approval.

Mag held her arms out again.

"And how rough her voice?" asked Rozhanitsy.

Mag cawed an imitation of the Queen Crow.

The witches collapsed in laughter, howling and slapping one another. Mag watched them, her face hot from their teasing.

Parca and Norn, still shaking in amusement, went through the kitchen door and down the hall. Rozhanitsy stayed a moment, and said, "Mag, I hope your friend does return. But crows are tricky, and if she does come back, you should catch her and let us bake her into a pie."

Four Small Losses

Rarely was Mag tempted into an act of disobedience, but in her longing for the Queen Crow to return, she found herself in a sour and disagreeable mood. She burned the cooking and dragged her feet around the garden. forgot the herbal lore she knew in her sleep and mixed up cumin and fennel for the first time in her memory. She did the washing and mending, but so slowly and so ill that she had to do it all twice. She answered the witches' questions in surly tones or grunts.

It went on for weeks, until Rozhanitsy came into the kitchen and asked her what was wrong. Mag shrugged and continued to scrub the stew pot without vigor.

"Dear, pretty Mag." Rozhanitsy drew her away from the sink to sit at the table. "You know that we three care for you, and feed you, and provide for all your needs. All we ask in return is your unquestioning obedience. You understand that, right?"

Mag nodded.

"Well, child, I'd like to believe you, but from the way you've behaved lately, I'm not sure that settles things. What is for dinner?"

Mag had a bit of dough rising for bread; she hadn't thought beyond that. She'd spent the morning reading a tale of a hedgehog who was secretly a prince and tricked the nearby king out of his daughter.

"I see." Rozhanitsy patted Mag's hands, there before her on the table, and then in a quick motion, cut off the little finger of Mag's right hand. The knife had appeared and disappeared so suddenly it might have been magic. Mag stared, numb, at her blood and her pinkie, lying separate from the rest of her.

Rozhanitsy scooped up the finger and studied it for a moment, then tidied it away into her pocket. "Mag, I want you to remember this. It's a moment to help you focus. We're doing very important work and we can't be bothered with cooking and cleaning. We depend on you."

Rozhanitsy bustled out of the kitchen.

Then the pain started, and Mag wailed.

Though the witches had punished Mag before, they had never done anything so permanent. Mag, shocked at this betrayal, gave up thoughts of black birds and night dances. She grew accustomed to the loss, regaining her dexterity once the pain faded. Norn put her finger bones on the mantel, and it was enough to remind Mag of her place. She did not even need to consult the books, once she recalled herself to focus, to concoct a balm to stop the ghost of her finger from itching.

She did have company, an occasional robin or blue jay, but never a crow. She worked up the nerve, finally, and asked for news of the Queen Crow. A sparrow told her that she'd given up her crown and was dancing with ladies-in-waiting in a distant palace. Late one night, an owl told her that the Queen Crow had married a prince, the youngest son of a faraway king.

"Yes, yes indeed." The owl blinked down at Mag's astonishment. "The court of crows flew for seven days, to a kingdom of spiraling towers and bright flowers. A sunny place, with too much daylight. Warm, though."

"I don't understand," Mag protested.

"Oh! Well, the farther south one travels, the warmer the seasons."

Mag crossed her arms. "I meant about the court of crows, and the wedding."

"Ah!" The owl shuffled in her feathers, settling into the crook of the branch. "There was a ball at the grand palace, a three-day extravaganza, where beautiful ladies and handsome men were dancing together, wearing shimmering garments and feather masks. The Crow Queen flew down to join them, and took the form of a woman, and wore her feathers as a magnificent cape. At the end of three nights, the prince was to choose a bride from the revelers."

"I think I know the story," said Mag. Or at least she had heard one like it.

"I did not attend to the details," the owl admitted. "The Crow Queen, however, danced with one lord more than all the others. He wore raiment of gold, radiant as sunlight. His mask was made of the feathers of the crows and the ravens, all the darkest birds, and on the third night as the prince claimed his bride, the dark lord slipped off his mask and asked the Crow Queen to be his wife. For he too was a prince of that land, and needed a bride of his own.

"That was many seasons ago, of course. The rest of the court of crows scattered, and it was some time more recent that I heard these tidings."

Mag felt foolish. She had longed for the Crow Queen, who, it seemed, had not given Mag a second thought. She left the owl to watch for mice and voles in the garden and went back to her kitchen hearth.

Mag wept all night, surrounded by the scent of the thyme and rue she'd bundled to dry above the hearth. At dawn, she crept back to her bed in the corner of the kitchen and recited herbal lore to herself until she fell asleep.

Norn was not pleased. She woke Mag, shaking her until the girl sat up and stared at her, blinking in the light.

"Mag," she said, "There was nothing for breakfast, and lunch looks to be missing, too. The kitchen is a mess, and the clothes in the mending heap haven't been touched all day. What do you have to say for yourself?"

"I was sleeping." Mag lay back down and shut her eyes; she was not sleeping, in truth, but dreaming of a life where she was a princess in a tower instead of a servant in a kitchen.

She heard Norn sigh. "Has it been a hard night, child? Have you trouble waking?" Norn took her uninjured hand and gave it a gentle pat. "Let me aid you."

Mag cracked her eyes open in time to see the witch lift the hand to her mouth and bite off the smallest finger.

It hurt immediately this time.

Norn pulled the finger out of her mouth and wagged it at Mag. "You look more bright-eyed already. Now see to your chores."

Mag found her focus once more, and soon after, the new bones were added to the mantel. She grew ever quieter, afraid to lose any more of herself, and continued to do the witches' bidding. When she gathered herbs in the cold light of the full moon she would, sometimes, think of flying away over the garden wall, but no matter her dreams, she did not grow wings; in all the witches' books, the only spells that granted such transformations came at too permanent a cost.

It was a spring evening, more than a year later, when she saw a single sooty black crow winging across the sky. It was too far away to see if it had been the Queen, but Mag waved and called to it. The crow fluttered and dipped, landing on the branch where his queen had alighted the night she danced with Mag.

"Stay a while, rest," she said, holding out a handful of dried plums. "Tell me of your queen."

"Oh, our queen, hmph, she is gone quite mad, or so they say." The crow plucked the fattest plum from Mag's palm.

"Mad?" Mag prompted; the bird took his time over the fruit.

"Well, in the way of a creature who cannot be herself," he clarified, chortling over another choice plum.

Mag sighed in sympathy.

"She cannot be cured of her humanity." The crow eyed her suspiciously and then gulped the last plum. "Her husband stole away her feather cloak when she bore him a son, and when she demanded her feathers back, he told her that he couldn't have a wife who would fly away on a whim. She has been searching for her cloak ever since, and has all of us, her *true* court, seeking for another way to change back into her true self. She has tried tinctures and ointments, and consults with wise-women and witches alike. The human courtiers think her quite touched."

The bird cocked his head again, but seeing no more plums forthcoming, bunched his feathers to fly again.

"Wait!" Mag cried, but he was already off, over the garden wall and out of sight. Free as she never could be, the bird awakened a bitter longing in her heart.

She wanted to follow the crow, to find its queen. For the first time, Mag was desperate to leave, determined to go. She wanted to see more than a tiny garden corner of the world. She wanted more than witches and potions and a tidy little kitchen. She wanted to find her friend.

In front of the cottage was a dark flagstone path. It was not so very long, and then there was the road, stretching into the forest in either direction. Mag set out without so much as an apple for the road, but stopped at the garden gate, unable to decide which way to go, and then a thousand protests clamored in her mind: where would she go, how would she eat, how would she earn her way? *Foolish girl*, she scolded herself.

She sank to the frigid stones, lost within sight of the garden wall she knew so well.

When morning came, Rozhanitsy, Parca, and Norn found her still at the end of the path, shivering in the misty sunlight. They brought her back to her hearth and then Rozhanitsy and Parca left her alone with Norn.

Norn sat beside her. "What's gotten into your head?"

"I want to fly away." Mag hid her face in her hands, felt the ghosts of her smallest fingers tickling her cheeks, and wished she hadn't spoken.

"Don't we feed you, and keep you safe? The world is a hard place, and you're safe here, so long as you do what you're told. You understand that, don't you?"

Mag nodded, but did not lift her face.

"You are part of our great work, Mag," Norn told her. "One day we will find our answer, and that will be because you have assisted us. That gives your life meaning. You will find no answer so easy as that in the wider world."

"But I want to see it!" Mag burst out, then clapped her hands over her mouth. She looked at Norn, fearful.

"However much you may wish to fly away, you haven't got wings. Remember your feet? There on the ends of your legs? You'll do better to stay solidly planted, and keep to your work."

This time, Mag was ready for the knife. She jumped away as Norn moved toward her.

"Sisters," Norn said. She did not raise her voice, but they appeared as though they had been waiting for her.

Mag fought them, kicking and thrashing, but she had nowhere to go, and soon they had her trapped. Rozhanitsy and Parca held her, and Norn cut the smallest toe from each foot.

Mag screamed.

Norn took no notice. Mag nearly missed the witch's words over the throbbing of blood through her ears and face. "One for grounding, two for obedience. Remember, Mag."

She remembered, but it was not the last time she attempted flight.

Five Years

On the fifth anniversary of her flying away, the Queen of Crows returned as though only days had passed. She sat on the kitchen mantel, next to Mag's tiny bones, and cawed impatiently at Mag when she did not look up from her chair beside the fire.

"Go away, bird." It was evening; she was nearly finished hemming Norn's new skirt and she wanted to go to bed early.

"Why do you hunch over your work, and speak like an old woman?" the crow asked her. "Your face is not lined, your hair is not gray."

Now she glared at the Queen with the full force of her anger and despair. "Why should I be young and happy? Is my life so wonderful? Is my life worth anything at all?"

The crow fluttered, but settled again. "Your life is hard, and I owe you an apology, for leaving you and more. Will you listen to my story, and decide if you can forgive me?"

Mag pushed herself out of the chair and hobbled outside. There was now a shackle on each ankle, and the chain between them was short. Her missing toes ached as winter bowed to spring.

She sat on the stoop. The moon was already in the sky, glowing orange on the horizon. The witches were gone to some revelry or mischief. Mag did not know when they would return.

The crow followed her and landed on the garden path, inky against the pale flagstones.

"Do you remember the night we danced in the moonlight?" she asked.

Mag laughed; not happily.

"When I watched you dance, I learned how to take off my feathers and stand as a woman." From her place before Mag, she shook herself. Then a cloak of feathers fell away, and she held it in human hands. She sat cross-legged on the stony path. "I flew far away that night, afraid of what I had, for that moment, become. Humans are tricky, confusing creatures, and I had felt things I did not understand. I flew until the sun rose, then I slept. When I woke, I did not know where I was, only that I was far outside my territory."

She told Mag of her young prince, who had seemed a brilliant novelty but had twisted her life into a cage. Of her search for a restoration, and the hedge-witch who had advised her. All this Mag knew, but now the Queen told her in greater detail, and her heart twisted as she remembered her own longing to go to her friend's aid.

"For a time, I was lost in despair. But news came to me that the Queen was, at last, expecting a child. When the babe was born, my husband said to me: 'Destroy the babe, wife, and I'll return your cloak.' This was the first proof I had that he knew where it was, and I became furious. I called him an evil wizard. He said there was but one way for me to get what I wanted, and at last I told him I would do as he bid."

Mag startled at this, horrified.

"I went by night to the Queen's chamber, and stole her little daughter. The child was peaceful in my hands, and as I gazed at her, I conceived a great love in my heart. I could no more harm her than I could hurt my own son. I took the girl deep into the forest, to a hedge witch I had met in my quest to return to my true form.

"When I told my husband the deed was done, he clapped and laughed, and I saw the shadow of the beauty that had drawn me to him. 'Now fulfill your end of the bargain, husband.'

"He tore his pillow from our bed. Black feathers fluttered in the air around him. 'What have you done?'

" 'I used the life in them to conceive our child.'

"I knew, then, of one magic to try, though I did not know if it would work."

Mag watched the Queen's gentle fingers close into fists. She continued, as though she dare not stop now.

"I went to the Queen and revealed all that I knew. She called the king, who was grieved at his brother's treachery, but when his eyes met mine I could see that he was not surprised.

"In the morning my husband was tied to a stake in the courtyard. I carried my son forward, and then drew from a sack all of my beautiful black feathers. I spread them on the ground around him while my child watched.

"I raised my head, and called out in my true voice. My lord's face turned to fear as I summoned my own court. First a single crow appeared, and then two more, and then a whole murder. They dove at the man I had married, pecking and clawing at him. As he bled, each drop fell upon a feather, restoring the vitality he had stolen from me. The king and queen clung to each other, turning their faces away. Our son cried and reached forward to touch my cloak, and in that instant was transformed into a crow.

"When the last breath left my husband's body, my cloak was complete, but for a ragged corner which had formed around my son. At last I could stretch my wings again. I took to the air, and my son followed, and the other crows too, and we did not look back."

Mag touched the cloak. It was sleek and smooth; no trace of the blood-magic remained.

The Crow Queen gestured, and Mag made out a fluttering in the trees outside the garden fence. There was her court. One of the birds was smaller, his feathers not quite as black; bits of baby down still showed in patches.

"Why did you come back?" Mag asked.

"When I was only a crow, I didn't understand why you were here. Now that I have been trapped, I know what it looks like. I have come to set you free." She stopped, then, almost shyly, "If you wish to come with me."

Mag touched the shackles at her ankles. "How?"

The Queen raised her arm, gave a signal, and the crows left the trees. They flowed past in a rush of wings and wind, and flew into the house.

Silence fell while they waited.

The first crow returned with a hair pin from Rozhanitsyi's dresser, a bit of metal gleaming in the moonlight. Mag picked it up and looked at the Queen Crow.

"Wait," she assured Mag.

The second crow flew out and dropped a coin at their feet. Mag had seen Parca twiddling with it, shining it through her fingers, a few evenings earlier.

A third crow came back with Norn's little mirror, the one she used to look at faraway places. Mag caught it before it broke on the flagstones.

The three crows looked at their little collection, then at the Queen. They ruffled their feathers in a kind of shrug, and flew back into the house.

The crows of the Queen's court repeated this until Mag had a little pile of glittering objects at her feet.

At last, the Queen's son returned. In his beak he carried a tiny key, duller in color than the other objects. Mag recognized it.

The little bird landed in her lap and held it until she took it from his beak. She fit it to the lock at her ankle, and the Queen Crow reached forward and turned it.

The shackle opened with a crack.

Six Days

"Come away, come away," the crows urged. "Before they return."

Mag took nothing with her. She followed the crows' singing; they cawed to her from the trees ahead. She found she was able to keep a steady pace, in spite of leaving her toes on the witches' mantel.

They walked all through the night and into the next day. Mag felt lighter with every step away from the witches' cottage. Every new sight refreshed her, whether it was a beautiful lady rushing by in a gilded coach, or an old man ambling along with a load of firewood, or a young lad guarding miniscule treasures in his wary fists.

They passed through the woods, and then a little hamlet, and then onto a broader road. The Crow's son joined them for a time, utterly silent, toddling along, then took to the air again. The Queen Crow herself seemed content to walk with Mag, watching her take in every scene along their way with as much delight as she took in watching her son discover new things.

They stopped for the night, and the Queen Crow paid for a room, telling the innkeeper that Mag was her sister. Mag could not imagine where she kept the coins when she changed to a crow. She winked at Mag as she shone the money through her clever fingers.

Though she was exhausted, Mag was too full of the day to sleep. So the Queen told her stories, from her life, or that she had heard, long into the night. Mag fell asleep dreaming of distant places, cottages on chicken's legs and magic lamps.

Five days more, they continued in this fashion. The farther Mag got from the witches' cottage, the more certain she became that this was real, but even so, she did not ask where they were going: a destination was too much to believe.

Then she heard laughter.

Seven for a Secret

The witches came sweeping over the land in a dark wind, finding her as easily as if she were still in the kitchen. They stole her away from the Queen Crow while she slept, head tucked under her wing, and brought Mag back to her little kitchen hearth, and all her fighting and thrashing and cursing made them laugh more.

"Mag, Mag, we must have you! We are almost at the end of all our hard work! Don't you want to know what happens?"

"I want to leave," Mag said. She would run farther this time.

They pulled her into the kitchen and sat her at the table. She waited for them to chain her, but they did not. Instead they pointed to the cauldron, where a murky stew was brewing.

"There it is, my dear," said Rozhanitsyi. "The key to our immortality, at last. Everyone dies, but we will break our fate. After all our long preparations, we have only to test it."

"I don't want to be immortal." Mag leaned away from their gazes.

They cackled. "Oh you won't, pretty Mag," said Parca. "We have undergone intense rituals, sacrificed many things, and prepared our bodies. The potion will not make you immortal."

"Then why do you want to test it on me?" she asked. She wondered if she could bolt for the door. One look at their faces killed the thought; they would catch her before she made it outside.

"If you take it, we can observe the effects, and match them with our studies. Then we will know the potion has been properly prepared," Norn explained. "It is very delicate; a single wrong ingredient will unbalance the whole thing. But I promise you, Mag, you will smile if you taste it. And after you test it, we will never ask anything of you again." She looked at the other witches. "What say you, sisters? This last task and Mag may go wherever she wills?"

They smiled and nodded. "Yes, Mag," said Parca, and Rozhanitsy added, "Nothing more will we ask of you!"

"I may go freely if I test your potion?" Surely it was a trick, some mischief, but they gazed at her earnestly.

Rozhanitsy nodded. "We will have no more need of you."

"How long will it take?" Mag asked, suspicious.

They hesitated. Then Norn said firmly, "One day. We must observe the effects for a full day, to be certain."

"And it won't hurt me?"

"It will make you smile," Rozhanitsy said again.

"Very well, I will test it. Then I never want to see you again," Mag said.

"You won't have to," Parca said. She looked a bit hurt.

Norn dipped a spoonful of the stuff and brought it to Mag's mouth, feeding her like a babe.

It did not taste as bad as it looked; bitter, but with the sharpness of fresh herbs. She swallowed, and waited.

It started in her stomach, a cramp, a slight discomfort. She pressed her hands against her belly. Norn, Rozhanitsy, and Parca were nodding, smiling: pleased.

And it spread, a hot cramping pain, worse than anything Mag had ever known. She tumbled out of her chair, collapsing to the floor as fire and chills raced through her body. She gasped at the shock of it and crumpled beside the hearth.

"Very good," Norn said, checking the sheaf of notes she held. "It is going as I expected."

"We will check on you soon," Rozhanitsy said, patting Mag's head. Each touch sent daggers through her skull.

The witches left her alone. They didn't need to chain her; she couldn't even crawl.

The Queen Crow flew in through the window. She transformed in an instant and knelt beside Mag. "What have they done?"

Mag could not answer.

The Queen touched her face with feather-light fingers. She studied the cauldron, the spoon resting on the table. "They are killing you."

Mag nodded and squeezed her eyes shut.

"Come away," the crow said. "Hurry," she said.

Mag could not move. "Stay," she pleaded.

An hour later, Rozhanitsy returned. The crow flew away before she entered the room. "Another dose, my dear. This one should go a bit better." She fed Mag another spoonful.

The effect spread through her body again. She grew heavy, as though the earth had decided to draw her closer. The pain chasing through her body thumped its now-familiar rhythm. It was harder still to move.

When Rozhanitsy left, the crow came back.

Mag knew, then, of one last magic to try, though she did not know if it would work. "May I have a feather?" Mag asked.

The Queen plucked one, long and dark as night, from her cloak. Mag pointed toward the cauldron, and the crow dropped it into the potion.

"Come back here," Mag whispered, "if you will. It helps, I think." She reached out a leaden hand. The Queen returned and held her fingers carefully until they heard Norn coming into the kitchen.

Each time Norn fed her a sip, the potion grew clearer, as though Mag were draining the color from it. Mag sank and then floated, was sick and then hot and then numb. Sometimes Norn asked her how she was feeling; sometimes she was able to answer.

After each dose, the Queen Crow or one of her court added a feather, which disappeared with no more than a sizzle and wisp of light. It was, she reasoned, no more risky than doing nothing; she did not believe the witches would let her leave alive.

"One more taste after this," Norn said, late in the night, and fed Mag a spoonful that made her tingle all over.

The Crow returned, and prepared to drop another feather into the potion, a downy feather from her son. "No," Mag said.

She tipped her beak at Mag quizzically.

She pointed at the mantel. The Queen found Mag's finger- and toe-bones where the witches had left them.

"Yes," she managed.

The Queen added them to the concoction, which hissed and boiled for a moment before settling again to the clarity of fresh rainwater. "What do we make, Mag?" she asked.

Mag tried to explain the muddled lore in her mind; the thoughts chased around each other and would not leave her mouth. She was not even certain that her idea would work, if the witches' potion was too strong for her to change — but another potion of transformation, another spell to change the form of a life — it was all she could try. The crow watched her and then nodded thoughtfully. "You need not speak, then, my dear," she told Mag. "I will wait and see."

At sunrise, all three witches returned. Norn gave her one last dose. "How does that suit you?"

Mag took an easy breath. The last of the aches and chills faded away, and the various discomforts dissipated. Pleasure — and then euphoria — filled her senses.

"It's ... wonderful," she said, and felt a grimacing smile grip her cheeks. The room faded; she could not focus her eyes.

"We'll be back in an hour," Parca said, "to move the body."

The others shushed her, and they left Mag alone again.

She felt glorious: as though light were pouring out of her, as though she were drinking honey-wine gone to her head.

She realized that the Queen Crow was weeping into her human hands, dark hair spilling over her face. "Why are you crying?" Mag asked.

"Because you are dying, and I have just begun to know you."

She looked down at herself in wonder: was this dying? Then she realized that she was truly looking down at herself from above. Her skin was turning gray, her eyes were growing dull. There was a smile on her lips, but the Queen was right: she was dying. The witches would let her go because they had no use for the dead.

So then, if that body did not hold her mind any longer, where was Mag? She shook herself, felt the soft rattle of feathers tested for the first time.

The Queen Crow held out a hand to her and she alighted. "Hello there, Maggie," she murmured. "You are still here."

"Did you not know why I asked for your feathers?" Mag asked.

"No." She stroked Mag with her other hand. "I thought you were lost."

Mag preened, testing her feathery body. She was spirit-light; a wisp of a creature, hardly more substantial than a cloud. It was all she had left, but it was a body, and one that could fly. She did not know how long it would last; but then, no one ever did. "Hurry," she said. "Help me."

She flew out to the garden and plucked elderberries, evil's bane; they bled red on their white blossoms as she tugged them free. She winged back and dropped them into the cauldron. They disappeared in the clear potion, with nothing but a wisp of steam to show they'd ever been.

Next, flax and horehound, for purification. The other crows, under their queen's command, followed her lead, around the garden and back again. Now rue and vervain, cleansing herbs, the potion still and clear as water. Rosemary: distinctive, purifying. And last, ague root, also called crow corn, hex breaker, ritual uncrosser. Her beloved kitchen and garden had never loved her back, but she knew every herb and its effect. With every gleaning from the garden and from her years studying their books, she bent the potion to her own purpose.

The witches returned to the kitchen, a dead girl, and a new potion.

Mag lingered under the eaves. "See how she smiles, even in death," Norn said. "See how her skin is like stone. The potion has worked as described on an unprepared mortal. It is ready for us, now."

"I thought she'd grow smaller," said Rozhanitsy.

"I thought she'd be wrinkled," said Parca.

"And I thought our preparations would be done decades ago," Norn said sternly. "Let us finish this thing, sisters."

They drank until the cauldron was emptied.

Mag fluttered to the trees, where the Queen was waiting with her court and her son. They welcomed her into their murder as the witches steamed and shrieked. Mag's spell scoured them of the death they'd twisted back to life, cleaned them of the wrongness they'd collected and clutched over the years. She did not think there would be anything left of them after that.

She did not stay to see.

The Queen Crow's court flew away: one as white as a dove, as there-and-gone as a wisp of cloud. Housewives and hedge witches watched them pass overhead. Some counted six and some counted seven, and all kept their secrets to themselves.

"Queen of Crows" originally appeared in
Metaphorosis on 5 August 2022

About the author

Rachel Ayers lives in Alaska, where she writes and hosts shows for Sweet Cheeks Cabaret. She has a Master's in Library and Information Science, which comes in handy at odd hours. She dabbles with oil painting, knitting, and making burlesque costumes. Her fiction appears in *Metaphorosis, Lady Churchill's Rosebud Wristlet,* and *Electric Spec* and she is a regular contributor at *reactormag.com*. She shares speculative poetry and flash fiction (and cat pictures) at patreon.com/richlayers.

About hope

I hope for science to triumph over all forms of cancer!

The Song Lives On

Louie Sullivan

"Where are we going, Granna?" the girl asked, trailing a few steps behind her grandmother as they crossed the empty street.

"To see an old friend." The old woman pulled back a broken section of a chain-link fence, leaving an opening just wide enough for both of them to fit through. "Now go ahead of me."

"Okay, but where *are* we? And why couldn't we take the train? Or the bus?"

"Where we're going, Cor, there aren't any trains or buses. In fact, there's very little out here at all anymore. Someone, I don't even remember who, bought it for construction years ago, before you were born. But after they cleared the land, the company didn't have the money to build, and I don't think anybody knows what to do with it these days."

"This looks like a dump. There's garbage all over and my feet hurt. Are we almost there?"

"Patience, child — we will get where we need to soon. I know this hill has seen better days. But you have to understand what it once was, what it could be again.

"All of this used to be a forest. It was long ago, back in *my* granna's time. Look around and imagine it. The trees grew taller than the buildings are now, their branches thick with thousands of fluttering leaves, and the rivers swelled with water that shone like polished steel. Every morning, the birds gathered to sing, and the air was full: not of the rumble of trains, but of vibrant music. Their song was joy, and love, and life. It echoed through the air and gave rhythm to the buzz of the insects, to the howl of the wolves. This faded gray road was lush and green back then, a tangle of sprouts and shrubs and dirt, and the deer strode calmly across without fear of guns or even arrows. In the springtime there were flowers and fruits, radiant with a rainbow of color and ripe with fragrant and delicious juice. In the winter, pure snow fell softly in delicate flakes and blanketed the earth in clean cotton, while the bears slumbered deeply in their caves. The work of the skies was of no consequence to them, and they dreamed for months on end.

"Did you know, child, that in those days you could look up and see the heavens with nothing but your eyes? They say the sky was bright and blue in the daytime, traced with wispy white clouds, and that at night its inky darkness glittered with more stars than you or I could ever count. Even now there are programs that struggle to compute the number. When I drift off into a deep, long rest like the bears, I am sometimes able to dream of it all, imagining what it could have been like to live among such wonders. They must have been beautiful to behold."

Granna could see that the story was doing anything but motivating the child — Cor was lagging behind, her eyes unfocused and distant ... and upset.

"I don't wanna hear one of your made-up stories, Granna! You promised no more baby stuff!"

"One never grows too old for imagination, sweet girl."

"But I'm *eight* now! Which is almost *ten,* which is *way* too old to like baby stuff."

"It's not a made-up story, Cor."

"It's not?" Tears welled in the young girl's eyes. "Then why isn't any of that around anymore? How come none of it's here now? It's not fair!" She could no longer hold back the dam of her eyelids, and Cor's face flooded. Granna scooped her up, cradled her in her arms.

"Shhhh, shhhhh ... it's okay. I know that it hurts. It hurts me too, to never have seen what I have told you. But I want you to understand that we are still lucky, still blessed. There are great things around us today, more than those who took the old ones away want you to believe, I promise.

It may take more than it used to, but you can still find the wonder. I know you can, and I will prove it to you."

Granna reached into her pocket, removing something vivid and colorful that seemed to almost glow, even in the dim predawn.

"Do you see this? Dry your eyes, and look. Take it in your hand if you like, feel how gentle and light it lands on your fingertips. Do you know what that's called?"

"That's a feather! I learned about them in school."

"Yes, clever child, a feather. It has been a long time since I've seen the bird that it came from, but I know that she was called Euterpe, and that she was a friend of our family many, many years ago. They loved her colors — see how fluidly they blend together, how rich and deep dark blue gives way to a lighter shade and then bright green, like the earth and sea — and she loved their birdseed! It's no surprise that a bond grew from that, and she became a trusted companion, decorating the days with her music. Together they would join in song, the bird and our ancestors, and it would make the burden a little lighter. This feather reminds us of that bond, and when we find our old friend Euterpe I have no doubt that she will grant you one of your own."

"What if," she said, still stifling a sob, "what if we can't find them? What if the birds are gone, the wonders are over, and they never come back?"

"I understand how you feel. I know that was very long ago, and it feels like such things have been lost to us, but I have something else to show you, something that proves the wonders of the past are not gone forever.

"Soon, most likely just as we meet our friend, you can watch the sun rise, its light breaking over the horizon and ushering in a fresh start to the day. It still does, every day, without fail — no one can take that from us. You will see how strongly its first rays pierce the dark, feel the gentle warmth it brings. I swear to you, it is nothing like the harsh heat that bears down on us at noon.

"And if you listen closely as the sun comes up, you *will* hear the birds sing — believe it or not, they still do, just as they used to. Despite all that has happened, they never stopped. It is a different song than before, one touched by the losses some of us have faced, the losses that others of us created. It is a more somber melody, an echo reaching back and grasping at the last time that things were safe and warm and comfortable. I am sure that it must pain them to sing this way, to pollute the memory of their ancestors with such a dirge. But they sing anyway, because singing keeps the memory alive. They are out there somewhere, waiting, surviving just like us."

Cor's eyes were shut, a strained expression on her face. Then they opened wide.

"Wait ... I hear the birds *now*!" she exclaimed, pointing. "Over there!"

Suddenly she took off, dashing away with the lightning speed of a young child powered by the energy of excitement. It was a pace that Granna could not match.

"Wait! Cor, come back!" she shouted, but it was not enough. Her plea fell on deaf ears, if it even reached the girl at all. And after a moment, Granna was alone.

"Cor!" she yelled again and again, scrambling ahead in the direction that the child had run off in. But there was no sign of her, and Granna soon grew tired and unable to press on. She let out a deep breath and sat, using some nearby rubble as a resting place. She knew she would find the girl soon, but doubt began to plague her tired mind. She thought of the dangers out in this uncultivated land — just because it was no longer naturally wild did not mean that it was safe. There were still animals here, not to mention the unstable ground, the sharp debris, the refuse left carelessly in towering piles ... this was no place for a child to be alone. Granna stood again, her head fraught with worry as she tried to get a sense of where she should search for her granddaughter.

But then she heard something, low and distant, but distinct. A whistling of sorts, faint and familiar. She found the strength to get up again, and began to follow it. Twisting and turning through heaps of wrecked refuse, Granna struggled forward. The sound grew louder and louder as she went, following its siren call. As she began to hear it more clearly, she suddenly recognized the song, and the child's laughter mixed with its ancient melody.

"Cor!" she shouted once more, this time with relief rather than desperation. Her lips curled into a smile as she beheld her granddaughter, surrounded by not only Euterpe but a vast flock in a rainbow of colors, joined together in their morning song.

"I think I found our friends, Granna!" she giggled.

"You most certainly did." And then, to a wise-looking deep blue bird flecked with green, "Thank you for looking after her, Euterpe."

The bird nodded in assent, and as she did a single feather fell from her plumage. It fluttered gracefully through the air and landed directly in Cor's hand.

As the dawn rose, with the feather held tightly in her hand, Cor began to understand a concept that she would hold true throughout her life, just as her grandmother had:

The birds believe, deep in their fragile hearts, that one day it will all grow back again. The trees will again take root, and the flowers will bloom. The smell of lavender will overtake the ash. We will be among wonders again.

It will not be the same as it once was — nothing ever can be. But like the birds, we must believe. We, too, must sing, each in our own way. One day the things that trouble us will be over, and at last we will all be able to go back home.

About the author

Louie Sullivan mostly writes about what scares him, but decided to take a more positive turn for this one. He is a graduate of Fordham University and Saint Peter's University, reads about a hundred books a year, and goes to the movies as often as humanly possible. You can find his work in the anthologies *Doors of Darkness* and *Doors of Darkness II: Trick or Treat* by TerrorCore Publishing, and in issues 62-64 of *The Sirens Call*.

You can find him on Instagram at @howdoyoulou or on the web at louiesullivan.com.

About the story

This story started with the line "All of this used to be a forest" and bloomed out from there — I found it very poignant to juxtapose nostalgia and longing for a lost past with hoping for a better future. It's frequently given advice to write the story that you want to read (or that you need to read) and I feel like there have been several points in my life where I've needed a story like this one. A story that, if I've done it right, reminds us that while the past may be a foreign and unreachable land, that doesn't mean that what's coming has to be worse.

About hope

There is always a pull toward romanticizing what has been lost, but if we work toward the future we want to see, it will come. My hope for the world is that we as a global community can more peacefully unite and understand that we can do better things together than apart. We are not alone, and even when things look dark for right now, the promise of the future always shines on brightly ahead.

The Trash King

Maggie Slater

The guy with the seagull head waggled a cold French fry in my face. "Do you know how much food people in this country waste on average? Thirty-eight percent! Take this fry —"

I scrunched up my nose as he dropped it down his gullet. "Mmmm." His beak clattered with pleasure. I'd never thought of seagulls as being dangerous, but when their beak is human-sized, it does make you worry about losing an eye.

"Salty, fatty. So good." He threw himself over the side of the dumpster again, rustling through the trash bags. "I take it you've never dumpster-dived before?"

"Um, nope." I'd heard of people finding perfectly good food tossed out behind supermarkets and restaurants, but the quad cafeteria? Even the salads were greasy.

"I'll find you something you'll like. Gimme a second."

"Knock yourself out."

I glanced at my phone. Christie had said she'd meet me behind the quad at seven, yet here I was, *forty minutes later*, stuck awkwardly conversing with a half-man, half-gull. The strangest thing about it? I wasn't even freaked out. The fact that his existence clicked so neatly into my universe was probably a sign of some as-yet-undiagnosed mental illness. Christie would laugh her head off at me. *Of course something like this* would *happen to* you, *Steph!*

I sighed and texted, [where u at?] before immediately regretting it. She was probably with Rachel. I could just see her, slumped on the couch, phone in hand, rolling her eyes.

Oh my god, it's Steph again. Jesus, can't she get a life? Rachel was in the theater department, too, and since we'd gotten back from summer break, Christie spent every free second with her. All I got were the scraps.

I stuffed my phone into my pocket. The breeze tickled my nose with the scent of rain and blooming flowers. The sky over Oahu glowed a deep, Pacific blue behind the cylindrical freshman towers. The moon gave me a Cheshire Cat's smile.

The floodlight behind the dorm building snapped on, flattening the landscape with harsh, industrial light. I gave my head a savage shake.

I couldn't blame Christie. She had a packed schedule and a lot of pressure. Her dad kept insisting she quit art and major in business; her stepmom only wanted to parent her half-brother Niko and basically treated her as hired help whenever she visited them; and her bio-mom had died when she was eight. Sure, I hated how she got mean whenever she spent time with Rachel, but I wasn't a pathetic, jealous friend who clung to people. I could deal with a little flakiness.

From the dumpster, the guy squawked. "Jackpot!"

He popped up clutching an armload of burgers in greasy wrappers and a zip-top bag of M&Ms, which he held out to me. "Here. Try these. They won't make you sick, I swear."

How rotten could M&Ms get? I took a palmful.

"There you go. One more convert in the battle against consumerist waste. I'm Dom, by the way." He readjusted the burger stash to stick out a hand.

"Stephanie."

His palm was rough like a surfer's, chafed raw by the sea, warm like he'd been baked in the sun. He wore a leather wristband. Between his thumb and forefinger he had a small tattoo of a hook constellation.

He noticed me noticing the ink. "I'm a Scorpio." Peering at me with one bright, yellow eye, he asked, "Waiting for someone?"

"A friend. She's just running a little late."

"Huh. I'd never be late if I were hanging out with you."

My ears went hot. The remaining M&Ms went into his gaping beak, clattering like jackpot coins. This close to him, I got a whiff of his cologne, and immediately realized it wasn't cologne at all: he smelled of brine and wet sand. Clean, like the sea. I shivered.

My phone buzzed.

[srry class ran late. Hang tmrw?]

Disappointment pooled in my stomach. How long had it been since we'd hung out? A week? Two? Had we spent more than a couple of hours together this whole month?

The night pressed down on my shoulders. It felt later than it was.

"Everything okay?" Dom asked. Was my disappointment that obvious?

Don't freak out, I warned myself. *We'll hang tomorrow. It'll be fine.*

"Uh, yeah. My friend had to bail. It's no big deal." I punched back: [no worries. get some sleep]

I shoved my phone in my back pocket. "Anyway," I said lamely, unsure how to excuse myself from this bizarre situation.

"Anyway," Dom said, and I felt sure he was teasing me a little. "We should hang out again sometime. If you ever have a hankering for dumpster food —"

He reached into his pocket and pulled out three small white feathers. He held them out to me like cards in a card trick.

"— just drop one of these, and I'll drop whatever I'm doing."

It seemed rude not to take them, so I did. They were softer than I'd expected, almost downy. He didn't wait for me to say anything, but gave a little wave and strolled off. As he passed through the shadows beyond the floodlight's reach, I swore the seagull head faded, replaced by shaggy hair and a human jawline. Then he was gone, around the corner of the building.

I tucked the feathers in my pocket and went back to my dorm alone.

Christie and I didn't hang out the next day. Or the day after that. In fact, I didn't see her until Thursday, when I happened to catch up with her on the campus mall. She jumped when I nudged her shoulder, dismay snapping into a squeal of joy. We hugged, and I asked how she was.

"*So* busy!" Her head fell back. With her black eyeliner smudged under her eyes, she looked exhausted. "Oh my god, Steph. You're so lucky you're not in the art program. This open gallery show is going to kill me. I should just drop out and go into business like my dad wants."

"What?" I gaped at her. "No way! You can't!"

She snorted, unconvinced.

"Chris, seriously. I can't even draw a stick figure, but you? I mean, that sketch you did of Critter? Or the portrait of Mrs. Dufresne? I mean, it was like a photograph!"

She waved dismissively. "Realistic representation isn't that hard. I mean, it's not art with a capital A. The *masses* like it, but real artists try to capture Truth."

"Sounds like Dame Palette Knife's been getting to you."

Dame Palette Knife was her Introduction to Oils professor, a reedy woman who wore ankle-length cardigans and started class with a prayer to the universe for creative inspiration. She was the one organizing the show, too.

"It's not just her, though, you know? The other kids in my classes are *crazy* good. High school totally inflated my ego because everybody else *sucked*. Here? I'm totally average."

"Come on. You're better than Freya, right?"

Her teeth peeked out between smirking lips. "You are *such* a bitch."

My stomach sank. How many times had she told me Freya's work sucked? Not that I'd seen any myself ... Had I been too mean?

"I dunno." Christie sighed. "It's not like you need a degree to do art. Rachel's friend in advertising said he could get me some gig work. At least then I'd earn my own money. We could get an apartment somewhere and stop having to go home for the summer. God, I hate flying."

She'd mentioned getting an apartment before. While I delighted in the idea of launching my adult life here with her, I withered at the thought of not seeing my parents at the semester's end. Christie was the brave one; me, the grounded one. She pushed me to do new things, like going to school in Hawaii all the way from Massachusetts; I did my best to be her rock. She'd never been all that good at picking people who treated her right, and it felt like my calling to be stable when those other friends and her awful family dragged her down.

"Oh, by the way! I've got a theater thing tonight," she said. "It's at seven in the Kennedy building. You don't have to come, but …"

The sourness in my gut melted away. She needed me, my support. "Wouldn't miss it."

Christie hugged me. "You're the best, Steph. So tell me about this guy, the one with … what was it? A seagull head?" She cackled. "Leave it to you to find the weird ones."

I shrugged, suddenly uncomfortable talking about Dom. I'd forgotten how odd he must look. We'd bumped into each other by accident a couple times on campus, and I enjoyed walking to my classes with him while he rambled on about all the things you can do with leftover bottlecaps and the edibility of carrot tops. But the way Christie said it, *this guy*, like he was *my guy*, made me itchy.

"I dunno. We're just friends. Actually, I don't even know if we're friends."

"He likes you, though, yeah?"

I forced a laugh. *I'd never be late if I were hanging out with you*, he'd said. But he'd been joking, for sure. "Uh, no."

Christie scoffed. "God, Steph, you're so naive. When do I meet him?"

"I guess I could invite him to your show. We could all go grab a bite to eat afterwards?"

"Oh my god, do it. Do it! Please!"

I'd put the three feathers in the desk drawer of my dorm room, and forgotten about them until now. I wasn't even sure if they'd work, but I had no other way to reach him.

I promised Christie I'd try.

I went to the theater a little early and slipped around the corner from where the audience was beginning to gather by the doors. I took the feather from my pocket. It was small and a bit crumpled in my palm.

This is dumb, I thought. *It's not going to work. You're going to look stupid, and Christie will think you didn't want her to meet him.*

I didn't have any other option. Either it'd work or it wouldn't, and I'd have to deal with it. I shifted the cellophane-wrapped poppy bouquet in my arms. Christie loved poppies.

Taking a deep breath, I released the feather, thinking it would fall to the ground. Instead, a sudden breeze caught it up and whirled it away into the sky.

"Hey. Thought you'd never call."

He strolled up out of the warm darkness wearing an old denim jacket with a tear in the shoulder seam and an ancient Three Dog Night T-shirt under it.

"Want to see a show?" I asked. "Christie's in it. She wants to meet you."

He shrugged. "Sure. Why not?"

We moved back to the crowd waiting to enter the theater. People stared at him, though he didn't seem to notice. It wasn't long before the auditorium doors opened and we funneled inside.

Twenty minutes into the play, Christie's part came on: one of six rolling eggs in heather grey sweatsuits, curled up in balls as a dancer in red tulle and a cheap Mardi Gras bird mask performed thumping leaps around them. I glanced at Dom, afraid he found the bird thing offensive, but he sat with his beak low on his chest, eyes squeezed shut, sound asleep.

Christie's egg rolled to the side and cracked, splayed on the stage, dead. The red bird rocked her violently from side to side as she mimed eating her. Only one egg made it, receiving a clumsy on-stage costume change into pink tulle and another bird mask. I stifled a giggle as they funneled offstage.

Afterwards, I nudged Dom awake. "Was it good?" he asked.

"Your nap was better." He clucked with amusement.

We made our way backstage. Christie stood huddled with the other girls in the drama group, Rachel foremost among them dressed — as it turned out — in pink tulle.

I waited by the back door, trying to catch Christie's eye as she laughed with the other girls. She had to see me eventually. The poppies crinkled in my arms. People from the production flowed past us, congratulating each other, giving us puzzled looks as they disappeared into the night. My stomach churned.

Dom sniffed, head cocked to one side. "Are we going to go over?"

The theater girls burst into laughter, Christie's shrieks rising high above them. I shifted the flowers in my arms. "She'll be done in a second."

"It's been twenty minutes. Pretty sure she's seen us."

Had she? Was she waiting for me to come over? Were they all laughing at how long I'd wait by the door?

Two sweatsuit girls vanished into the back halls, leaving Christie alone with Rachel. I steeled myself.

"Yeah, okay. Hold on."

Rachel pouted at me as I approached them. "Oh, Chris, you've got an admirer. Wish someone had gotten *me* flowers!"

Christie slapped Rachel's arm. "Oh my god, you *know* David would bring you flowers if you asked him to."

"He used to bring me flowers without being asked," Rachel said with a sigh, dropping her head back as if exhausted. "Ugh. I should break up with him, shouldn't I? But I hate being alone. And at least he's a great kisser."

Christie rolled her eyes as I handed the flowers to her and made a little *aw* sound.

"You guys were great tonight," I said.

Christie shook her head like I'd just said the stupidest thing in the world. "It sucked," she said. "I mean, the *bird* costumes? You must have been so bored."

Rachel squawked just like a bird, and I glanced back at Dom. "It wasn't so bad from the audience side."

"You are such a liar." Rachel's smile was cold. "My friend Nick attended a Broadway Camp last summer and he said this was the worst thing he'd ever seen in his life, and that includes a high school production of *Cats*."

"Nick was here?!" Christie shrieked, clapping her hands over her mouth. "Tell him I owe him ten bottles of Di Saronno for suffering through that, okay?"

"He's a cheap date. You could probably get away with two."

They burst into cackles and Christie whacked her with the bouquet. Red poppy petals fluttered to the ground.

"Stop! Stop! Stop!" Christie gasped, blinking away tears.

Before Rachel could start again, I said, "Hey, you wanted to meet Dom, right?"

Christie stared at me like she had no idea who I was. Then, with a shiver, she plastered on the fakest grin I'd ever seen. "Oh my god, is that *him*?"

Rachel pinched her arm. "I'll see you at Jerry's, m'kay?"

"Wait, can I get a ride with you?" For half a heartbeat I thought Christie might actually walk away from me. "I'll be two minutes. Promise!"

"Whatever, bitch," Rachel called as she headed down the hall. "It's going to take me thirty minutes to chip off this makeup, anyway."

Christie giggled. It died in her throat as she turned back to me, gaze skipping to Dom as he strolled over. "Wow, he really does have a seagull head."

"I do," Dom said, holding out his sunburnt, tattooed hand. I felt a twinge as Christie took it, her thumb tracing the inked constellation.

"Ooo, Scorpio." She tilted her hips, softening her posture. "Nice. I've wanted to get my sign somewhere for *ages*, but my dad would flip out."

"Ah. Daddy's little girl, huh?"

Christie gave him a narrow smile and slipped her arm through mine. "Something like that. Let me just chat with Steph a second, and then she'll be all yours."

My face caught fire. I glared at her as she drew me towards the stage doors. Right before we passed through, Christie turned, growling, "I don't like him. Not for you."

I tried to scoff casually. "What do you mean, *for me*? We're just friends."

"Don't do that." She was all business, no smile now. "You need to be careful, Steph. You come off as desperate, and some guys feed on that."

"Okay. Whatever, weirdo." I tried to draw back, but Christie clawed at my sleeve. Her fingernails scratched against the skin underneath.

"I'm just trying to protect you. Anyway, I can't join you guys for food. Jerry — he's the teacher — anyway, he wants us to come to his house for an afterparty, and it's for our grade, so ..."

A gap inflated between us. Once again, I was left behind. I tried to swallow the lump in my throat, reminding myself to be cool, to be flexible. "Oh, sure. Of course. Hang out tomorrow?"

"Yeah, maybe."

Yeah, maybe, like *no.* Had I pissed her off? "Hey," I started, but she'd already stepped through the stage doors.

"Thanks for coming, you guys!"

"She's ... interesting," Dom said as we headed outside. "How long did you say you've been friends?"

"Middle school. Eighth grade."

"Huh."

The way he said it nettled me, dug a pin into my sternum and lodged it there, festering. We walked in silence. The sky was grey towards Honolulu, black behind the shadowed hills that encircled the campus. The stink of wet asphalt clogged my nostrils, making my eyes sting.

Huh. What was that tone supposed to mean?

Because Christie's interesting. Christie's cool. He probably wishes I'd stepped aside so he could ask to go to the afterparty with her. It'd have been more interesting. I bet she'd go dumpster diving with him. She's always looking for new experiences, always living life to the fullest. And me? I'm just tagging along like a loser.

"Hey." Dom bumped a shoulder into me as we walked. "You okay?"

"Yeah. Fine." I coughed to clear the phlegm from my throat. "I'm sorry Christie couldn't join us. School stuff. She wanted to come."

"I don't mind."

"She's really amazing. You should see her art, it's ... She could be a professional *now*."

"Good for her."

"What's your problem, huh?" I whirled on him, surprised by my own frustration. "Why don't you like her?"

"Steph, I don't even know her."

"So what was with the *huh*?"

Dom shrugged. We walked on.

"Sorry," he said after a while. "It just seems like she doesn't appreciate you."

"She does, though. And if she comes off as gruff, it's ... it's just how she protects herself. She's got this really sensitive side she doesn't show to anybody but me." My teeth ached as I ground them, unable to articulate the building pressure within me. "You have no idea how cool she is."

"You're cool, too."

I burst out in a sharp laugh. "Not like her. I mean, in high school, every guy I had a crush on liked her. My junior-year boyfriend was her ex, but when we broke up he admitted that he'd only dated me to stay close to her."

"That sucks."

Why was I getting teary? I wanted to shake Dom, get him to understand that Christie didn't deserve his scorn. I'd seen her sobbing in the girl's room, drunk on lemon extract, threatening to kill herself because her dad had called her a whore. Nobody else witnessed Christie's walls down. She needed me.

"I'd never have come all the way out here without her." Tears cinched my throat tight. "I mean, I'd probably be at a dinky community college living at home. I'm a total coward, but with Christie, I *live*, you know? We're practically sisters, and sisters can be jerks sometimes. It's fine!" My voice cracked as tears bubbled up in my eyes, turning the night into a spray of colored stars.

"Hey. Come here."

Before I knew it, Dom's arms were around me and I was crying into his jacket, enveloped in the musty scent. When I drew back, palming the tears from my cheeks, I saw stains on the denim.

"Shit. Sorry." I forced a laugh, shaking my head like *wow, I can't believe I just did that*. Deep in my chest, the tears threatened to surge up to my eyes again. I needed to get back to my dorm before they spilled out and Dom realized I was a psycho hot mess.

The warm night air hugged us as we made our way down the sidewalk. I chewed on my cheek, forcing the well to hold.

"Crying's healthy," Dom said, gazing up at the sky. "Sometimes we need to purge emotions we can only express through tears."

"You sound like a cult leader."

He laughed. "More like my therapist."

"You have a therapist?"

"Yeah. It's helped a lot."

I scoffed. "I can't imagine anything bothering you enough to need therapy for it."

"Oh, trust me," he said, looking down at his shoes, "there's plenty."

The following Wednesday, Christie and I stood in line at the Campus Center sub shop. She stared at her phone, tapping another text to Rachel. They'd been carrying on an extended conversation ever since we'd entered the winding line, and she only looked up when the guy behind the counter told her to put the phone down and order.

"I forgot my meal card," she said as we slid towards the register. "Pay you back?"

Never mind that it was the end of the month, and I was low on points. My parents had warned me they wouldn't pay for extra stuff I didn't need. I sighed. "Sure."

"I mean, you don't *have* to," Christie said, louder than necessary. "I'll just tell the guy I can't pay and get out of line."

"No, it's fine." I nodded at the guy squinting at us from behind the counter. "I've got it."

No 'thank you'. No smile. Her eyes dropped back to her phone, thumbs pattering away.

Outside, heavy clouds pushed down on the campus. A light drizzle slicked the pavement in streetlight shine. My maroon sweatshirt turned wine-dark across the shoulders where the damp soaked in; red dirt, churned into mud, squelched between my toes, making my feet slip sideways off the foam soles of my sandals, ankles twinging with each step. The plastic sandwich bags dragged like too-tight handcuffs on my wrist.

I reached into my pocket and touched Dom's second feather. I'd taken to carrying it around with me since that night after the theater. Something about just having it there, with me, reminded me of his hug, his smile, and gave me a little jolt of energy. *You're cool, too.* He'd been teasing, probably, but it was nice to hear it.

I glanced at Christie. Her eyes glowed in the glare from her screen as she smirked.

"So ... how's Rachel?" I asked.

"Ugh. Terrible. She's got this audition later tonight and is *freaking out*, and her boyfriend might be cheating on her, and it just ... her life sucks. She's in a bad place right now."

"Sorry to hear it."

Her phone pinged, and she looked down. I sighed.

"What?" She squinted at me, hunched low in her shoulders.

"Nothing."

"You just did your martyr sigh. I really need to focus on Rachel right now, okay? Don't be jealous."

I shifted the bags to my other arm as we passed under a sputtering streetlight. Ahead, dorm windows glowed over silhouetted treetops. "I'm *not* jealous."

Christie rolled her eyes at me. "Seriously? You've been jealous of Rachel since Day One."

"I'm not *jealous* of her. I ..." I bit my tongue, trying to find a way to say what I need to without sounding pathetic. "You see her every day in class, and I just ... I miss spending time with you."

"You need to get a life, Steph. I can't be your *only* friend."

"You're *not* my only friend."

Christie's head dropped back, face upturned. "Ugh. Name one."

I thought for a moment. "What about Deanna?"

"Horse-face from Japanese class? Please. Do you even know her last name?"

"Megumi?"

"Are you asking *me* if you're friends?"

"We went shopping together at Ala Moana a few weeks ago."

"And have you talked outside of class since?"

My face tingled. *She's right. You're a loser. You don't have any other friends.*

I thought back to high school, searching my memory for people I would have considered friends, and came up blank. There were some girls I'd hung out with, but they had their own friend groups. I had Christie. I wasn't sure why none of those relationships evolved, and thought of grey sweatsuit eggs flopping open on-stage, dead.

Walking suddenly took focused attention, like I'd forgotten how the muscles worked, how the bones supported each step.

"There's Dom."

Christie snickered. "Oh, right. Seagull boy. Nice."

"Why don't you like him?"

"Why do *you*?" Christie stared at me, teeth bared. "Seriously, you have the *worst* taste in guys."

"It's not like that."

"Whatever." Her gaze dropped to her phone.

Sharp words bounced around in my skull, threatening to break out between my teeth, to snap back, but I knew if they did, I might not see her for weeks until I caved and apologized. So I did what I always did to avoid lashing out: I thought back to weekend sleepovers, laying on my bed while we watched *Outlaw Star*, teasing each other about boys and gossiping about the popular girls; I thought of the crazy bosses we'd had during summer jobs, the delusional — and probably dangerous — cruising we'd done senior year, flirting with guys, leaning out windows to grab event fliers from cars at stoplights. Everything had been better between us in high school.

Had it? The thought zapped me, and I took a deep breath and shoved it down.

On a whim, I drew out Dom's feather and dropped it behind me. A gust of hyacinth-scented wind swirled around us, caught up the feather, and was gone.

"Is everything okay?" I asked. "You seem a little on edge."

Christie shrugged.

"Is it your dad, again?"

"He told me he doesn't want me coming for Christmas this year. Whatever. It's not like I *like* spending the holidays with him and his bitchy wife. I'll miss Nicky though."

She sniffed, and I realized she was about to cry. Shifting the sandwiches, I squeezed her shoulder. "Hey, I'm sorry. If you need a place, you're welcome at my house."

When we rounded the corner, there was Dom in front of my dorm. Hands in pockets, surveying the building, he turned as we came into sight.

"What's *he* doing here?"

Christie stopped, glaring at Dom.

My throat seized up. I shouldn't have called him. I wasn't even sure why I had, only I was annoyed with Christie, and it was nice hanging out with Dom, and —

"I could tell him we're having a girl's night," I said weakly.

"No." She straightened up with a huff. "No. You know what? You want me to get to know him better. So, let's do it. Let's all hang out. Maybe I can figure out what his angle is."

Because he needs an angle to want to hang out with me, I thought, stomach clenching. "Yeah, okay. I really think you'll like him if you give him a chance."

She followed me over. Dom waved. "Hey Steph. Hey Christie."

"We were going to have dinner and watch a movie or something," I said. "Care to join us?"

"You bet."

"Great!" I gave Christie an encouraging smile.

As we tromped up the stairs, Christie hung back with Dom.

"I hear you and Steph are spending a lot of time together," she said. My stomach flip-flopped at her flirty tone.

What is she doing?

"We hang out occasionally."

"Oh! Maybe I got the wrong impression ..."

"Chris!"

She gave me a shit-eating grin. Iridescent disks flashed in her pupils as we passed into the third-floor hall.

"What? It's not *my* fault you made it sound like you guys were ... well, you know."

I snagged her arm, dragging her to the door. "What are you doing?"

Christie's eyebrows arched. "Nothing! Geez, relax."

I unlocked my door as she pivoted back to Dom. "So, what are you guys?"

"Friends." Dom peered at her, squinting. "What are you?"

Christie tittered and swatted him. "Touché! Okay, Steph, I *do* like this guy." She gave him a long side-eye, biting her bottom lip. I shoved my shoulder against the sticky door.

We hung out for about an hour, though it felt like the whole night. Christie sat close to Dom, touching his knee, leaning into him as she chattered incessantly, punctuating her narration with suggestive jokes, usually at my expense. I sat on the floor, numb, picking at my sandwich, my appetite fading each time Dom chuckled at something she'd said. At no point did Christie pull out her phone and start texting, though I heard it buzzing frantically. I wondered how Rachel was holding up. The air in the room thinned minute by minute, until I couldn't get a breath deep into my lungs. It was hard to stay awake.

"Oooooh my god, you're so bad!" Christie burst into giggles. "Well, if you ever want to go downtown, I know some great food trucks to hit up. Seriously. Text me anytime. I'm always up for a falafel. Here —" She dug out her phone, swiping away the notifications from Rachel. "Gimme your number and I'll call you so you have mine."

Dom stretched. "I don't have a phone. Anyway, I don't kick around with much cash."

"Oh, that's no problem! I'll pay. You have to try these falafels. Doesn't he, Steph?"

I flinched at her sudden attention. "Oh. Yeah. No, they're really good."

Dom's fingers brushed my arm. They were so warm. I glanced up to see if he'd done it on purpose, and found him watching me. It sent a jolt of energy through me, enough to enable a single, steadying breath.

"Could be cool," he said, standing. "Anyway, I should probably head out."

Christie jumped up. "Oh, me too! Are you heading back to campus? We could walk together!"

"Nah, I'm actually heading to my pal's place. See you around, though, yeah?"

I dragged myself to my feet. As I walked them to the door, Christie pinched my arm right where Dom's fingers had touched. "You're coming to help me with the paintings tomorrow, right?"

"Yup."

"Good. I don't think I could bear going by myself. You're the best!" She dragged me into a quick hug, fingers stabbing into my back. "Okay, I'm going!"

She pushed past Dom in the doorway, bumping her chest against him. "Whoops! Sorry!"

He hung back as she headed for the stairs, calling behind her, "Have Steph text me when you want falafels, okay? And get a phone!"

Her footsteps scrabbled in the stairwell, filling the air with the rustling of her movement, until the door at the bottom screeched as she slammed out. I sagged against the doorframe, light-headed, the last bit of energy sucked out of me. I wanted to crawl into bed and cry and sleep for days.

Why am I like this? Why can't I just be fun like Christie?

Dom turned to me. "She kind of dominated that hangout, didn't she? I wish we'd had more time to talk."

A flare of energy crashed over me, washing away the images of her fingers tracing the tattoo on his thumb slowly, hypnotizing, of her sultry glance as she pressed past him in the doorway. It hadn't hooked him. He'd seen through it.

"You ... you don't have to go," I blurted, immediately mortified at myself. What was I doing? "I mean, if your friend won't be upset, we could just hang out a little longer. But, I mean, it's fine if you can't. Whatever."

He peered at me with a piercing yellow eye. "I'd like that. Sure. Whatever you want."

Digging around in my dormmate's movie stash, I found *Van Helsing*. I popped it in the DVD player. Halfway through, he slipped a heavy arm around my shoulders, and I nuzzled into his downy throat, inhaling salt and sand and the tang of dried out crab shells. I kissed the corner of his beak, smooth like sun-warmed porcelain. He wrapped his other arm around me.

We moved from the common-room couch to my bed. He was lithe under his shirt, his chest speckled with tattooed shells and dead fish, winged skulls, crab claws, and mermaids. I thought of ancient, animal-headed gods and wondered if he was a symbol for something.

"Do you like me?" I whispered as he nibbled gently at my ear. "I mean ... *me?*"

He sat up. "I do." It should have sounded cornier.

We made out for a while and then snuggled close, eventually dozing off. I awoke a few hours later to find him lying on his back, arms behind his head, beak open, breath rattling softly. I'd wedged myself into the five inches between his elbow and mattress edge, afraid to fall and wake him in case he decided to leave.

As the sky blushed with sunrise, he stirred, beady eyes opening. He sucked in a breath like someone resurrecting.

"Morning." He nuzzled his beak into the crook of my neck, cool and smooth like melting ice. I shivered.

"Did you sleep well?" I asked.

"Mmhmm."

I stroked his ruff as he wriggled closer, his arm cinching around my waist. The popcorn ceiling turned rose, then gold, then white. Outside, palm fronds swayed in the breeze, clattering against my window. I wished we were closer to the sea, right on the shore, listening to the thundering surf.

Why does he like you? The thoughts came unbidden, as always, turning me cold from the inside out. *What could he possibly want from someone like you?*

Doubts congealed in my chest, fossilizing until I had to cough them up in order to breathe. "Christie thinks you're using me."

His chuckle vibrated against my throat. "I'll bet she does."

My stomach went greasy as an oil slick. I rolled towards him. "What makes you say that?"

He grunted, propped himself up on one arm, careful to keep his beak away from my face. An octopus curled its black tentacles from his shoulder to his wrist.

"What do you think I am, Steph?"

"Huh?"

"From the first moment we met, you've just rolled with the fact that — let's be honest — I'm a pretty strange-looking dude. Why do you think that is?"

I frowned. "I don't know. It's just never bothered me."

"But why? It bothers other people."

Just that little detail: it popped up and tripped me over my own nonchalance, putting me off balance. It *was* strange, wasn't it?

"Okay, different question," he said. "Why do you think we bumped into each other that night at the dumpster?"

I shook my head, thoughts whirling like smoke, too unformed to grab. "I — I was just there, and you happened to be —"

He shook his head, pity in his yellow eye. "I followed your scent, Steph. I'm a scavenger. But I don't just eat dumpster food. I eat self-loathing. And you? You reek with it. I picked up your scent trail from all the way downtown."

"Wow. Okay." I got up, crossing my arms across my chest. Had I seriously just made out with a guy who said I smelled like trash?

Christie was right. You are *desperate! He never liked you. It was a game, a ruse. He* is *using you. Oh my god, you're so stupid.*

"Steph." Dom sighed. "I'm sorry, it's hard to explain."

"No, I think I've got it. I'm, like, trash."

"No. You treat yourself like trash. And there are people out there, like me, who feed off that energy. The more time you spend with us, the worse you feel about yourself until we drain every ounce of self-respect you have. You give up on yourself and let the years slide by, too afraid to try anything, marinating in regrets. It's an awful existence. Some don't survive it."

It was just like Christie had warned me: *You come off as desperate and some guys feed on that.*

Except, I *didn't* feel bad when I was with Dom. I watched as he slung his legs over the side of the bed and stood, catching up his T-shirt.

"But you're not feeding on me, are you," I said.

"Nope."

"Why not?"

He threaded his beak through the neck and wrestling it down over his bare stomach. "You caught me in a transition. Six months ago, I would have gorged myself on your self-esteem. But I got sick of making the world a worse place. My soul is bleached, decaying. It'll kill me, too, eventually, if I don't change. And when I smelled your trail, I knew you were in trouble. You're too nice to hate yourself so much."

The sunlight cut a glaring stripe across the desk and floor, imprinting my vision with purple bars. "I don't hate myself."

"Yeah. You do. And I'm not the only one who knows it. People like me, we can hide in broad daylight pretty damn well. Next time you start feeling really shitty about yourself, look at who you're with. Start with the eyes."

He took me by the shoulders, gave me a gentle peck on the cheek. "You can still save yourself," he whispered, his breath smelling faintly of crab and cigarette smoke, "but you don't have much time."

Christie stood in front of her dorm with three canvases propped up against her knees, tapping furiously into her phone. She didn't even look up when I came over, just thrust one of the canvases at me.

"About time! What took so long?"

I thought of all the times she'd been late or blown me off entirely, but kept them to myself. She was stressed about the show. I could handle some saltiness.

I took the canvas, and she clicked her tongue, scrunching her pointy nose. "Careful! Geez. I only finished these a few days ago and the paint's probably still wet."

She, I noticed, held them the same way I had grabbed mine initially, but apparently she knew what she was doing. A scratching irritation started under my skin as I followed her down the sidewalk.

The sun microwaved us through breaks in the clouds as we made our way to the art building. The rays evaporated the morning's moisture so fast, it formed banks of mist that clung to our knees. My jeans absorbed it, turning tacky and damp. The inner seams chaffed against my skin, raising welts, but Christie kept a brisk pace and I had to scramble to keep up with her.

Pigeons scattered as we cut across the courtyard, abandoning the bits of trash they'd been fussing with. Christie reached the door first and whipped through, not bothering to stop and hold it for me. A wave of icy air billowed out behind her, sucking the breath out of my throat and jolting me with a flash of anger.

She was already almost at the staircase before I got inside. "Hey! Could you wait for me at least?"

She only cast a glare over her shoulder. My face started burning; my heart hammered. I jogged to catch up, and managed to come up behind her as she reached the second floor.

"Are you mad at me?" I asked.

Christie scoffed. "Oh my god, Steph. Not everything is about *you*, okay?"

It felt like a slap to the face. "What the hell, then? Why are you being like this?"

Christie whirled on me, glowering. "I'm stressed, okay? I spent last night hanging out with that freak you like, bored out of my mind, and I didn't sleep because I'm sick to death about putting my work up in a public space. God, Steph, how can you not *get* that?"

"You didn't seem bored last night."

"What's that supposed to mean?"

"You know what I mean." I tried to catch my breath, the alarms in my head blaring for me to stop, to shut up, but now that I'd started, it boiled up under my skin and burst out of my mouth. "You spent all evening flirting with Dom, touching his arm, laughing at everything he said. That stunt by the door?"

"Oh my god, Steph. Do you honestly think I'm trying to steal him from you or something? Grow up!"

"I didn't say you were trying to steal —"

"Oh, come on." She gave me a deadpan glare. "That's what you meant, though, wasn't it? Get a life, Steph. Seriously."

She hurried on, shoulders hunched, shaking her head. I trailed behind, struggling to keep up her pace. I was a bad friend. I was making this about me, but it wasn't. This was Christie's day. I was insecure and immature and jealous and so incredibly selfish.

I trailed her through a propped-open pair of double doors into the dimly lit gallery space. Dozens of paintings were already up on the walls, glowing under spotlights. An abstract painting caught my eye; its slashes of thick, white paint against blue made me think of a flock of seagulls wheeling above the ocean. Below the canvas, I caught a glimpse of the nametag: the painting was Freya's.

I stared at the artwork, at how beautiful it was. How could Christie think this was *bad?* It was wild and free and — if I was totally honest? — I liked it better than Christie's pieces. I felt like an idiot for all the times I'd just assumed Christie was right, that Freya was a hack loser. But there was nothing wrong with Freya's art. She was gifted. Inspiring, even.

Dom's words came back to me: *When you start feeling bad about yourself...*

Christie propped her canvases against the wall in the back corner and stood frowning at them.

"Great. The color's all wrong under these lights."

The spotlight on the blank wall cast a slash of shadow across her face. *Start with the eyes ...*

She'd always worn a lot of mascara and eyeshadow, but today she'd really caked it on. It feathered out across her cheekbones like fur, whisking back towards her ears.

Ears? She didn't have any, not where a human would have them. Nausea swelled up in my gut when she glanced back at me, and I caught those bright, iridescent eyes full-on. Tufted ears on top of her head, needle canines, pointy nose, silver-brown whiskers. It was impossible not to see it.

I gasped for breath. "You *are* like him."

She stared at me, and then with a little shake, her surprise switched off. "Ugh. He told you. Asshole."

I couldn't believe it. We'd been friends for years, yet here she was, visible for the first time: a girl body and a raccoon head. A scavenger like Dom. *That* was what he'd meant when he asked why I didn't find him strange. Because I'd been exposed to someone like him for years. My brain just accepted that these were the kind of people who liked me. Or liked preying on me.

The nausea roiled, and I set the canvas against the wall, swallowing the sudden rush of saliva to keep from puking on the floor.

"Why didn't you tell me?"

Christie shifted her weight to one hip and sneered. "You could have seen it anytime you wanted to bother opening your eyes."

As if by her command, my thoughts turned against me, pummeling me with shame and doubt. *Why didn't I see it? Was I just stupid? Nobody else was dumb enough not to see her for what she was. But me? I was too desperate for a friend, any friend. That was it, wasn't it? I was a lonely loser who would cling to anybody who pretended to like me.*

I clenched my eyes against a sudden rush of tears. In my pocket, something pricked me through the fabric. Reaching in, I felt Dom's last smooth feather. *He'd* never hidden himself from me. With Dom, what you saw was what you got.

I could call him. I could drop that last feather and he'd be right there beside me in a moment. But what if I never saw him again after that? My heart ached, but it helped the nausea pass.

I stood to face Christie alone.

She combed her fingers through her fur. "Look, I get that it's a bit of a shock. Okay? But it's not like I've *changed*, you know? You accept Dom, so why can't you accept me?"

"Because you're feeding on me." My voice was stronger and angrier than I'd expected.

"So?" She grinned through sharp teeth. "It didn't bother you before that asshole showed up. He's trying to break us apart. Can't you see that? And after he does, he'll eat what's left of you until you're nothing but a pathetic shadow of regret. Is that what you want?"

"Friends don't lie to each other. You used me."

She hunched into her shoulders, her smile shifting into a grimace. "How is this *my* fault? You practically jam your self-doubt down my throat! *Oh, I'm so bad at art, Christie, and you're soooooo good. You're the cute one; I'm just a boring old blob of wasted skin.* You think you're doing it to lift me up, but the truth, *Steph*? You're just fishing for compliments. *No, no, Steph, you're soooooo smart! You're cute, too! You're totally talented!*" She tittered. "It's pathetic. How can I *not* eat when it's served up like that? Nobody else will put up with you self-deprecating bullshit."

You are so pathetic, the voice in my head whispered. It sounded like Christie. Ever since we'd become friends, I realized, that little voice had burrowed into me, seeding doubts, tearing away at my confidence. And yes, I *had* wanted her to tell me I was worthy, to validate and encourage me, but that was only because I liked validating and encouraging her, because that's what friends *do*.

She'd weaponized that against me, and blamed *me* for it!

A whiff of something stale crept into my nose. It bloomed around me, smelling of mold and rotten grease. It took me a moment to realize it was *me*. I could smell it, now, the decay of my self-respect. It was so strong, my eyes watered.

Christie pouted. "Aw, don't cry. You can't help it that you're boring and lame."

I gripped the feather in my pocket as her words clawed into me, hooking something deep within that dragged me towards her, a gravitational tug I'd never noticed before.

"Come on," she said, expression softening. "I promise I won't feed on you anymore, okay? Rachel's so insecure and self-centered, I don't even really *need* you. Let's just go back to the way things were. It's so much better not knowing, isn't it? I can do that. I can make this all disappear if you want me to."

She held out a hand, but I clenched my teeth and took a step back. Her hold on me snapped. The gallery brightened suddenly, chasing the shadows back, and air swept into my lungs. It felt like the first breath I'd ever taken.

"I'm done being your trash," I said.

Christie cackled. "Whatever, loser. No one else will ever like you. You're plain and stupid and boring. You'll be all alone, and you can't bear that, can you? I give it a day before you come running back."

Later that night, I thought of a dozen burns that would have wiped that smug grin off her rodent face and sent her scurrying for the bushes. But in the moment, all I could come up with was, "Goodbye, Chris," and walking away.

The skies were on fire above Waikiki Beach that evening. I stood in ankle-deep sand under a banyan tree bower strung with fairy-lights, listening to the hushed whisper of the waves and letting the gold and scarlet and plum clouds burn verdigris, emerald, and daffodil shapes on the backs of my eyes. The breeze tugged at my shirt, running warm fingers across my empty palm where the feather had been just a moment ago.

I heard him coming, a certain lazy lilt in grit-covered sandals, the friendly squawks of the seagulls near me as they lifted into the sky. His warmth settled in beside me and we stood shoulder to shoulder, watching the sunset fade.

"We don't get sunsets like this in Massachusetts," I said. "They look like paintings."

He didn't say anything for a bit, and then, "I can't smell you anymore."

"I confronted Christie."

"Good for you."

The lights in the banyan branches overhead cast a soft glow on his feathers. The breeze riffled through them. He blinked and looked at me, smiling in that seagull way, beak slightly ajar, eyes twinkling.

"Thank you," I said.

He shook his head. "For what?"

"For seeing something worth saving in me, I guess." I frowned, peering out across the darkening waters. "I think I just needed to hear it from someone else. To know the way she made me feel wasn't all in my head."

"An outside perspective can be good like that," he said.

We strolled down the walkway along the curve of the beach, hands in pockets, not talking. Ahead of us, Diamond Head's hulking shoulders stood out black against the evening blue. The scent of the ocean finally gave me the strength to speak.

"I've really enjoyed hanging out with you," I started, then felt my throat tighten up.

"I sense a 'but' coming ..."

I sniffed, willing back the urge to cry. "I think I need to work on myself for a bit, you know? It's been so long, I need to learn how to trust myself again, and ... Sorry, I hope you understand."

"I do." He nudged our shoulders together and peered at me with one of those twinkling yellow eyes. "Never apologize for taking care of yourself."

I threw my arms around him and squeezed tight. "Where are you going to go now?"

He clucked as we parted. "Plenty of other folks out there could use a good outside perspective. And my soul's got a long way to go before it's healed. But maybe we'll bump into each other at a dumpster sometime."

"I'd like that," I said.

"Me too. Good luck, Steph. You've got this."

With that, he tucked his hands into his pockets and strolled off into the night. I watched him lift his beak to taste the air, and wondered whose scent trail he'd follow next. Whoever they were, they were lucky. They just didn't know it yet.

Then he was gone, and I was alone.

I caught the bus back to campus, and strolled alone down the dormitory plaza. There was a lightness and joy in my step that I hadn't felt in a long, long time. I was free, I realized. Like a feather on the breeze.

About the author

Maggie Slater's speculative fiction has appeared in *Apex Magazine, Metaphorosis,* and *Redivider,* among other venues. She lives in an 1800s farmhouse in New England with two half-tamed boys, one half-trained dog, her husband, her parents, and at least one benign ghost. When she has an almost quiet moment, she enjoys Haruki Murakami novels, sampling craft beer, and hoarding cheap notebooks. For more information about her and her current projects, visit her blog at maggieslater.com or find her on Instagram: @maggiedot_writes or on Bluesky: @maggiedotwrites.

Magic Is Given

Jacy Morris

The thing about magic is that it works, but people don't have the patience for it. They are greedy, want it to happen right away. A spell, a real working spell, takes time — in fact, it might take your whole life.

The elders had told her as much, regaled her with tales of those who had given their lives to an impossible task. They had warned her not to go the same way.

"It might never happen."

The words of the elder rang in her ear as she pulled herself awake. Coals hissed in the fire, embers floating away on the wind like fireflies before blinking out. Haven stared into the dying light exhausted and lonely, with only the world around her for company. She studied the glimmering remains of the night's fire, tried to unravel the message in their shifting luminescence. A large part of her wished to return home to her tribe, to give up the quest she'd set out upon, to hear the laugh of her brother once more. But Haven knew that without her mother, she could never be happy.

The coals whispered of the brevity of life. Like the fire, Haven only had so much time on this earth, and she had already wasted too much of it camped on the side of a mountain with only her memories and her desires to keep her company.

Haven scowled at the coals. *You don't have to tell me.* An image unfurled in her mind — her mother slipping on a mossy stone in the river, her arms spinning in the air, the back of her head cracking upon a submerged rock, blood in the water.

Out here, camped under the shadow of the sacred mountain, the world constantly reminded Haven how quickly her life, and her quest, could end. Every time she scaled a tree, clambered up the mountainside, or braved the chill night air in the hopes of spying that dark shape in the sky — the one she needed to complete the spell — she knew the fear of death. One broken branch, one mistimed step, one loose stone, and she would cease to be — as quickly as her mother had. And then what hope would there be for her brother and her father?

Am I doing more harm than good?

Is this worth it?

It wasn't only her own life she had to worry about. When her mother had died, so too had Haven's entire family. Her father pulled into himself like a turtle retreating from the world, leaving Haven to comfort and raise her brother. She knew nothing about raising a child, and despite her efforts, her brother seemed to be growing up odd. None of the other children played with him, and he grew prone to long bouts of silence. He needed a mother just as Haven did. Haven's mother was the key to her entire family, and thus her entire world.

Without her mother, Haven couldn't live her own life, couldn't think of starting a new family until her old one was healed. Until her father could smile with his eyes as he'd used to, until her brother knew the pure love of a mother, Haven's next life could never begin. The river of Haven's life had frozen over, trapping her the moment her mother's skull had split upon that treacherous stone.

After years of failing to fill the void her mother had left, Haven had informed the elders of her quest. They'd told her not to go searching for the components of the spell, that she might waste her whole life searching for them. "One death should not lead to two."

A person couldn't just take the components of a spell. If they did, the spell would be tainted, and nothing would work. The components had to be given freely or found in the wild. Her friend Joonski had discovered this the hard way when she'd tried to perform a love spell on the object of her affection. She hadn't shown the patience, had taken the reagents from nature without their blessing. In the end, her spell had worked but with unintended consequences. Her beau had loved her — for all of a month — left her with child and then disappeared into the wilderness. At least Joonski still had the child, so it wasn't all a loss.

Success *was* possible. She knew it from the stories the elders had told in her childhood, the stories they tried to ignore now. But she remembered the spell components, the distant locations requiring months of perilous travel through wastes, swamps, and mountains.

She ignored the elders' warnings. Without her mother's embrace, without the possibility of a family of her own, she might as well be dead already, she'd argued.

The elders wearied of trying to change an unchangeable mind. Instead, they gave Haven one last piece of advice: "For a spell to work, you must gather the components yourself. They must be imbued with the pieces of your life you dedicate to acquiring them. Magic is a consuming thing."

But Haven had already lost the pieces of her life she cared about. All that was left to her was time.

She had spent a year in the wastes waiting for a serpent to lick her lips, another year in the southern reaches wading through the bogs to find the leaves of the Heaven Tree, and another month waiting for the season to change and a leaf to drop into her hand.

Haven knew patience. She would not allow herself to succumb to greed. If the world meant her to bring back her mother, it would give her the last item she needed — a feather of the great bird — or else she would die waiting on the side of this mountain. She might fail like those others the elders had mentioned, might become a cautionary tale herself, but at least she would have tried. Sometimes, that was all a person could do.

Patience was the key. Haven didn't want to think of the consequences of what would happen if she used a tainted reagent, what cruel joke the world would play on her and her resurrected mother. In her mind's eye, she pictured her mother standing in front of her, dark and twisted, alive but not alive. Shuddering, she poked at the fire, tried to bring it back to life, to take away the morning chill. But the fire was too far gone, and she had work to do, so she buried the ashes and prepared for the day.

The great bird hadn't been seen since her great grandfather's time. But Haven believed, and she hoped that would be enough. Belief is a magic of its own, given freely with no consequence. She'd listened to the stories of the eldest in her village, watched as she mentally traveled back in time to her youth, her face softening with wonder as she recalled falling under the all-encompassing shadow of the bird flying in the sky.

The elders said the great birds were magic themselves, and that the world was changing. Some elders feared the birds had already gone on to the next world, but Haven believed. She had listened to the elders' tales, interrogated them until they begged her to leave them alone and let them rest.

Now, here she was, camped at the foot of the sacred mountain, her tribe's traditional homeland, abandoned after a wildfire had ripped through its forested slopes two generations ago. The trees had come back, healthier than ever, growing strong in the charred soil, reaching for the skies. Around her, the forest's boughs danced and swayed as she wandered and picked their bounty, feeding herself, keeping her energy strong. The tart berries she gathered exploded in her mouth, and she washed them down with water. As the forest awakened, she reveled in the songs of the birds, imagined they sang to her, blessing her every step.

In the middle of the day, with the sun shining overhead, she climbed a pine tree to survey the land. The rough bark of the tree scraped against her hands as she wended her way up and up until the limbs began to bend under her weight. She scanned the world around her, wondered what her brother was doing back at the village. It had been months since she'd seen him. In truth, she'd only ever returned to the village to check on him. She could have continued on her quest for the rest of her life without seeing anyone if it weren't for him. Her brother's desperation, his need to be loved, pulled at her heart, but even when she spent time with him, he didn't seem right, was missing the spark of life the other children had. The other children knew it, too. They avoided him because he didn't know how to love. The cold duty of her father was no substitute for what her mother could provide.

Her brother had grown in the time she'd been away, begged her to let him come with her in a voice that was a treasure all its own. She wanted nothing more than to allow her brother to come with her, so they could learn everything about each other, so they could grow as one, like the vines use the trunk of the aspen to reach up to the heavens. But he was too young, didn't yet have the ability to believe in his heart. When you're young, you're flighty, and this is why children can't do magic, and why many adults believe it's not possible — because it didn't work when they were children.

"Is Momma coming home?" he'd asked her last time.

"She will," Haven had said with conviction. "I will bring her home, and she will be pleased to see you, to know the man you're growing into. And she will love you, and you will love her."

Her brother had never known their mother, as she had died when he was still stumbling around the camp in diapers.

"How do you know?" he'd ask, the doubt of youth tainting his heart.

"I just do." She could have explained the process of magic to him, but that would only increase his desire to join her.

She had hugged him, stayed with him, checked on her father who was quiet now, but who still looked after her brother. He didn't believe her either, had been so tainted by the loss of his wife, that if it weren't for Haven's brother, she believed he would have given up on living a long time ago.

Haven shook her head, scanned the skies for the shadow of the great bird. The elders said it was tricky, that it wouldn't show itself to just anyone.

After another mouthful of berries, Haven sighed, lashed herself to the branch for her long watch, and leaned back against the crook of the tree — recalling her mother's face, the curve of her cheekbones, the crooked smile, the gleam in her eyes. She fell asleep that way, lashed to the tree, swaying back and forth as the wind soughed through the treetops and the birds sang her to sleep.

She awoke to a clap of thunder, lifted her head to discover not a cloud in the night sky. She thought maybe she had dreamed the thunder, perhaps jerked herself awake with a memory from the dreamworld, but then the sound came once more, physically assaulting her.

Her head turned of its own volition, locked in on the spot where she thought she'd heard the thunder originate. In that spot, the stars didn't shine. A great shadow appeared to be blotting out the sky. And then it struck her … the great bird. With shaking hands, she undid her lashings, and began descending the tree, moving carefully in the dark though her heart hammered in her chest. Every second she spent in the tree, she worried the bird would escape, vanish, and she would have missed her opportunity.

Risking her own life, fully aware the massive bird could swallow her in one gulp, she pressed forward. The elders had never mentioned tales of the great bird feeding on humans, but she supposed if it did eat people, they wouldn't be returning to tell the tale.

Another crack of thunder hit her halfway down the young pine, and she knew it came from the flap of its wings, just as the elders had said. The force of the massive wings sent a wind rushing through the tree, almost causing her to lose her grip and tumble to the ground. It was close now.

She leaped from the bottom branch of the tree and landed roughly. The tree's old, dead pine needles stabbed into her hands, drawing blood. She rubbed her hands against each other, removing the needles, and then she sprinted up the slope of the sacred mountain, her head craned backward, trying to spot the part of the sky where the stars didn't shine. The great bird seemed to be in no hurry, just spun round and round, as if searching for prey. *What if it eats me?*

The thought frightened her, but she had come too far, knew if she lost sight of the great beast now, she might never find it again.

"Oh, great being!" she called. "See me! I am down here!"

She scrambled up the slope of the mountain where the pines had not yet reclaimed their land. The sky opened up before her. She stumbled up the sacred peak, falling, her hands held out to the bird, beseeching its favor. She didn't know if it heard her, but it stayed, circling and circling in the moonless sky.

Haven climbed, calling out to it, leaving her skin behind on the stones of the mountain, dripping her blood into the soil clinging to its rocky sides. She proffered her sweat, her blood, and then her tears as exhaustion consumed her. Up and up she climbed, growing dizzy as the great bird glided in lazy circles above her.

Close. It's close. But really, it was as far away as it had ever been.

The slope grew steeper, and she climbed with one eye on the sky, pressing upward, trying to launch herself into the air, not for herself, not for her mother, but for the brother who had never known his own mom and the father who had lost all joy in life. She used their faces to stoke the fire in her breast, and the night grew longer and darker, more and more stars appearing, but for the patch where the object of her need soared.

She tried to send her desires to the beast, to impart its importance to her, to beg of it the gift she needed to complete the spell.

"Oh, please, please, please," she repeated as she ripped the fingernails from her hands and tore her clothing to shreds on jagged spurs of dark stone. She offered herself to the mountain, to the bird, and still it merely hung in the sky, judging her.

When she reached the peak of the mountain — a flattened, broken surface with centuries of charred sage burned into the stones by her ancestors — she reached up to the sky like a child wishing to be picked up by a parent. Her hands opened and closed, and she shouted at the bird, hoping it could hear her over the rushing wind.

"Please!" she shouted. "It's not for me! It's for my brother who has never known joy and love! It's for my father, who lives only out of duty!"

The shadow rotated in the sky, seemed to drift away. The great bird was leaving.

"I will give you whatever you want! Anything!" she called, her voice cracking in her throat, tears pouring down her cheeks.

Another rotation, and the shadow receded, more stars appearing in the sky as it flew farther away.

"If you leave, we will all die! My father will wither away, my brother will grow hard and crooked, and I will lay down on these rocks and give my body to the earth! Oh, please!" Haven's blood ran from her wounded hands and down her arms in dark ribbons to land upon the rocks.

The great being in the sky roared, its screech making the top of the mountain tremble, and Haven's eyes shut in pain, as if they were connected to her ears and could stop the abuse, but still she stayed on her feet.

When next she opened her eyes, a patch of stars appeared and disappeared above, and a moment later, she felt the flap of its wings. The wind knocked her backward onto the stones, bringing forth more blood from her scraped arms and legs. The thunder of the being's wings deafened her, and she held a bloody hand up to it. This close to it, she felt its magic, felt the sentience in the buffeting wind. It spoke with its wings, with the air it cracked and sent radiating outward.

"*Why should I?*" it seemed to say.

Haven, still lying on her back, clasped her hands together and squeezed her eyes shut. *Because I believe.*

A great peal of thunder flowed over her, rocking her and stealing her hearing. The gusts from the being's wings threatened to drive her off the side of the mountain, but still she held her hands together, chanting, "I believe," over and over.

One last rush of air buffeted her, and she felt something drift across her supplicating hands. And then, with a great crack, she lost her hearing for good. Something fell upon her. When she opened her eyes, the stars were gone.

The feather lay on her like a blanket obscuring the world, and for a moment she thought she'd died, that she lay in the belly of the great bird. But then a gentle breeze slid across the mountain top, ruffling the feather atop her, allowing her to see the skies above. She sat up, and the human-sized feather slid off her. She ran her hands across its velvet vanes, marveling at their suppleness. The rachis of the feather, as thick as her wrist, reflected the stars above.

She pulled the feather to her chest, bowed her head in thanks. Tears dripped from her eyes, ran off the waterproof feather, and dripped onto the stones of her tribe's sacred mountain.

"Thank you," she whispered, though she did not hear the words.

She lay this way for some time, not quite believing she'd succeeded in her quest. Then the sun rose and revealed the truth of her success. The pitch-black feather turned iridescent in the sun's rays, and Haven longed to show its beauty to her father and her brother.

Haven descended the mountain, no easy feat with a massive feather clutched in her hand. At her camp, she packed her gear for the return trip home. Though she could no longer hear the song of the birds or the rustling of the trees dancing in the wind, she could hear other sounds in her mind — the memory of her mother's voice soft and filled with love.

"I'm coming, Mother. We will be a family again."

As she entered her village, the villagers rushed to greet her, marveling at the massive feather in her arms. The normally stoic elders eyed her with pride, smiles on their faces as the gift of magic returned to the village once more. Haven rejected their misplaced pride, knowing she hadn't earned it. After all, magic is given. All she'd done was hold out her hand.

Her father embraced her, his hand gently touching the feather as tears wetted his cheeks. Her brother gazed up at her with wonder in his eyes.

"What is it?" his lips seemed to say.

"A gift. The way to bring Mother home."

About the author

Jacy Morris is an Indigenous author. He is a registered member of the Confederated Tribes of Siletz. At the age of ten he was transplanted to Portland, Oregon, where he developed a love for punk rock and horror movies, both of which tend to find their way into his writing. He has written several novels, including the *This Rotten World* series and the *One Night Stand at the End of the World* series. His latest novel *We Like It Cherry* will be published by Tenebrous Press in August 2025.

About hope

I hope the world comes to the same realization I have: that all lives are valuable and worthy of protection, and that we continue to fight for the rights of everyone, and not just those we identify with. It might seem like an impossible task, but as I show in my short story "Magic is Given", sometimes the impossible is worth working toward.

Shiver Soft Feathers

L'Erin Ogle

Jake was halfway through his sandwich, the mustard making the bread soft and mushy against his molars, squeezing in the spaces between his teeth to fester until he brushed them. He hated the mid-shift, two to ten PM, sitting in a hot car letting the Kansas sun bake him crisp all day long. When the sun set, the calls would start pouring in. People sat around and got drunk and angry in the summer heat, then night cooled it down enough for them to find the energy to beat their wives, rob their dealers, and get into bar fights that spilled out on sidewalks and pulled bystanders into their orbit.

He put his sandwich down and took a drink of water, swished it around to get rid of the spare bits. His radio clicked, about to broadcast. He ran his tongue over his teeth. The radio crackled to life, the dispatcher requesting a unit to respond for some kind of domestic situation called in on the side of the road. Jake sighed, hit the lights, left the sirens silent, and began driving, gravel scattering from under his tires.

The request had originated between 1300 and 1350 Rd, on Turner Road. He knew all these roads, even this one, one of those little lanes that was mostly mud, with a sign that read NO MAINTENANCE.

He arrived at the scene, where there was an SUV parked on the side of the road with its flashers on. A silver-haired man in blue jeans and a collared T-shirt was standing in front of the open driver's door, and he looked relieved to see Jake. He backed away from the open door, said, "I came up on her walking just back there." He pointed a few yards away. "Had to stop real quick. She was walking right in the middle of the road. She's got blood on her, but only her feet look hurt."

The girl sat in the driver's seat, maybe four or so, skinny legs dangling off the seat, the air conditioning blowing her dirty blonde hair around. It looked greasy and ill-kept, the ends uneven and frayed, like the strings of his hooded sweatshirts. She had bloodstains the color of rust on her clothes: a tiny pair of shorts and a threadbare Royals T-shirt that was too big for her, her arms swallowed by the sleeves.

"Hi, darlin," he said. He crouched down to look her in the eyes. She had pale blue eyes that looked out past him. She acted like she didn't hear him, so he patted her knee. "Hello, I'm Deputy Jake. I'm with the police." He tapped his badge, the silver star. "Are you hurt anywhere?"

The girl's flat eyes never moved. She shook her head.

"Where'd you come from?"

She pointed back down Turner, still silent. He felt the rumble of the ambulance coming.

He radioed in to update Dispatch. The medics would take the girl, who still wasn't talking, to the local hospital. Jake would start looking down Turner for where she'd come from. But, really, how far could a barefoot kid have walked in the sun on the hot dirty gravel?

Two miles, apparently. Two miles from the stop, he spotted a small dirt driveway about thirty feet long that led to a small rundown tan trailer. He eased his car down the ruts in the drive, came to a stop behind an old dusty Ford Ranger. The plates were expired by a month, not that uncommon. The trailer was a double-wide, had seen better days, big flaking rust spots dotting the sides. He radioed in his location, opened his door, and stepped out. He flicked open the strap that crossed the top of his gun, put his hand right on the butt. The smell drifting out of the trailer was the smell of copper and chemicals, and it meant one thing to Jake — the same thing it meant to every cop, medic, coroner in rural counties. Death and meth. Meth brings death, he thought, standing outside his unit, lights on, no sirens. Just silence and smell, lit up blue-red-blue-red. He waited, watching the door to the trailer swing in the wind. There were small bloody handprints on the door, where the girl had come out.

He approached the door after he saw and heard nothing but the wind whispering across the flat land. Here, the copper death meth smell was thicker, choking him, closing up his airway. He kept his hand on his gun, felt it solid and cool against his palm. He had a bad feeling about this whole thing, that maybe a body or bodies in there had been in the August heat for days, rotting and swelling until they burst along the seams. Maybe the guilty party was still there, lips wrapped around a glass pipe or with a needle dangling from their arm, waiting for suicide by cop.

It happened more than people thought. He knocked loud and sharp on the door, the boom boom boom that made anyone who knew the law go quiet and still. It said cops. It said, open up or run, but down you go either way.

There was no answer. He was sweating heavy under the vest and the belt and the Kansas heat. The trailer was silent, no views through the window, all the cheap shades pulled down. Some of the slats were snapped off at the edges. All the dopers had the same blinds, always broken at eye level. The paranoia was real after a day or two without sleep. They'd run to the blinds and lift them up to check for whatever demons they thought were out there—cops or thieves or ghosts. Course, the real demon was always right next to them.

He used his foot to catch the swinging metal door and keep it open. "Police," he called. "Coming in!"

He was quick through the door, a little two-step dance, scanning right to left. The trailer went both ways from entry. To the right was a little spot with a fold-down table and booths, both splashed with rust-colored blood spread over scattered white crystals and ashtrays and crumpled cans. He turned his back on it and went on to the little living area. There was a space for a TV that held some paraphernalia, needles, spoons, an empty two-liter bottle with the top sawed off. And a mattress saturated with blood.

It was here the copper chemical stink stopped being heavy and became impenetrable, the sheets stained black.

No bodies yet.

The soft hair on the back of his neck stood at attention. There was something crawling around in his stomach, making it clench like a fist. He listened, but the booming of his heart echoed across his eardrums. This was a bad place, where something bad had happened, and bad places where bad things happened had histories that repeated themselves.

He passed through the narrow hall, cleared the tiny shower stall. There was a different smell now, a stale smell, that reminded him of his grandma's assisted living place. It wormed under his skin and hummed like an air unit, kicking up gooseflesh all over.

There was another door that he pushed open with his foot. The bed there sagged heavy with stains, but no blood. Just neglect. There was a torn Tinkerbell blanket and some broken crayons on it, empty juice boxes and chip bags on the floor. Some kids' clothes, all pinks and purples, folded in a pile on the floor. Someone had cared a little at some point in time.

On the left side of the bed, there was one of those little rectangle doors that you could pull out of the wall, where it led to a space used for storage, a few feet that unfolded between the trailer siding and the wall. The opening was dark, and there wasn't any blood, but his heart beat loud in his chest as he approached it.

He put his head into the dark. The smell in there was shit. Human shit. He gagged on it, at the collection of feces piled in the corner. And then his eyes moved to the opposite corner.

The cleanest thing he'd seen yet. White ivory bones gleamed at him — dozens of them, stacked in piles.

Human bones, he knew. Big bones.

And feathers the size of sunflower petals, littered everywhere, white as the bones. He reached out and dragged his fingers against one, felt it shiver soft against the soft pads of his fingerprints.

He went back out. Radioed in. Asked for a run on the Ranger tags.

The tags came back to a Spencer Myers, 37-year-old white male. Previous arrests for drugs, DUI, domestics. Current warrants for probation violations and failures to appear.

Who'd you drag into your shit, Spencer? Had to be about drugs. Meth addicts were notorious for violence.

The picked-clean bones, though? How'd that happen? Was it a message? Jake hadn't heard of anything like that round here. More like slash and run, or shoot and run, that's what the locals did. Quick, violent, and bloody.

So, who was the girl, and why leave her?

That was what bothered him, as the horizon lit up with the familiar red and blue lights of the other deputies arriving. Whom did the bones belong to, where had the adults who had been living in this trailer gone, and how did the little girl fit in?

The little lost girl goes to an older couple for emergency placement. They call her Kate, after their stillborn daughter from decades before. They're quiet Methodist folks. They have no other children. It would be dangerous to place her anywhere else, the social worker whispers. Not without knowing what happened.

Kate sits with her knees pressed together. She is now half of a whole. Half of her left in a flutter of feathers. She still remembers how bones sharpened and carved through skin and muscle to fly free, a blur of snow-white wings and bloody droplets. She remembers. She just doesn't talk about it.

She draws pictures. Bird after bird after bird, wings spread, towering over the sheets of construction paper. She wants to be free. Everyone watches her, and she feels restraints drawing tight around her. The dust and the people close in on her and she focuses on the ticking in her mind, the sound of a clock shaving away time. Counting down.

From that foster home she goes to another, and another, and another. She's not really any trouble, but she's not quite right either. She speaks when spoken to. She has school and therapy appointments and updated immunization records. But the silence that surrounds her bulges out at people, increases the pressure in the room. Makes folks uncomfortable. Kate never gets to stay in one place very long. She travels the local foster homes like a salesman, hawking stock no one wants.

Inside her skin, her bones remain formed and solid. There isn't a whisper tiptoeing along the edges. Normal, normal, normal.

There is a boy named Matt who sits next to her in school. He has blond hair that looks soft as the feathers she wants to touch. He doesn't talk much either.

But he watches her draw birds in the margins of her books, watches them soar across the pages of her composition book. When she looks over and catches him, he just looks back. She thinks she might be able to ask him things, but she never can find the words to ask the right way, to properly explain what she means. The ticking never stops long enough to think. Tick-tock, tick-tock.

"You can do better than this, Kate," the guidance counselor says. She's thirteen now. She's gotten used to the ticking, the heaviness of her bones stiff and unbending in her body, to the body itself, all female with the heaviness of hips and the fat deposited on her chest. The body is foreign and clumsy and yet people stare at it, men and boys and the occasional woman. She's stuck here, in this dirty, dusty town, held down by her own treacherous form.

She doesn't answer. The counselor, like all adults, will eventually go away. She waits them out, flat-eyed and mute. She's already found booze, how even though the whiskey scorches her throat, it floods her with numbness, makes her feel silk-soft feathers tickling insider her skin. Already she can feel saliva flooding her mouth at the thought of it, of sneaking into Matt's dad's stash and drinking fire-water together in his room. His mom's never home and his dad's laid off from the plant, all fucked up on pills and booze. They can do whatever they want.

"You ever think about your future, Kate?"

Kate picks at a thread on her frayed shorts. She doesn't answer.

"What are you thinking, Kate?"

About hollow bones, about the sky, about the moon.

The counselor lets her go. They're both going through the motions anyway.

Later, she and Matt are drinking and watching X-Men, when he asks her what her superpower would be. "Flying," she says. "Invisible flying."

Matt lives just down the road from where they found that messed-up trailer with all the bones in it fifteen years ago, when people started going missing. It was big news at the time, for a year or two, but people get used to things. Kate spends most of her time at his place. She doesn't have anyone who really cares where she's at anyways.

Matt loves Kate and Kate knows it, but she doesn't love him back. She isn't quite sure what love is, but she knows it is something other people have, something they hold in their chests and their hearts. There's a tickle of something inside her sometimes, when she curls up against Matt and feels okay, for a moment. Then the shutters close over her heart and she turns to something more familiar. She goes with guys who cheat on her, talk shit about her, call her names. It's easier that way.

Kate and Matt get drunk and talk about the places they'll go. To the ocean. To the city, sparkling lights. Every weekend they sit in his room and watch movies in the dark, drink Natty Light, and talk about who they could be.

Kate drinks a lot more than Matt. She talks about the Spotted Girl when she's drunk.

"One day, she'll come for them," she says. She has nails bitten down to pink flesh that weeps scarlet. "Then, you'll see."

Boys and men go missing around here. Everyone pretends they ran off and they don't talk about the thing that flies at night, wings spread inky on the light of the moon. They don't talk about the curfew that isn't law but that everyone follows. They talk about fuel points at the grocery store and the local ball team, about how bad the meth's gotten, about the dropping price of soybeans.

But not talking won't stop the wings of the night.

"They kept her in a cage," Kate says.

She'll tell how the girl's skin was soft and slick but covered in dark purple spots. Mongolian spots, the girl's mama said. Meth spots, the mama's boyfriend said. And they caged her and fed her scraps, but you couldn't blame them. They were possessed by demon crystal that made nothing matter but the rocks. The rocks they'd start melting in spoons and pulling up in syringes and shooting into veins.

"Meth ain't cheap," Kate will say next. Matt's got the story memorized. They sold the girl. A hole's a hole, no matter what it's surrounded by. And meth doesn't care, it makes your teeth fall out and your skin grow spots. Men ain't picky when that wicked crystal fogs their brains like a windshield, makes everything too sharp and not quite real. Nothing hurts in meth land.

Maybe that's how they missed the way she began to change. The bones under her skin, sliding around, grinding themselves into new shapes and patterns.

"Her shoulder blades split her skin right open," Kate will say.

"Ssshh," he'll tell her then.

The telling hurts. He knows that.

Kate will shake her head and seal her mouth around a bottle, drinking to forget.

She never finishes the story. It always ends with the splitting skin, the carved shoulder blades springing free.

Jake's had women. Single women, women with children, pretty women, hard women, all kinds of women. He's not a bad guy. Not one of his exes complains about him. He was just — absent. He said all the right things and did all the right things, but part of him was always somewhere else.

He's always thinking about that goddamn trailer, full of blood and feathers.

He only forgets when he goes up to the city and gets lost in another place, in five o'clock stubble and flat chests. He goes there to be himself and home to be someone else.

There are places where he could go to be himself, but those places aren't here. Home is home. Even when it hurts.

"I'm a nobody," Kate always says.

And maybe Kate's a nobody, but she doesn't need anyone either. She made herself that way. Every time someone pushed her away, anger burned in her, a hard, hot coal in her chest. I'll never need a fuckin' thing from anyone, she'd whisper to herself. One day, I'll be somebody, and they'll all be sorry.

That's not how it happens, though. Maybe some girls have stories that end like that, but not this one. Kate's just a pretty girl who will fade into a bitter old woman with cracks around her eyes and mouth from her pack-a-day habit, and drink cheap whiskey on the front porch of a shitty rental, wondering if this is the day her cigarette will set fire to her oxygen tank and blow her right out of this world.

She hasn't forgotten the end of the Spotted Girl's story. How her shoulder blades gleamed ivory and lavender as they emerged. Wings, feathered white, pulling free from her spine, the sound of corn kernels popping in the microwave. The Spotted Girl, her teeth long rotted out of her mouth, yawing her lips open, gums blood-red lined with new teeth of needles bursting through the empty sockets. The new teeth snapping right into the back of the man on Kate, who wasn't Kate then. She doesn't even remember what her name was back then.

The man screamed. Kate doesn't remember his name either, but she recalls his blood hot and wet falling in hard drops on her back. Always face-down, because most of them didn't like to see what they were doing. Not in the eyes, anyway.

She'd watched the Spotted Girl turn to bird of prey with her cheek pinned against her fairy blanket. She never did like fairies after that.

The Spotted Girl didn't ever have a name. Kate thinks of her now as the huntress, tearing men from limb to limb. Her sister, but not, not really.

When things get too thick to breathe, Kate imagines the ropes of her own DNA shifting. Some trigger pulled that lets the mutation free. She checks her body for spots every day, but the purple she finds are just ordinary bruises. Maybe it's just bitterness inside, rising to the surface.

Kate likes to sit outside late at night, watching shadows. She lives for clear night skies. For a glimpse of widespread wings and blotted out stars. There's hope in the huntress stalking the night.

There's none in the daylight, where Kate watches her life unspool before her. The late nights, the shit jobs, the men, all of it. The dust, the fucking dust everywhere, always. Booze makes things manageable, sands down the sharp edges of living. Makes it go down smooth.

Sometimes she thinks back to the day where that cop, Jake, rescued her. She wonders if she had kept walking, if no one drove by, if she could have walked into another world. If she could have become a fairy tale, the one where the girl was raised by wolves and eventually became one.

Kate watches the Spotted Girl's shadow spread like ink across the moon. She hears the call that sounds like screaming. She can feel her real teeth humming below her gum line — but she can't make them come out.

Jake handcuffed Kate the first time in 2019, when she was sixteen, twelve years after he saw her sitting in the driver's seat of that SUV. He hoped it wasn't her, but the eyes, they were iridescent blue.

The same eyes looking at him as he told her to turn around, put her hands behind her back.

He didn't have a choice. She was high as a kite, pupils ballooning in and out every time she breathed.

Always the goddamn meth.

Always followed by death.

"What's your name, darlin'?" he asked.

"Blow me," she said back.

He cuffed her, pushed her up against the cruiser, but gentle. He asked her for her ID, she refused, and he fished it out of her back pocket, touching her as little as possible. And that's how they meet up over and over. Over five years, he's put her in cuffs probably two dozen times. Always ends up letting her go. She thinks it's because he wants to fuck her. She knows how to work men.

"You're going down the wrong path, honey," he tells her every time he uncuffs her and lets her go. Then he goes home and drinks and thinks about loneliness, and how a woman's the last thing he wants, how every time he's been with one, he's thought about how he doesn't want soft skin but rough stubble against his cheek. That everything soft reminds him of feathers and bones. He wants something different, but you can't want something different when you grow up here and play football. You just can't.

"You want a fuckin' blowjob, or what?" she'll answer, not the same words every time but the same message, and he'll look into her eyes, scarred-up crystals in her hollow face, and he'll think, yeah, god yeah, I want a blowjob, I want to fuck someone's mouth, but not yours, darling.

"I don't," he tells her every time.

It's fifteen years before he tells her he knew her.

"Why you keep letting me go?" she asks, her eyes so fucking dead it kills off a part of him to look at them.

"I was there that day," he says.

She stands there, letting the wind whip her long, white hair around. He's touched it, put his hand on top of it the way you do when you put someone in the back seat. It's the same as the silk peeled from sweet corn, soft as downy feathers.

"Don't know what you mean," she says at last, but she does. The knowledge sits there between them, vast and impenetrable as the darkness that lives inside her heart. "What do you want from me?"

"Not a damn thing," he says, and he gets back in his cruiser and drives away.

She's just a young woman, he tells himself, lit up by the moonlight in his rearview mirror. But the shiver-soft hair under his fingers, the shiver-soft feathers at the fucking trailer ... Something wrong with her hair the way something was wrong with those fat white feathers. The feel of both of them runs cold along his skin. He can't explain it, but the softness was cold to touch, the kind of cold inside glaciers. Something wrong and different and the memory of the sensation sits in his mind and snows.

Kate always has Matt. He shows up at jail to bail her out, he picks her up from the bars when she passes out. Everyone in town knows when Kate's in trouble, to call Matt, who will ride to the rescue. He covers her rent sometimes. He borrows trucks to move her from place to place, he listens to her, sometimes he sleeps over.

Then the accident shatters her life. Matt's driving down one night when a drunk driver misses the dividing line and smashes into his little pickup. Kate will have nightmares about it. She can see Matt, hand laid on the horn, blaring a warning. See his arm crumple accordion-like, long bones of the humerus and ulna and radius melting into one gelatinous blob of splinters and marrow bagged together by skin.

It's a closed-casket funeral.

If she could see his face.

If she could climb in the coffin and go to sleep next to him.

There is a great big hollow space inside Kate where everything aches. You have lost the only person who ever cared about you, it whispers across the canyons inside. Who are you now?

That night, she drinks and drinks and drinks, but she can't get drunk. She gets high enough to chatter her teeth. She can feel something itching inside her shoulder blades, she can, she can. She uses the shower door to scratch her back, carving bloody ribbons of flesh.

No wings.

Nothing. There is nothing.

There is a blackness that comes rushing up that swallows her whole. Her vision narrows. All she can see is the road ahead in her mind, a whole bunch of days just like this one stretched out in front of her. It isn't that everything sucks so bad now.

It's that it will always be like this.

There is a knife, and blood, and she does it the way you're supposed to, long vertical notches in the elbows instead of horizontal wrist lacerations, and she goes to her bed and curls up and allows herself to fade out.

She sucks even at killing herself. She wakes up to a sheet crusted with blood and clotted blood caked on her skin.

So it goes.

Jake's gut is spilling over his belt. He's gotten fat somewhere along the way. Not noticeable in his legs or arms, but the gut doesn't lie. He stands in the mirror hungover and pinches white flab, watching it ooze between his fingers. He thinks he should have left this town when he was young and strong, when the years of aching and longing hadn't eaten him whole. He could have been someone else, but time waits for no one.

He dresses and leaves the house. The moon is coming out for his graveyard shift. Some towns, that spells doom, but it's quiet around here most nights, unless it's cloudy. And tonight is clear and lit up by pale, washed-out moonlight, painting everything dull and shadowy. He might see the winged woman, but she doesn't cross the moon as much anymore. Maybe she's eating less or she's moved on. Maybe she's dying of loneliness somewhere. Being one of a kind must be a desolate, aching existence. But the threat remains, heavy over all of them.

He starts his patrol.

Kate made a little mistake. Or a big one. She's out of money and out of dope, got this dude to front her a gram of crack. Crack's not her thing, but any port in a storm, or whatever the fuck the saying is. She's blasted, can't hardly speak, which is the problem with crack. Everything loses focus.

Meth sharpens things. Now she's jonesing her ass off, looking at the white specks on the floor, wondering if they might be a spare rock, and the guy's giving her shit, telling her he can't do no more credit.

"Come on," she says, tongue thick and heavy, a foreign object immobile in her mouth.

"Gonna have to pay one way or other," he says.

He lets her have a hit, and when she falls back on the couch he turns into an octopus. He covers her and she can feel tentacles pinching and pulling and prodding, kneading the flesh that feels loose on her skeleton. It's the thought of squirting ink that does it, makes her fists clench. She hits him hard, right in the jaw, hears his teeth crack together. The sound tickles something inside her. There's a mass she finds inside, a seething pool of rage, and it starts to boil and rise, little wisps of smoke curling out of her mouth. Her eyes fill with wildfire.

"The fuck's wrong with you?" the dude says. He doesn't have a problem slapping a bitch, but this shit is getting freaky, the curl of drool coming out of her mouth. He hits her closed-fisted and she screams, a sound that cracks across his eardrums and shatters them. It rises and rises, curls up and away, slices across the shitty rundown apartment complex.

Everywhere, people stop, even the tweakers.

Jake's the first to respond. He's still hungover when he pulls on the scene. There's no screaming, it's silent, and there's a smell. It's copper and burnt crack. Not the same as meth/death smell, but just as likely the same result.

Something comes staggering out of the door. It's the shape and height of a person, but missing pieces. An eye, for sure, and an arm. A large ragged part of its face, torn by serrated teeth. It falls to the concrete, whining with the remnants of vocal cords.

Behind it, he recognizes Kate only by her eyes and hair. Something has happened to her face. It's grown longer and thinner, developed sharp angles coming to a sharp pointed mouth shiny with blood. She's smiling.

Jake gets out. What other choice is there? It was always coming down to this.

"Don't, Kate," he calls. "Honey."

She cocks her head.

"Don't," he says, but it's already too late. There are things in motion that cannot be stopped.

Kate's bones shifting sound like feathers beating. Her heart squeezes faster, faster, faster, as her shoulder blades sharpen. Then the fire of shoulders knifing through skin, the separation of wings from spine, joints separating rapid-fire like a microwave popcorn bag at full heat. Being high pales compared to the feeling of spreading wings for the first time. It's electric and it's buzzing and Kate would throw her head back and shriek, if she had a voice. Instead, she unfurls her wings, spreads them wide.

He aims, but he can't shoot her. He should, and he knows it, but he can't pull the trigger. He lowers his weapon. "Fly away, Kate," he whispers.

She's in motion. Wings spanning four feet each beat winds of fury that blow his thinning hair against his skull. He has to squint as the sounds quickens.

The actual take-off blasts him to the ground.

He looks up and sees a beautiful shadow spread across the moon. Ink against bone. Then it's blotted out by the white shiver-soft feathers falling like rain.

The Spotted Girl isn't a girl anymore, and she's more bird than woman. She's curled into a soft, snowy ball when she hears the faint cry of another, feels something turn over inside her heart, warming her. She calls back shrill, and hops to her feet. Then she takes flight, until she finds her sister, circling the sky, still clumsy in her new body.

She leads her back to the cave, deep in the shadows. They curl against each other, burying their long beaks under each other's wings.

"Shiver Soft Feathers" originally appeared in
Score: an sff symphony in 2019

About the author

L'Erin is a nurse and a writer living in Kansas. She spends her free time enjoying reading, writing, and working with her daughter and horse. She has numerous short works published in *Metaphorosis, Pseudopod,* and others. She is currently working on a collection of dark superlative fiction.

A Touch of the Wind

Frances Pauli

The first time he saw her, she wore the feathered cloak. Iridescent jewels lapped like scales around her slim body. Golden hair fell over the cloak, gilding its layers. She regarded him with wide eyes, pulled the garment tightly about herself and giggled.

Considering he'd donned his finest armor, that he wore the regalia of the king whilst on patrol, and that he'd bathed and groomed himself to a polish fully representative of his status, he did not appreciate being laughed at.

"Come down from there," he ordered, head craned back to see her among the branches. She must have come from the castle but had wandered to the very fringe of the king's grounds. "You'll be hurt, and then I'll have to carry you back to court."

"I'd ask you to come up ..." Her voice had a musical edge to match her beauty. How had he never noticed her among the kingdom's ladies? The tone turned achingly sad when she continued, "But you're far too heavy."

He frowned at that. Of all the king's men, he was the most spry, the strongest and the leanest. Just the day prior, in fact, his captain had hinted at promotion. His devotion had been noticed, could earn him many rewards. He was going places, and all of those places were upwards. "Where are you from?" he demanded. "I shall escort you home in safety."

"My home is the wind's kiss and the sun's caress," she answered merrily.

"Still," he tried. "Squatting on a tree branch is no place for a lady."

"You should try it," she said. "But not with all that metal weighing you down."

Then he saw her for the trick she was. His gaze fixed on the brush below her tree, and when nothing stirred there, he turned a slow circle. There was an ambush here, of course. And he was not so foolish as to remove his armor for the sake of a beautiful woman. It was such caution, he believed, which had caught the king's eye. His practical mind and his good, fast thinking. Of the king's men, he was the least likely to be swayed. Also the least likely to win hearts, perhaps, but what time did he have for wooing anyway?

His hand hovered above a gilt pommel. His steel-clad fingers twitched, and his heart raced to attention. But when he found no enemy and turned once more to the tree branch, the feather-woman had vanished.

The next time he found her, she was walking along the riverbank. Her feathered cloak hung loose about her shoulders, fluttering like a great wing. She wore little. A few scraps of fabric that left her lithe limbs exposed to the weather. They were tan like the inside of tree bark, freshly peeled.

He looked away.

"Where is all your metal?" she asked.

"Perhaps," he said, "I thought I might climb a tree today."

This time when she laughed, he heard bells tinkling, the distant jingle of his abandoned armor. The sound drew him, and he slipped down the bank to stand on the stones beside her. "What is your name? Where do you come from?"

"Names are heavy, too," she said.

"I don't understand."

"It's the weight." Her eyes widened, filled with dark secrets. "It makes everything difficult."

"Listen." He had no desire to fight, nor any wish to scare her off again. Her insistence that he was heavy still made his face burn. He wore no armor, came before her in nothing but cloth and good intentions. "I am strong and limber, and there isn't an ounce of fat on me anywhere."

"Yet you are heavy," she repeated sadly. "Weighed down by the flesh in your bowels and the deeds in your past, by your oath to a king, and by the thoughts in your mind."

"And you are not?" he asked. What deeds he had done had always been in the name of justice. Always at his king's command. It was not his place to question. If a few orders sat uneasily on him, it was only the price of fealty. Kings kept the peace, and good men served faithfully.

If she swore to no king, she might be foreign, dangerous. He sensed a trap again, but when she whispered, "Walk with me," he went willingly beside her.

"Are you an angel?" He sat on a stump, watching her dance a circle in the clearing ringed by brambles. They had met every afternoon for a week straight. Today, she held her cloak wide, spun it like a flag above the grass.

"Beliefs are heavy, too." When she smiled, the sun brightened.

The feathers gleamed, sparkling and casting rainbows across the clearing. Even the shadows at its edge seemed to step back from the light they made. He'd begun to suspect it was not really a cloak. Just as he'd come to suspect his companion was no lady of the court.

Perhaps, no woman at all.

But when she twirled in the sunlight, when she giggled her merry song, his chest constricted with it. His hands trembled, and he could care about nothing else.

"I think I am under a spell."

"Heavy," she said, and let the cloak flutter to the grass as she came to him.

He knew about selkies and swan maidens. The ancient stories had been sung in the King's halls all his life. While she slept, as easy in the long grass as a newborn fawn, he crept to the cloak and bundled the feathers into his arms. As quiet as he could go, he carried it into the forest and tucked it beneath a mossy log, covered it in a deep layer of leaves, and when it was absolutely hidden from view, returned to their makeshift bed.

She sat up the instant he returned, eyes shining in the morning slant of sun.

"Marry me," he said, and when it came out too much like a demand, he squatted beside her, lowered himself. "Please."

"What is this *marry*?" she asked.

"Well," he began. "When two people are in love, they exchange rings, they make a promise before the king and ..."

Her head began to shake almost immediately. Her answer was a sharp sparking in her wide eyes. "Heavy, heavy, heavy," she said.

"It doesn't have to be."

"I make no promises, and I wear no rings." She stood, then, naked, her strips of cloth forgotten as if they were no more than cast-off leaves. "I'm going now."

"You cannot." Desperation made the words a growl. His fists caught at the grass, digging. "I have taken your feathers. I know the rules."

Her laughter was daggers then, a sharp series of barks that cut at him.

"You won't find it," he whispered, afraid suddenly that she would. The stories never, never ended well. Inevitably, the fair knight died or was turned into something horrid. Always, he lost the love he'd found. Magical beauty was a wild thing. But the thought of entering this wood one day and not finding her turned his belly sour. Left him shaking each night as he tried to sleep inside his king's walls.

"You think I am a fairy tale," she said.

"Aren't you?" He looked up, faced the bright sky and the fury of a woman.

She backed from him, one slow step at a time, and though he might have reached for her, caught her easily, he could not move. As he watched, dumbstruck, she threw her arms wide. She arched her neck, gazed into the sunlight, and lifted.

Feathers bloomed from her naked skin. Her arms became great, wide wings, stretching toward the brambles, rising and falling until she hovered in the air a man's height from the ground.

I could still reach her.

The thought was a stone in his belly, an anchor pinning him to the earth.

"You are a heavy fool," she sang. "And I am a touch of the wind, as light as the mountain air. I need no feathered cloak to be free. I am light enough to go my own way."

He wept as she ascended, hot tears slicking his cheeks. His eyes marked her, holding her as she flew away. He watched in silence, and when she was no more than a speck upon the sun, he found he could stand again. He could think again, and he remembered that every story is a lesson.

Shaking and cold, he staggered into the forest to retrieve the trap she'd left behind.

He wore the cloak always, and nothing else. The only things in his belly were the berries and roots he found, the clusters of seeds which crowned the rushes beside the creek. He forgot his king, learned to dodge the scouts that came to find him, the soldiers that searched, and the hunters who brought heaviness and murder.

His thoughts stilled. His heart lifted. In his mind there was only hope, and as time passed, a gentle knowing that it would happen. Eventually, it would happen to him. And though it all began with her, he believed he would not seek her out at all. His love, his obsession, had been heavy too.

With the feathers warm and moving around him, playing at being wings, he climbed a tree. He swam the river. He walked among the trees, and each step he took was lighter, lighter. And on the day his toes no longer reached the earth, he barely even noticed.

About the author

Frances Pauli writes about animals because she finds them infinitely more interesting than people. She's not terribly sorry about this, though she understands it might cause some of the latter distress. Still, when given the choice between a starship piloted by a human and one with a hippopotamus at the helm, she will inevitably lean sharply in favor of the hippo.

Once upon a time she wrote about people, and you can still find those works milling about at large, but for the foreseeable future, expect pangolin pirates and savvy sword-swinging armadillos.

If that sounds appealing, you can find her work on her webpage at francespauli.com and at most retailers who sell that sort of thing. You can find Frances herself in the general Washington State area, often at writing, science fiction, or furry conventions. She is also, against her better judgement, present on most social media platforms.

But she'd rather be writing.

About the story

"A Touch of the Wind" owes its origin to a little song I wrote while plunking about on my ukulele. Don't be fooled by this, I am no musician and my ukulele playing is highly suspect. Still, the little string of notes captivated me, and being a writer at heart, words were quickly added, and a story was born. Until the submission call for Hope, that story remained as a simple chorus and four brief verses of dubious merit. When I read the anthology guidelines, however, it became clear that it was time to expand the idea into something that was lucid and captured more firmly upon the page. I hope the reader enjoys it, and if you'd like to imagine the song whilst reading, it goes, "tum tum tum, te tum tum". Or something along those lines.

The Sky was Made for Wings

Michael A. Reed

My sister Ava crouched by the window, her eyes tracking the red lights that split the sky. She couldn't hide her longing as rainbow shimmers burst from behind the clouds. Her fledgling wings, only a ruffle of black and cardinal-red feathers, quivered whenever we heard an explosion from the protesters' bombs, but she never stopped staring at the crack in the universe and all the winged sylphs who soared to it.

"Will you go one day?" I asked. I wasn't brave enough to watch the Exodus, the brief moment the sky opened and the sylphs slipped into the glowing unknown. I huddled in the corner of our bedroom, hugging my knees to my chest.

"When it's time, I think I will," Ava answered. "Look at all those beautiful people going somewhere better."

I believed I would be a sylph, too. I pictured myself draped with handsome feathers, flying out the bedroom window and joining the other winged people as we escaped to a better reality. I dreamt of leaving this doomed city and disappearing into the beyond.

I felt my back for evidence of wings: a bulge of bone, a prick of feather, a patch of raw skin, but there was nothing. Always nothing. Quiet, I watched my sister's wings stretch and flutter with mindless ease. Though small, they were as much a part of her body as her hands and feet, an extension of her heart, a gift sprouting from her shoulder blades.

"Did you know?" I asked her, even though she had answered the question before.

"I had a feeling I would be a sylph, yes." Ava pressed her head to the window and counted the ones who wouldn't return.

"What kind of feeling?" I tried to hide my jealousy — my fear — but it was painfully obvious.

Ava tilted her head and smiled. Strands of dark hair drifted over her face. She brushed them away so I would see her clearly.

"You will have wings, too," she said. "Don't doubt yourself."

"Mom doesn't have any," I said. "Or Dad, wherever he is now. What if I'm not meant to ..." I waited for the latest explosion to fade. "What if I'm destined to walk the earth forever?"

Ava returned to looking out the window. One day, when her wings had grown strong enough to fly, she would join an Exodus, and I would be left to fight for food and shelter. Like the many wingless people who killed one another in the streets tonight, I might learn to hate my sister and all the sylphs like her.

I hoped she wouldn't see me crying. I didn't want her to think I was unhappy, even though I wished she would stay with me. After a deep breath, I mustered the strength she deserved.

"I'll miss you when you're gone," I said.

I joined my sister at the window as the searing rip in the sky dimmed and the path beyond our world closed. Before long, the Exodus ended, and the city was dark again. The sylphs had gone away. Below, the angry mobs groaned and yelled and cursed the sky for leaving them behind.

In the morning, the city was silent. The birds didn't sing and the trains didn't run. There was no distant noise, no perpetual television program bantering in the living room, no hissing pipes in the apartment ceiling, no clocks hanging on the walls, urging their minutes to pass.

After an Exodus, the world stopped to recreate itself. Every time, the sylphs left behind their jobs, their families, their responsibilities. I remained to fill the holes the sylphs had dug. People like me, at least. And Mom, who set our breakfast on the table, her hands still shaking, her skeleton vibrating from the endless ring of last night's explosions.

It had been three years since the first Exodus, and people were furious. The more sylphs flew away, the more the rest felt forgotten. Unworthy. With every Exodus, the violence intensified. The protestors set off pipe bombs or detonated C4 or leveled apartment buildings with Amatol. They did whatever they could to make their own fire and distract themselves from the crack in the sky.

"It isn't much, but it should fill you up for now," Mom said, pushing our plates toward us.

My sister and I scarfed down the cold chickpeas and browning celery sticks. Perched on her chair, Ava looked like a raven. She held the food between her teeth before chewing it. Maybe it was intentional. Maybe she was playing the part.

"Don't worry, Mom," I said between bites. "When Dad sends us more money, we'll be able to afford mushrooms. Portabella. Trumpet. Maybe even Porcini."

Mom shifted uncomfortably. I hadn't noticed until now the crumpled paper in her hand, the same lifeless stationery Dad always used. She tightened her fist, but her thin-lipped smile didn't waver.

"Dad won't be sending any more money," Mom said. She spoke so matter-of-factly I didn't register what she meant. "He hasn't sent anything for a long time, actually."

Ava and I exchanged a glance. We had never expected Dad to come home — he had made that point very clear when he left — but now he was cutting us off?

"Alec can get a job," Ava said. "There will be plenty of work now that the Exodus has passed."

She mouthed a silent apology to me. We both knew she couldn't get a job. To keep herself safe from scalpers, she had to stay home. Even so, I was bothered by how quickly she volunteered my time.

"Me?" I asked. "What am I supposed to do? I'm only thirteen."

Mom nodded but didn't hear us. "We'll be fine if we can keep the apartment," she said. "In a few days, I'll speak with Mrs. Garcia about extending our lease. She likes us. We'll take advantage of that."

My sister touched her feathers incessantly, more nervous than I'd ever seen her. If we lost the apartment, Ava wouldn't have a place to hide the fact she was a sylph. Too many wingless people would do anything to join the Exodus and escape our miserable city. Terrible things, even. She couldn't be homeless and survive.

"Alec," Mom said. "Why don't you see if Ron needs any help? The bombs didn't bother us much, but he had a rough night."

"Can you come with me?" I asked, hoping for some company.

"Not this time." Mom beckoned Ava with her hand. "Your sister and I need to discuss a few things."

I shuffled the short distance across the hall to Ron's apartment. The front door was ajar, so I poked my head inside and found our neighbor sweeping up broken glass.

"My mom sent me to help you," I said as I walked inside.

"Oh, good," Ron said. The old man gave me the broom and sat in a rickety chair. He rubbed his shoulder with his knotted hand.

The windows along the wall of Ron's apartment had been blown out. From this side of the apartment complex, I had a better view of the city. Smoke billowed above high rises as fires still raged from last night's chaos. Seeing the city burn made me realize how lucky we had been.

From his chair, Ron looked beyond the shattered windows. He nodded as if he understood what I was thinking.

"People are angry," he said, waving a lazy hand. "They'd rather blow the world to pieces than accept reality."

"And what's the reality?" I asked. I had a pretty good idea of what he meant but wanted to hear him say something I didn't already know.

"We can't all be sylphs flying in the sky." Ron mimed sweeping with his hands. I resumed my work. "Some of us have to stay behind and suffer this life."

"I don't want to stay behind," I muttered. I reached down and picked a bit of glass out of my shoe.

Ron pursed his lips and bobbed his head as he considered my complaint. "Any word from your dad?" he asked.

"No," I lied. "But money has been tight. I hate to ask this of you, Mr. Ron ... could you pay me to do this job? It doesn't need to be a lot. Anything would help us. It's okay if you say no. I mean, you have your own —"

"Are you afraid you'll lose the apartment?" Ron fiddled with his thick fingers as he formed his thoughts. "It wouldn't be good for Ava, would it?"

I stopped sweeping and examined Ron with a newfound wariness. There was no sign of malice in his expression. He looked almost sad, like he understood my family's dilemma.

"Why did you say that?" I asked, squeezing the splintered broomstick.

"Because your sister is a sylph," Ron said. He held a finger to his lips. "No worries, Alec. I won't tell a soul. You're my neighbors, so of course I noticed a change in your family's behavior. Like the way your sister dresses differently as of late. Longer coats. Bulky bags. Too many layers. Your mom shifted her daily schedule. You kids stopped going to school."

"Protestors destroyed our school," I retorted. I tightened my jaw and tried to look mean. I needed Ron to understand I would hurt him if I must. It made me even angrier when he looked amused rather than afraid.

"Can I tell you a secret? Ron asked. He kept talking before I could answer. "It's only fair I give you a secret, since I know one of yours. Don't you think so?" Slowly, he lifted his dirt-stained tank top and revealed two scarred nubs protruding from his shoulder blades.

"What are those?" I asked.

"I was a sylph, too. Three years ago, just after the first Exodus, my wings sprouted. I was terrified, of course. I'm an old man. How could I possibly fly? I didn't know my wings could've saved me from what this world would become."

I tried not to stare at the flesh mounds that looked more like balled fists than wings. But I couldn't stop looking. I imagined the color of Ron's missing feathers and, oddly enough, envied him, a rugged old man and his destroyed apartment. Even he had had wings once. What did that say about me?

Ron let his shirt down and smirked. "I fell on hard times," he said. "I needed money. Like you. I sold my wings to scalpers and had enough cash to last the year."

"Why would you do that?" I asked, not bothering to hide my frustration. "Who the hell would sell their wings?"

I wanted wings so badly that the thought of willingly selling them seemed as abominable as murder.

"Stupid, yes." Ron coughed and patted his chest until his throat was clear of mucus. "But it's easy to be stupid when you're afraid. Especially when you're a teenager." He looked me in the eyes until I turned away.

"I'm not afraid," I said. I counted the glass shards on the floor and tried to re-form the pieces in my mind.

"Nobody knows what's beyond the rip in the sky," Ron whispered. "When it first opened, a woman ranting on the streets claimed it was a portal to hell. That all the sylphs, all the self-important people, were flying straight into eternal flames. The red glow. The unbearable tearing of time and space. She said we were like moths drawn to a flame. That image frightened me. I sold my wings because I'm a coward, Alec."

Ron walked to his small kitchen and returned with nearly moldy carrots stacked on a warped paper plate. He handed it to me. I set aside the broom and took his gift.

"I've got no money to give you for your help, young man." Ron squeezed my shoulder. "Do me a favor. Don't let your sister make my mistakes. Keep her safe from the world. From herself. From your own mother if you have to."

"I will, Mr. Ron," I said. I hated that my eyes watered. I wasn't going to cry over something as stupid as carrots, but Ron didn't know that. More than that, now that his food was in my hands, I was ashamed I had yelled at him. I felt foolish for thinking he didn't deserve wings and I did.

"One more thing, Alec," Ron said. "It won't be long until Ava is ready for the Exodus. Wings grow faster than you think."

Over the course of a few short months, Ava's wingspan grew longer than her height. Ron had been right. My sister's feathers came more quickly and beautifully than we could have anticipated.

Many sylphs had gray or white wings and could be mistaken for an overgrown pigeon. Beautiful sylphs had feathers like the blue jay or the peacock. Yet only the rarest sylphs could boast of Ava's royal black and rose-red blend. When she slept, wings curled over her body, she resembled a pristine lady-bug shining on a blade of grass.

For a sylph of her caliber, leaving the apartment was especially dangerous. So I complained to Mom when Ava got a new job. Every other night, Ava slipped out of the apartment and didn't return until morning.

Tonight, she was late.

"Should I look for her?" I asked. "Could she be in trouble?"

My mom, chewing on her fingertips, shook her head. Ever since Dad's money stopped coming, she had been unable to relax. She was always listening to sylph horror stories on the news and writing out manic lists.

"It has only been a few hours," Mom said.

"I'm going." I stood up and Mom jabbed a finger in my direction.

"You're going to stay." She took a step toward me. Her thin back, like a threatened cat, curved as she came closer.

"Ava shouldn't have a job," I barked. "Why are you sending her out there? What does she do at night?"

"Maybe if you could get a job, your sister wouldn't need to take care of this family." When the words left Mom's mouth, her expression was tinged with regret, but she didn't take it back.

To make it worse, Mom was right. I hadn't been able to find work. I had no skills. No education. I lied about my age to look older on paper, but whenever I landed an actual interview, I was scoffed out the door.

"What does Ava do?" I asked.

I had been concerned, especially at first. But there was money again. We weren't going to lose the apartment. The fridge was lined with lentils and coconut milk. Every day, there was something delicious on the table. Quinoa. Fresh bread. Raspberries. Our new comforts had diminished my worries.

Deep down, I knew the answer. It made me sick to my stomach.

"She does what she has to," Mom said. The words caught in her throat. It pained her to speak them aloud, yet she managed to squeeze them out.

"Scalpers?" I asked.

Mom gave me no indication whether I was right or wrong. She simply stared past me as if she could escape my question by disappearing into her mind.

"Are we selling her wings?" I asked, my voice cracking.

"Only the feathers. One or two every few nights. Nothing she can't spare." A tear rolled down my mom's cheek. "Until her Exodus arrives."

"Why does she have to go in person? Send it in the mail or deliver it yourself! You've put her in danger!"

"Her buyers need to ensure authenticity." She said it as if it was common sense. "Plucking the feather in person leaves no doubt."

After that, we said nothing else to each other. For hours, tortured by the silence, we waited for Ava to return. When I thought I would find a payphone and call the police, I heard a quiet knock.

"Help," Ava croaked from the crack beneath the door.

I ran to the door, ripped it open, and found Ava, wrapped in her oversized coat, lying on the floor. Carefully, I brought her inside. She was pale and could hardly keep her eyes open. I was afraid she would faint, so I propped her against the wall. She cried out in pain.

Mom shoved me aside and took Ava's chin in her hand. "What happened, baby?" she asked. "Where does it hurt?"

"My wings," Ava sobbed.

I held my breath as mom rolled Ava onto her stomach and gently pulled away her coat. When Mom saw Ava's wings, she gasped before calling to me for help. I came closer, but recoiled when I saw my sister's injuries.

Her once-beautiful feathers had been ripped from her skin. One of Ava's wings had been mostly plucked. With time, the feathers might grow back, but her other wing had been badly burned. All that remained was singed flesh and the semblance of melting feathers.

Mom went to the kitchen and returned with warm water and a towel. We didn't have any medicine for burns. When the water touched Ava's deformed wings, she howled as if Mom were tearing the feathers out her back. It wasn't going to help her, but I understood Mom had to try.

I took hold of Ava's legs. She thrashed against me, her bare feet brushing against my face. I hadn't noticed her shoes were gone.

"Why?" Ava called out. "Why me? Why my wings?"

Unable to answer the question, Mom took Ava into her arms and cradled her. She buried her face into Mom's shoulders and wept.

But I knew why. I thought back to the bomb explosions and the fires and the hatred and the murderous riots taking more people than the Exodus ever could. Ava's wings had been too painful a reminder of the difference between sylph and man. Humanity couldn't bear her beautiful gift. So like all good things, they ruined it.

"See if she will eat," Mom said.

She pushed a meager plate of food in front of me then returned to the shadowed corner of the living room. The days after Ava was attacked, Mom had refused to see her. She was ashamed, I thought. She had used her daughter for money and Ava paid the price. It must have been easier to ignore her mistakes than be Ava's mother. I cared for her in Mom's place. I fed her, cleaned her wounded wings, and listened to her cry at night.

Wordless, I took the plate. I walked to our bedroom where Ava had been caging herself since the night she was attacked. I took a deep breath.

"It's me," I said. "I'm coming in."

Ava lay on a thin mattress, a blanket strewn over her wings and her head turned to the window. A red line, long and angular, hung in the sky. It was the Exodus, threatening to leave Ava to wilt with the rest of us.

"You have to eat today," I said. I didn't bother trying to convince her she could die of starvation. Instead, I took a small handful of stale rice and plopped it into her mouth. Brainless, she chewed but didn't swallow.

"I thought being a sylph made me different than other people," Ava murmured, stray rice tumbling from her lips. "But I'm stuck here like everyone else."

Part of me wanted to leave the room. I wasn't ready for this. I didn't know how to help my sister live any more than she cared to try.

"You're still a sylph," I said. "Your wings will grow back, I'm sure of it. Some of your feathers have already returned."

"You love me, Alec." Ava rolled onto her side so that she could see me. There wasn't a smile left inside her, but I knew she appreciated my feeble attempts to bring her back from the dead. "That's why you lie to me."

I sat down on the mattress beside her, and we studied the red line in the sky. I put my arm over her shoulder, careful not to touch any part of her wings. She winced, but didn't recoil.

"Before, when you asked me if I knew I would have wings, I lied." Ava said. "I had no idea, but I wanted to feel important. I wanted to believe in destiny."

"Yeah, right," I said. "You and I both know you were made for wings."

Ava looked sadder than ever before when she said, "The sky was made for wings. And I wasn't made to fly. It was a trick. I believed it, too. I actually thought I had been chosen. By what, by who, I didn't understand or care to understand, because I had feathers. I was actually going to escape this place."

Determined not to cry, Ava pinched the bridge of her nose and closed her eyes. She bowed her head and took deep breathes to keep the tears away.

Before Ava's wings had been plucked and burned, I had secretly hoped she would stay on Earth with me. In my imagination, scalpers taking her wings was an acceptable outcome as long as she wasn't permanently hurt. Those ideas had felt justified. Like she owed me her future just because we were siblings. Selfishly, I had believed that I deserved her.

But now?

Angry crowds had already gathered in the streets below. Jealous because they hadn't grown wings and would never know what existed beyond this sad world, they prepared to loot, murder, and destroy. Whatever it took to minimize the pain of living on. For hours they had been chanting, lighting cars ablaze, shattering store windows, cursing the Exodus. Soon the bombs would start. Any minute, the red line in the sky would become the escape hatch for the sylphs, those lucky few, and Ava would be with them. I gritted my teeth. I would make it happen.

I tucked my arms underneath Ava's armpits and hoisted her up.

"Put me down," she said, though she didn't fight me.

"I'll drag you if you make me."

I waited for Ava to willingly stand on her feet. The blanket that had been covering her wings slipped to the ground. Her charred wing had not fully recovered. The once lush, red feathers had grown back small and gray. The wing drooped to the side like a withered flower.

Yet, many of the feathers from her plucked wing had grown back. I smiled for the first time in weeks. It meant she still had a chance.

Together, we walked into the living room where our mom sat in a ratty recliner, her hair unbrushed, her jaw set against the sight of us. She opened her mouth to say something, but her words were drowned by the familiar split of time and space. It was the seams of the sky wrenching apart and the beginning of the Exodus.

Like a pair of three-legged racers hell-bent on winning, Ava and I hobbled down the apartment building hall. We reached the roof-access door. I pushed against it, but it was locked.

"Forget it," Ava whispered. "Take me back to our apartment."

I had never been strong, but the will to pass through that door buzzed through my blood vessels. At that moment, there was no greater purpose, so I kicked with all my might. A rusty bolt erupted from the hinges, and the door went limp.

We climbed the short flight of stairs and emerged onto the apartment roof. Not even the clouds could dull the gaping rip in the crimson sky. I stood in awe as I watched hundreds of sylphs, with their many-colored wings, ascend toward it.

Ava had to yell to be heard over the people screaming below. "I won't make it!"

"You will!" I yelled back. "Fly, Ava!"

Cold wind tossed our hair across our faces as we started to run. Hand in hand, we sprinted the length of the rooftop. Ava's wings stretched out and caught the breeze but when it came time to leap, she hesitated, stopped.

"You'll be alone!" Ava yelled.

I shook my head, took hold of her hand again, and circled back to make another run. No words would change my mind. I feared she wouldn't have wings at all by the next Exodus. Mom might sell every last feather. Ava had to go now. She had to live a better dream for both of us.

Again, we ran. The wind pushed us back, our faces freezing, our eyes drying. My ankle ached from kicking the door, but I wouldn't stop.

"I said *fly,* Ava!" I yelled. "You fly now, or you won't fly ever!"

Ava squeezed my hand, and I felt her determination finally take root. She dipped her head, spread out her wings, pumped her arms, and looked to the sky. We reached the roof's ledge, and she leapt.

I held my breath. She plummeted at first, and I thought she would crash into the streets. Then she rose. Sloppy like an injured bird, Ava managed to keep herself afloat with her damaged wings. Every so often, she dipped back down and threatened to nosedive into the city. She needed inspiration. She needed to be reminded that she was destined to fly.

"I love you!" I yelled, not knowing if she could hear me. "I love you, Ava!"

Other sylphs saw Ava struggling and came alongside her. They took her by the arms and together floated into the setting sun like a celestial herald. She never looked back.

Eventually, Ava disappeared into the hole in the sky, like all the other sylphs who flew beside her. I had never been so happy to be alone.

Late in the night, while the city fires blazed, the Exodus ended. The hole in the sky had been stitched closed. I hadn't left the rooftop. I wanted to remember my last evening with Ava. I waited until dawn before I decided I should find my mom and tell her the news. Ava was gone, and she would never return.

I stumbled to the stairs, not sure if my ankle was seriously injured. And my back was inexplicably sore, too. I reached behind myself to inspect the mysterious pain. Hesitantly, I fumbled my fingers over a small bump of skin below my shoulder. I couldn't be sure, but at the center of it, only barely protruding, I thought I touched the tip of a feather.

About the author

Michael A. Reed is a speculative fiction writer and ironically dyslexic English teacher from Las Vegas, Nevada. He dreams of talking cities, robot rodents, and the sweetly dark. His other work has been published or is forthcoming at Tenebrous Press, Shortwave Publishing, Dark Matter INK, *Factor Four Magazine* and others. A history of his publications can be found at Mikecantreed.com.

About hope

"The Sky Was Made for Wings" represents the dream of escape. We are destined for better things than the chaos of this world. I imagine a future where we know our purpose, have clear visions, and have the chance to be beautiful.

Going Home

Martin Westlake

The eerie howl of the Ekranoplan's jet engines echoed around the city's early morning streets. Dimitriy's stomach lurched involuntarily. A ground effect craft, they called it, designed to be a troop carrier, now recycled as a passenger craft, plying the route between Derbent and Astrakhan. The relic, all stubby wings and a massive, V-shaped tail, howled there and back three times a day. He loathed it, but it was the only way he could get to the laboratory in Astra.

Every Monday morning for over a year, Dimitriy had suffered the same torment of emotions. Anastasia said nothing anymore as they kissed. "Think of the children," she had said in the old days, before she'd realised entreaties were useless. "They need their father." He missed the whole school week. Sasha, the younger, still greeted him with affection on Saturday mornings, but Andrei, now in his teens, had become increasingly sullen. Dimitriy wanted to tell him how sorry he felt, but the truth was that he didn't. Guilty, yes; sad, yes, in a bittersweet sort of way; but not sorry.

Then there was the Ekranoplan. Anastasia had been unable to leave Derbent when Dimitriy had taken on the Astrakhan job and he had accepted that. The car trip took ten hours in the summer and in the winter the roads were frequently impassable. No, the only viable means of getting there was the Ekranoplan. He would never get used to it, though. Whenever there was the slightest hint of a breeze, his heart dropped, for the monstrous thing could only take off facing into the wind, and that meant riding the incoming waves, like a ship. Once it was up in the air the ride was smooth, but how he hated the take-off! The only thing that made the mixture of sadness, guilt and fear worthwhile every Monday morning was a euphoric sense of anticipation; the knowledge that he would soon once again be where he most desired to be.

His path through the sleepy streets to the Ekranoport took him past his old workplace, the Caspian Gates Secondary School, reminding him of the day it had all begun. He'd stayed behind to help a group of fifteen-year-olds, then hurried home. A tall, thin, grey-suited, sallow-faced man was waiting for him outside the main entrance to their block of flats. A cigarette bobbed on his lower lip as he spoke. He seemed oblivious to the February cold, though both men's breath clouded about them.

"Semenov?" he said.

Dimitriy nodded.

"Could we talk?" said the man, gesturing towards a bar.

There was something about him — not furtive, but a sense of secrecy all the same. The man bought two vodkas and they sat at a scuffed table.

"To your health," he said, raising his glass. He stubbed out his cigarette in an old dented aluminium ashtray and lit another. "Ivanov," he said. "Rear Admiral Anatoly Ivanov, Caspian Flotilla, Astrakhan."

"There's been a mistake," said Dimitriy.

Ivanov shook his head. He gestured to a passing waiter and ordered two more vodkas.

"I shouldn't stay," said Dimitriy.

"Tell me, Dimitriy Semenov," Ivanov said; "how much do you earn?"

"Enough," said Dimitriy.

"Why are you a teacher?" Ivanov leaned forward over the table. "You are a brilliant physicist with a top doctoral thesis in Biology and Materials Sciences from Moscow State University and yet you hide yourself away at the Caspian

Gates Secondary School teaching low-grade mathematics to misfits."

"My wife ..." Dimitriy began.

"We know all about your wife," Ivanov said.

"It's time I left," Dimitriy said.

"Sit down," said the Admiral, gesturing with his half-empty vodka glass. "What I mean is that we know she has all her family here. That's why you're here, isn't it?"

Dimitriy said nothing.

Ivanov leaned over the table again. "The motherland calls, comrade."

Motherland! Comrade! Dimitriy knew immediately that the job had to be some sort of secret military work.

"It's not what you think, Semenov," the Admiral continued. "If I told you now, you wouldn't believe me."

Dimitriy inadvertently looked into his empty glass. Ivanov flagged the waiter down and ordered two more vodkas.

"No!" said Dimitriy.

"For the road."

The Admiral toyed with his cigarette lighter, an old-fashioned metal model with a flip top and a thick wick. Then he looked up at Dimitry. "Interested?" he asked. "We'll pay you four times what you are getting at that dump of a school."

"The catch?" said Dimitriy.

Ivanov drank off the remainder of his vodka and placed the glass down gently on the tabletop.

"You'd have to come to Astra, Monday to Friday. We'd cover your board and lodging."

"How would I ..."

As if to anticipate his question, the unmistakable howl of the evening return Ekranoplan came to them through the thin glass window.

Ivanov reached into his pocket, drew out an envelope and placed it on the table.

"Your ticket's in there. This coming Monday. The seven-thirty departure. When you get to Astra, make your way to the Moskva Hotel. A room has been booked in your name. I'll join you there for lunch. It's half-term. The school won't miss you."

Back home, after the children had gone to bed, sitting in the low light at the melamine kitchen table, he and Anastasia had discussed the offer in earnest whispers. He had doubts, but she was logical and reassuring. The money was important. With the kids growing, it would be good if they could rent somewhere larger. If he didn't like the work, whatever it was, he could always return to his teaching. What did they have to lose?

Dimitriy had been travelling to Astra for just over two months when Anastasia first put the question to him. He had known it must come. She had nodded and accepted so mildly when he'd first explained that he couldn't talk about his work, but who could blame her, now that the yearning had started? She chose a Saturday evening. The children were in bed. The classical music radio channel was on, and she'd put a cloth and a candle on the dinner table. They talked about Sasha and Andrei, and then about her family. At the end of the meal, Anastasia took Dimitriy's hands across the table. *Here it comes*, he thought. But she simply looked into his eyes and asked if he felt all right. She'd told him he seemed preoccupied, as if his mind were elsewhere.

He'd laughed. "I'm fine," he'd said.

How could he tell her? Even if he had told her, she wouldn't have believed him.

The second time, Anastasia had been more direct. Dimitriy had just returned.

"Did you miss us?" she asked.

"Of course!"

"Really?"

She went back to the kitchen. There was no cloth and no candle on the table. Over the meal, her replies were monosyllabic. Afterwards, he went to help her with the washing up, but she insisted on doing it alone. He sat on the sofa and waited until she emerged, drying her hands on a tea towel.

"Dima," she said, "are you sure you're not having a relationship of some sort in Astra?"

Astrakhan was on a broad river, not a sea. Its waterways gave the impression the city was floating. Unlike Derbent, there were no hills behind, and no citadel looming over the city. Rather, the great Trinity Cathedral soared upwards, with its gold-capped green domes. Astrakhan was flat and expansive. Being there gave Dimitry a sense of a new beginning. He hadn't realised, until he first set foot in the place, how oppressed he'd felt back home. That first Monday, still wobbly from the flight, he'd walked easily to the Moskva Hotel, a great block of fake chrome and smoked glass. A room had been booked, as Ivanov had promised. The clerk told him a table had been reserved in the restaurant for twelve o'clock. Dimitriy went to his room, unpacked the few belongings he had brought, then turned on the television and watched a programme without really following it. What was Ivanov going to offer him, he wondered?

The Admiral was sitting at their table when Dimitriy came down, a vodka in front of him and a cigarette on his lower lip. He nodded curtly.

"Welcome to Astra," he said. "A drink?"

"Thank you," said Dimitriy, "but I don't drink at lunchtime."

Ivanov beckoned a waiter over.

"Today, you'll make an exception."

When the waiter had brought their drinks, Ivanov raised his glass. He had ordered borscht, brought by another waiter. "Eat," he insisted gruffly.

"Thank you," said Dimitriy.

"Thank Mother Russia," said Ivanov, stubbing out his cigarette.

They started to eat, dipping into the rich red soup with their spoons.

"What do you know about Tunguska?" the Admiral asked.

"Siberia? The beginning of the last century?"

Ivanov nodded. "30 June 1908," he said.

"I remember the pictures," said Dimitriy. "All those felled trees. A meteor, right?"

"Da, da," said Ivanov. "That's what people think."

"Think? What was it, then?"

"We don't know." He lit another cigarette. "I've brought a file for you to read, but before that, I want you to sign this."

Ivanov tugged an envelope from his jacket pocket and drew out a folded sheet of paper. "Official Secrets Act," said the Admiral, unfolding the sheet. "I will only tell you more if you sign. To be clear, if you sign the declaration and do not respect it, you could be tried and imprisoned. Not even your wife. Got it?"

Dimitriy read the declaration, his hand trembling. He would have liked to talk to Anastasia. Suddenly, she seemed very far away. He read it again.

"I need to think about it," he said. "I need to talk to my wife."

Ivanov shook his head grimly. "It's now or never," he said.

Dimitriy sighed and thought about the money. With such a salary they could easily rent a three-bedroom apartment. He was sure Anastasia would have agreed. She would surely have wanted to know what work the Admiral was offering. He signed and dated the paper and handed it back.

"Good," said Ivanov, putting it in his pocket. He gestured to a waiter to clear their table and ordered two more vodkas.

"The Tunguska region wasn't as sparsely populated as people think," said the Admiral. "Quite a few people heard and saw something." He lit a cigarette. "It started with noises from the sky."

"Noises?"

"Da. You'll read the transcripts. Some of the witnesses said it was like trumpets."

"Heavenly trumpets?" said Dimitriy ironically.

Ivanov sneered.

"The noises went on for about a week," he continued.

"Then?" asked Dimitriy.

"There was some sort of *conflict*, in the sky," said Ivanov. "Some sort of *celestial* conflict."

"'Celestial'? You seem to be choosing your words with care, Admiral."

Ivanov stubbed out his cigarette.

"You'll read the file and see for yourself. As good scientists, we try always to keep open minds."

"The word 'conflict'," said Dimitriy, "suggests that more than one body or object might have been involved, right? And the word 'celestial' suggests this was high up?"

"There are drawings in the file," the Admiral said, "based on contemporary eyewitness accounts. The locals, the Evenki, were convinced they'd seen their god, Ogdy, in a fight."

"Fascinating," said Dimitriy, "but I am not sure why this should bring me to the Volga Basin and the Official Secrets Act."

Ivanov lit another cigarette.

"Leonid Kulik," he said. "A mineralogist. He came to Tunguska several times, starting in 1921. That was already thirteen years after the event. There was no crater — that puzzled him. How could there have been a meteorite impact if there were no crater, and if there were no fragments? He realised the fragments might have blasted out craters that had then got filled in. So, he kept digging holes to try and find filled-in craters with remains of one sort or another at the bottom — something, anything. No joy. Until 1938. His last expedition. One of his men found something, deep down, in a pit. Whatever it was, it blinded the man. He complained of an intense, searing light, then he lost his sight. Kulik's workers mutinied. For them it was proof they were messing with Ogdy. They dragged the man out and refused to get into the pit. Kulik had to shovel most of the earth back in himself. He measured the location as accurately as he could, and then returned to the Mineralogical Museum in Leningrad. He planned to return with his own men, but the Germans invaded in 1941 and he joined the fighting. The next year he died of typhus in a POW camp."

Ivanov drank some vodka.

"Whatever they found," he continued, "remained lost in the archives. For a long time, as you know, the motherland had more important things to think about than primitive superstitions. But in 2007 a group of archivists started going through Kulik's papers. When they got to the file about the 1938 incident, the team had the good idea of involving us."

"Us?" said Dimitriy.

"The security services," Ivanov said. "If another expedition to Tunguska were to be launched, they knew they'd need state resources. They dressed it up as being about some potentially weaponizable force. They weren't entirely wrong. Kulik's coordinates were accurate. They used a remote-controlled digger. Once they'd reached the depth Kulik recorded, they lowered a remote camera that relayed images of glittering metallic fragments. They sent down instruments, but the instruments measured nothing. A volunteer discovered that *reflections* of the fragments could be observed in a mirror. Using remote cameras and mirrors, the fragments were dug out of the pit bottom. It was all hit-and-miss. Somebody thought of lead, being a heavy metal, so they fashioned a lead-lined steel box and used a remote-controlled robotic arm to shepherd the fragments towards the box and seal the lid."

"Shepherd?"

"You'll learn about that," Ivanov said, "*if* you take the job." He stubbed out his cigarette, drank off his vodka, and continued. "The fragments were then brought to a ..." (he coughed) "... *facility* here in Astrakhan. The box was opened and the fragments were housed in a specially constructed room. That, Dimitriy Semenov, is where you come in. We want to analyse the fragments. Test their qualities." He leaned over the table as if to share a confidence. "And perhaps," he said, "replicate them."

Dimitriy felt the thrill of scientific discovery and the repulsion of a lifelong pacifist. But curiosity gripped him strongest. If only he could tell Anastasia! He was sure she would have been just as fascinated.

The Admiral got to his feet.

"I will be waiting outside tomorrow morning at seven," he said, "and will take you to the facility."

Dimitriy watched as Ivanov threaded his way steadily through the tables. That word, *comrade*, again. When he had gone, Dimitriy picked up the file and hurried to his room.

The Admiral was waiting for him on the hotel's esplanade in a sleek black chauffeur-driven limousine. He was in his uniform, his gold brocaded cap on the seat beside him.

"Is this a Zil?" Dimitriy asked, getting into the tobacco-fugged interior.

"The 4104," said the Admiral. "The Navy is determined to keep them going until they fall to pieces." He lit a cigarette. "You read the file?" he asked.

"Of course. Do you want me to believe that the Evenki saw angels?"

"*You* saw the drawings," said Ivanov. "*I* don't want you to believe anything."

"Yes," said Dimitriy, "I *saw* the drawings."

The Admiral gazed through the smoked glass window.

"Do you believe in angels, Dimitriy Semenov?"

"No," said Dimitriy, "I don't. But what else can be made of those drawings? And those sounds; if not something like trumpets, then what?"

Ivanov shook his head.

"I told you; we are trying to keep open minds. You have to remember in 1908 the Evenki were a primitive, superstitious people. When something they didn't understand happened, they naturally ascribed it to their god, Ogdy."

"You don't think there was a conflict?"

"Imagine if you were a primitive people and something massive exploded overhead," said Ivanov. "Wouldn't you extrapolate from what you knew? Battle, noise?"

"And those trumpeting noises *before*?" asked Dimitriy.

Ivanov chuckled.

"*You* called them 'heavenly trumpets', Dimitriy Semenov, but you don't believe in such things, do you?"

"Of course not, Admiral. But what are the alternative explanations?"

Ivanov tutted. "You are a scientist, aren't you? Because we don't know the answer doesn't mean there isn't one. We just don't know it yet — perhaps we'll never know it. What we *do* know is that we have seven fragments of an unknown powerful material that *may* have fallen from the sky about the time of the Tunguska event. We can, and must, try to know as much about those fragments as possible, using scientific methods, and not basing our judgements on superstition and hearsay and eye-witness accounts from long ago."

"Of course," said Dimitriy, chastened. "It's those pictures in the file. My imagination ran away with me."

The Admiral stubbed out his cigarette.

"We have arrived," he said.

Some five months after Dimitriy started the job, Anastasia stopped making dinner on Friday evenings. The first time, she told him she'd been feeling unwell, and he accepted the explanation unthinkingly. He ate alone in the kitchen. The next Friday, though, the new practice had been rationalised; she said it was too late in the evening to eat a full-blown meal — better that he snacked or had a bowl of soup or a salad. He again accepted the explanation. Then, one Friday, when he came to bed, he found her weeping.

"What's the matter, Ana?"

She rolled over and he saw that her eyes were puffed up.

"I just wish you'd tell me," she said. "About her, whoever she is."

"There is no her," Dimitriy insisted.

"You can't hide it from me," Anastasia said. "I see the way you look as though you have been torn away from someone."

"There is no other woman, Anastasia."

"Is it a man? I'd understand."

"There's nobody else, I swear!"

"You think I'm stupid? You can't wait to get back on Monday mornings."

She rolled away and wept herself to sleep. He stared up at the ceiling. She was right, of course. The weekends back home in Derbent had become a torment.

"Welcome to Astrakhan State Technology University," said Ivanov, checking his cap's position in the glass of the chauffeur's partition.

The Admiral led him through the glass-fronted entrance. Students milled about, seemingly unfazed at the image of a uniformed Admiral threading a path through the crowd.

"Where are we going?"

"The Institute of Oil and Gas." Ivanov led the way across the leafy campus to a nondescript red brick construction. They went through rotating doors and stopped before a block of lifts. When the lift came, the Admiral pushed the button for –2, but he kept his finger on the button a long time. Ivanov turned to face a small camera in one corner of the roof of the lift and gave a salute.

"Forgive the cloak-and-dagger stuff," he said. "Until the Union collapsed, the Caspian Flotilla was based in Baku, but a lot of the command structure was kept safely within Russia itself, including here, in Astra. The Americans knew that, of course. This place was just as much of a target, so special underground facilities were built for the command structures. That's where we are going now."

By then, the lift should have reached –2 level, but felt as though it were still in motion. After several minutes of slow movement, the lift stopped, and the doors slid open. In front of them stood two armed, uniformed guards. Behind them was a vast, brightly lit space. Ivanov produced papers and explained about Dimitriy. Once the papers had been stamped, the soldiers stood aside and let them pass.

"It's quite a hike," said the Admiral.

The vast space was devoid of human activity, but all around them stood massive columns of plastic-wrapped material.

"Thousands of men could live down here for years," said Ivanov.

On the far side of the bunker, Ivanov led Dimitriy into a complex of smaller spaces. Each entrance was a double-doored air-pressurized port. Finally, they came to a twin set of grey-painted heavy steel doors that had been swung open.

"Here we are," said the Admiral. "The playroom; the laboratory."

They were greeted by the head of the scientific team, Fyodor Babikov, a beanpole of a man wearing large tinted spectacles. Ivanov left them together, promising to return at the end of the day. Babikov showed Dimitriy to the changing room. There were sinks, lockers and benches. They scrubbed up together, then dressed in classic surgical gear. Afterwards, Babikov led Dimitriy into a small meeting room. The walls were lined with large drawings showing distinctive geometrical structures. Babikov gestured for him to sit down at a table and sat opposite.

"What has Admiral Ivanov told you?" he asked.

"The basic story," said Dimitriy. "And I've read the file."

"Did he tell you about their effects?"

"The blindness?"

"Well, there *is* that," said Babikov. "But you don't need to worry. The lab is rigged so that you simply cannot look directly at the fragments. You can only see them indirectly by using the mirrors we've installed, or by using the camera. But did Ivanov not talk about anything else?"

"Nothing," said Dimitriy.

"Mmm ... He was probably afraid he'd scare you off."

"Why would I be scared?"

"They seem to have an addictively euphoric effect on some people."

"Some?"

"It seems to depend. There's nothing chemical about it."

"How do you know this?"

"You're not the first expert drafted in. In fact, you are the third."

"The others?"

Babikov shook his head.

"They didn't last very long. The first was here for just over a year. The second lasted almost two years."

"Where are they now?"

"Locked away," said Babikov.

"And you?"

"Nothing," said Babikov. "But, then, I don't spend hours in the viewing room."

"All right," Dimitriy said. "What else did Ivanov *not* tell me?"

"There isn't a whole lot more to know."

"How long have the fragments been here?"

"Since 2008."

"And you have honestly learned nothing?"

Babikov grinned.

"Honestly, very little. I'll tell you everything we know, but it won't take long."

Dimitriy leaned back in his chair.

"Tell me," he said.

"We know they have properties, and powers. The power to blind people, for example."

"Are we sure of that?"

"You mean?"

"Well," said Dimitriy, "we've only had that one example, of the man down the pit, back in 1938. It could have been a stroke, couldn't it?"

Babikov coughed. "There have been quite a few accidents since," he said.

"Here?" asked Dimitriy.

"Yes," said Babikov. "People who didn't listen. People who didn't believe. An accident. A drunk."

"How many?"

"Enough for us to know that the fragments, if looked at directly, cause blindness in humans, as in animals. Even welding masks didn't help."

"You've tried reptiles?"

"Oh, yes," said Babikov. "We've tried reptiles *and* squid and octopus *and* insects. We've tried everything," he said. "The fragments have the same effect on any sort of eye known to us."

"Your instruments?"

"Show nothing. Whatever this effect is, it is produced in an undetectable way."

"What else?" Dimitriy asked.

"Oh, the euphoria business."

"Can you be sure of that?"

"Scientifically, no. But there must be a strong presumption."

"Two cases only? You can't presume anything from that."

"You are right," Babikov said, smiling ruefully. "Let me just call it a *hunch*, then. Two highly intelligent, balanced, reasonable scientists, both following a similar pattern of obsessiveness and increasingly frequent episodes of manic euphoria, culminating in madness and confinement in clinics. I agree with you, Dimitriy Semenov. It could be sheer coincidence, but I think not."

"All right," said Dimitriy. "What else?"

"We have found a way to manipulate the fragments," said Babikov. "Only one metal may touch them — gold. All others melt away as they get near. Once we realised that, we had special gold implements made up that could be attached to the arms of the robots — that is the main way in which you will be working with the fragments, if you need to manipulate them."

"But it is curious," said Dimitriy, "gold being so malleable — like the lead in which they were encased."

"In retrospect, the lead-lined box was a crazy risk," said Babikov. "Who knows what might have happened if they had melted their way out during the trip?"

"What else?"

Babikov shook his head in sudden exhaustion.

"We know next to nothing, and that is all we know."

"Now you are talking in riddles."

Babikov looked at Dimitriy for a few moments, as though brought back from a reverie.

"We cannot record images. Nothing works; film, X-rays, electromagnetic resonance imaging, transmission electron tomography ... Whatever sort of imaging we have tried to use, nothing shows up. They are definitely there; we can see their reflection, but we can't capture them as images, and that means that we can only study the fragments themselves."

"What about microscopes?" asked Dimitriy.

"Lenses work," said Babikov. "But you cannot record what you are seeing."

"You can't draw them?"

"No, no," said Babikov. "They can be drawn, at least — hence all of these ..." he waved at the drawings hanging on the walls around them. "Your predecessors' masterpieces."

"May I?" Dimitriy asked.

Babikov nodded.

Dimitriy studied the drawings for a while.

"I have an idea," he said. "But I'll wait until you've finished."

"Second," Babikov continued, "they are constantly levitating."

Dimitriy raised his eyebrows.

"They always hover, never touching any surface."

"Some sort of energy, then?"

"I think so, but we can detect nothing. We thought of magnetism or light but it's neither of those." Babikov smiled and shook his head. "Believe me, Dimitriy Semenov, we have tried and tested many ideas — all fruitlessly — so far."

"I understand what Ivanov was getting at now."

"Getting at?" said Babikov.

"We were talking about scientific method. He said we don't know the answer yet, and perhaps we never will."

That very first time Dimitriy came back from Astrakhan she'd known already, he realised — or, rather, she'd suspected already. Something had happened. He couldn't entirely hide it from her. For a start, there was the fait accompli of his decision. He had taken the job without first discussing the offer with her. It was so generous, he said, that he had decided on the spot. That wasn't the whole truth, of course. She asked about the work. He told her how he'd had to sign a declaration and was now bound by the Official Secrets Act. He saw her recoil.

"It isn't what you think," he'd said.

"What is it, then?" she'd asked.

"Something unimaginable," he'd replied.

She'd wrinkled her nose. "Can't you give me a clue?"

He'd laughed. "I promise you it's nothing sinister."

"I can see you are enthusiastic about it."

"Come with me to Astrakhan, Ana," he'd urged. "Bring the children. We can make it work."

"We discussed all that," she'd said, shaking her head. "My job, my family, the children's schools …"

He'd nodded his head slowly. Already, his thoughts were drifting back …

"Dimitriy?"

"I'm sorry, my love," he said. "I was daydreaming."

He'd listened patiently as Babikov listed the other properties his team had so far noted. The seven fragments were identical in appearance. Each was a convex oblong, about nine centimetres long by five centimetres wide. From a distance, they seemed to be golden in colour but, the stronger the magnification, the less colour there was. From very close up they seemed neither transparent nor invisible, and completely colourless yet iridescent. The fragments' default position was to hover vertically in an overlapping formation, like the defensive *testudo* Roman legionaries had sometimes adopted with their shields. If the fragments were separated, they immediately moved back to the *testudo* formation. Once again, Dimitriy studied the drawings on the walls.

"So, what's this big idea of yours?" said Babikov.

"*Lepidoptera*," said Dimitriy.

"Butterflies?" said Babikov, momentarily confused. "We'd thought of fish scales, but *lepidoptera*?"

"In appearance they seem similar to fish scales, it is true, but butterfly scales have three-dimensional lattices that cause iridescence, and I just wonder whether some similar effect is not at work with these scales — and they *are* scales, Babikov, aren't they? They're not just fragments."

Babikov blushed. He took off his glasses and polished the lenses.

"Ivanov doesn't like such talk. I think he's right. We shouldn't leap ahead of ourselves."

"But are we?" said Dimitriy. "We know — or we assume — that these fragments fell to earth in June 1908, right?"

Babikov shook his head.

"No," he said. "We know only that they were found in the area where that event occurred."

"Ivanov gave me to understand there was a probability."

"So there may be," said Babikov. "But he doesn't want us to start wandering off into anthropomorphism and zoomorphism and all the rest of it. We know only what we know. The rest is speculation. If the Admiral hadn't given you the file, you wouldn't have started thinking along these lines."

Dimitriy smiled.

"What lines, Fyodor Babikov? What lines are those?"

Babikov remained silent.

"All right," said Dimitriy. "I'm sure you have similar thoughts. These so-called fragments are themselves a fragment that fell off something much larger, probably during that 'event' of 1908 — off a wing, maybe?"

"Enough!" said Babikov, waving his hands in front of him.

But somehow, Dimitriy *knew*; the fragments *belonged* to something.

In February, just over a year after his first visit to Astrakhan, Anastasia put the ultimatum to him. He couldn't blame her. The Christmas period had been disastrous. Derbent was bitterly cold and the streets were littered with filthy snow and slush where the gritters had passed. The morning, midday, and evening howls of the Ekranoplan as it departed and returned punctuated Derbent's days just as accurately and regularly as a clock-tower bell. He couldn't wait to get back to Astra. He was constantly irritable with the children and mostly morosely silent with her. He felt dreadful. He needed to be back, to be back with *them*, in their presence. When the holidays were finally over, and he had been leaving for the Ekranoplan, she had said, "I can't say I'm sorry to see you go, Dimitriy. You have to get a grip on yourself. Whatever is going on in Astrakhan, you have to put a stop to it. It is ruining you and us."

That had been January. He had got worse over the following month. Then, one Friday evening in late February, she took the final initiative. Part of him felt she was absolutely right — he felt sorry for her and for Andrei and Sasha. But another part of him just didn't care. Or, rather, it only cared about *them*, the angelic fragments (which was what he called them now), and about being with them.

The children were in bed. The classical music radio channel was on. She'd even put a lit candle on the laid dinner table. It was the first time in a long time that she had cooked a meal for his return. At the end of the meal, Anastasia took his hands across the table.

"I am so very sorry, Dima," she said, "but I can't take this anymore."

"What do you mean?" he blustered.

She smiled and put a finger to his lips to hush him.

"You know what I mean. I have spoken to you so many times."

She was right.

"So, now what?" he asked.

"I'd like you to resign from your job in Astrakhan."

"But how would we ..." he began, blustering again.

She shook her head and smiled wistfully.

"We were fine before. We'll be fine again."

"But my work is important."

"I'm sure it is, Dimitriy but, please, let somebody else do it."

He burst into tears.

"I can't," he wept. "I just can't."

"What do you mean? What is it that has such a hold over you? If it is not a mistress, then what is it? Drugs? Is that it? You can tell me. Please."

"It's none of those," he blurted. "But I can't tell you."

"Of course you can!"

"I have signed the Official Secrets Act, Ana."

"I promise I won't tell anybody else. Who could I tell, anyway?"

Dimitriy shook his head.

"If you won't tell me," said Anastasia, her tone hardening, "that's it."

"What do you mean?"

"I'll leave you, Dimitriy."

His shoulders sagged.

"All right, I'll tell you," he said finally.

He told her about his second meeting with Ivanov, and the file about the 1908 Tunguska event and Kulik's 1938 discovery. He told her about his first entry into the thick-walled, steel-shuttered underground space where the plate glass and mirrors had been set up to enable scientists to gaze indirectly on the fragments. He told her about his indescribable feelings of ecstasy, of euphoria, when he was in the presence of the angelic scales, and how the obsessive feeling had grown until it had now overwhelmed all other considerations. He told her about the steel shutter inside the space housing the scales which Babikov had to operate every day so that Dimitriy could at least no longer gaze upon the angelic fragments, and the way he, Dimitriy, had to be dragged out of the space by orderlies and given sedation before he could be convinced to return to his hotel room in the evenings.

Anastasia sat patiently through his explanation.

"All right," she said when he had finished. "Suppose everything you've told me is true. Where do you think this will all end?"

"I have to finish my work," he said. "Nobody understands the fragments better than I do. I have a *feeling* for them, don't you see? I understand them, their need to return. You see?"

She looked at him with sad eyes. "Of course I do, Dima," she said, "but you need to take a break. You're working yourself crazy."

"I can't take a break, don't you understand? I *must* continue."

"Nobody would blame you for taking a break," she said.

"But the *work*," Dimitriy insisted. "I *must* be there."

She shook her head. "No," she said. "You must stop this nonsense. You *can* stop it, you know. Let somebody else do it."

"NO!" he shouted, startling himself as much as Anastasia. "I can't let someone else come in. *I* must be with them. You can't stop me now." He broke off and wept. "Don't you see?" he said. "It's stronger than me."

Anastasia shook her head once more.

"You must choose," she said softly.

"No!" Dimitriy sobbed. "Please don't make me choose."

"If you go back to Astrakhan on Monday, then we will move out."

"But the children need their father!" Dimitriy blurted.

"Don't be a fool," Anastasia snapped. "The children haven't had a father for over a year now."

He nodded and hung his head. "All right,' he said. "Where will you go? Your parents?"

She nodded.

Good, thought Dimitriy, with a sense of wonderment at his own callousness. *Now I can go back to the fragments.*

Anastasia didn't come to the doorstep with him. He'd kissed her on the head as she lay in bed. She didn't move, though he sensed she was awake.

"Goodbye, Ana," he said. "I still love you, you know. And I'm sorry. I just have to be there."

He closed the door and walked through the slushy remains of the snow to the Ekranoport. He was petrified of the take-off, as usual, but his heart had already filled with joyful anticipation. As the Caspian Queen approached Astra, the sea became agitated and the sky darkened. A strong wind blew up and Dimitriy could feel that the pilot was struggling with the controls. He was relieved when the craft slowed down and started its long taxi up the relative calm of the Reka Bakhtemir channel. Ivanov was waiting for him on the quayside.

"Something's going on," he said. "We've been hearing noises in the sky."

"Heavenly trumpets?" said Dimitriy.

"Noises in the sky," Ivanov repeated. "But, yes, not unlike the descriptions the Evenki gave in 1908."

"Could it be?" asked Dimitriy.

"Be what?" said Ivanov, drawing on his cigarette. The sky flashed. A long roll of thunder sounded. "And we've been having strange weather. Look at those clouds."

Dimitry looked up at the dark, corrugated formation hanging heavy and low over the city. Thunder reverberated above and around them.

"And the fragments," Ivanov continued, "have started to oscillate."

"Oscillate?"

"All right," said the Admiral, flicking away his cigarette and blowing out smoke. "They seem to have become agitated."

"I can't wait to see them."

Ivanov gave him a sour stare then lit another cigarette and leaned against the Zil.

"I'm not sure that's a good idea, Dimitriy Semenov. They are no longer stable."

"What do you mean? I've got to see them. You know that."

"Pull yourself together," said the Admiral.

"It's just that I've *got* to see them. Surely you have understood that by now?"

The sky flashed and flickered. Ivanov looked up and waited for the roll of thunder.

"This is not normal," he said. "Something is going on."

"There's a connection?"

"I don't know, but I have a sense there might be. It's almost as though the scales are trying to escape."

"Ah! Escape?"

"Babikov says they have already melted through the gold lining on the roof of the cell."

"No!" said Dimitriy. "Then we must hurry. They are going back. I knew it!"

"Back?" Ivanov drew deeply on his cigarette. "Take my advice," he said. "Return to Derbent. The Ekranoplan will be leaving very soon. Go back to your wife and children. Maybe it's nothing. We'll see. Come again tomorrow."

"There's no point," said Dimitriy. "They've left me."

"Because of this?" Ivanov asked. "Because of your ..."

"Yes," said Dimitriy.

Ivanov nodded slowly and drew again on his cigarette. They heard the distinctive whine as the Caspian Queen's jet engines started up.

"Go!" he urged.

"I can't!" Dimitriy sobbed. "I must see *them* again."

They leaned on a railing and watched as the gangplanks were drawn away and the aft and forward doors closed. The sky flashed vividly. A dockworker cast off the mooring ropes. When they had been entirely wound back on board, the jet engines roared, and the Caspian Queen sailed slowly out into the Volga. They heard the familiar howl as the captain increased the power and taxied the strange vessel down towards the sea channel.

Ivanov flicked away his cigarette, then opened the door of the Zil.

"We'd better hurry," he said.

"Ana," called her mother. "Come quickly."

Anastasia pulled the plug in the kitchen sink, wiped her hands on her apron and joined her parents in the living room. They were watching a Russian television channel and the news bulletin had just started. Sasha was playing on the floor. The newsreader was halfway through the headlines. A train had crashed just outside Vladivostok. The President had visited a new LPG facility at the port of Murmansk ...

"What is it, mama?"

"Ssshhh," said her mother, "you'll see in a moment."

The newsreader finished the headlines. Anastasia's mother turned the volume up.

"And now we go back to our main news item this evening. Reports are coming in of a massive explosion on the northern outskirts of the city of Astrakhan, at the premises of the State Technology University. The explosion is said to have occurred in an underground research facility situated beneath the University's parkland.

"As can be seen from these helicopter images, several buildings have collapsed and the police and the fire services are searching the rubble. Among those missing are the director of the Caspian Flotilla's scientific outreach programme, Rear Admiral Anatoly Ivanov, and the head of the Astrakhan State Technology University's Oil and Gas Institute research programme, Fyodor Babikov. An acclaimed Moscow State University materials scientist, Dimitriy Semenov, who joined the research team from Derbent, is also missing."

Pictures of the three men flashed up on the screen for a few moments.

"That's Daddy," said Sasha.

Anastasia nodded tearfully.

"Yes, darling," she said.

"Babikov!" Dimitriy cried. He staggered out into the remains of the room where he had first met the scientist. He could hear flames flickering. The air was heavy with smoke. A long, low groan sounded out. "Babikov!" he said, "Is that you?" Dimitry staggered over to where he thought Babikov's office had once been. He heard the groan again. "Babikov?"

"Dimitriy Semenov," whispered the scientist. "What has happened to your eyes, man?"

Dimitriy smiled, the charred skin wrinkling where his eyes had once been.

"The fragments have gone back to their rightful place," he said. "I'm going home now."

"Going Home" originally appeared in
Metaphorosis on 12 March 2021

About the author

The only thing Martin Westlake has ever always wanted to do is write creative fiction. Science fiction exercises a special, but not exclusive, attraction in that regard. His full-length creative historical novel, *Other Than an Aspen Be*, is currently on submission (Bill Goodall literary agency).

About the story

I admire the way Ted Chiang wove biblical elements into stories such as "Hell is the Absence of God". I wanted to do something similar, bringing together elements that had been in my mind for some time. What if the 1908 Tunguska event had been the result of some sort of celestial clash? What if feathers had, literally, flown?'

For All That Is and Still Lives

Lisa Fransson

Once there were the birds, and then there were none. Birds that filled the air with their trills and hoots and craws, birds that were only noticed after they'd gone silent.

"Do you hear that?" said Marissa.

"Hear what?" said Albie, the man she'd just hooked up with through *GreenerGrass*.

"That's just it," said Marissa. "Nothing. Even the old crow who always perched in the chestnut over there is gone."

"*Old* does tend to lead to *dead*," said Albie. "It's only natural."

Marissa spun round to face him, forcing him to a stop right there on the path so that his feet started to sink into the mud.

"It *isn't* natural," she said. "When was the last time you saw a robin? Or *any* other kind of bird?"

"How should I know?" said Albie, tramping on the spot as if to stop his feet from sinking any deeper, but soon the mud had reached over the top of his boots nonetheless. "I never was a twitcher."

"But you told me you liked birds," said Marissa. "In the chat."

Albie shrugged.

"You agreed to come on this walk in the hills with me," said Marissa taking a step closer to him, "to watch for birds."

"I thought I might get some nice photos of them, with you and me. For the socials, you know? I didn't expect to have to go yomping through all this muck to find them." Albie splayed his fingers wide as if afraid they'd get dirty too. "I'm going to head back before all this kit gets ruined."

"You're not going to come with me to look for the crow then?" said Marissa.

"I don't know why you're so obsessed with this one crow."

"Albie, that crow … Her craws and clacks have followed me on my walks in these hills for as long as I can remember, and I didn't even realise. What if she's lying injured on the ground? What if she's the last one? Ever?"

"I don't think I'd be of much use to a crow even if it were the last one," said Albie "But I'll see you later this evening, yeah?"

"Why?"

"We're having a date, aren't we?" said Albie, now grinning. "And you're just the kind of bird I like to watch."

"How come your kind aren't extinct yet?" she said and stomped off, leaving him there in the mud, wishing he'd keep sinking and sinking and sinking. She'd had her misgiving about him already when he'd met her earlier that morning in shiny new walking boots, a titanium walking stick showing no signs of wear and one of those Swedish jackets.

Marissa turned off the path and headed into the brush towards the chestnut. She scrambled through the thorny brambles, sliding in the mud until she came through with whipped cheeks to a clearing where the tree grew as if alone. Without the song of the crow, the silence seemed boundless, too large for her to hold, so she walked up to the tree, with its wrinkled and scored trunk, and put her arms around it.

So far the grass hadn't turned out to be any greener than what she was used to, and right now she missed the old crow more than any other kind of companionship. Much more, in fact — it was as if it had left its tree to perch inside her chest, where it pecked against her ribcage in time with the beat of her heart, its hoarse song a rasp in her throat, the slow beat of its wings her breath.

"Where did she go?" she whispered to the tree, surprised at the depth of her own sadness. But how else was she to handle this unfathomable thing, the flight out of this world of the crow, perhaps the last of its kind. Or the last of all feathered beings?

The thought overwhelmed her. What had she done? What could she have done? To save the birds.

There was a comfort in hugging the sturdy trunk, as if it gave off a slow-moving energy that smoothed the sharp edges of her grief, telling her that: 'There's no rush to feel it all at once. Let the grief not stab, but seep into you like sap. Let it become a part of you, a thing you can learn and grow your love from, for all that is and still lives.'

Marissa opened her eyes and looked up into the stark crown, the bare, criss-crossing branches stretching upwards, reaching for a hope that had surely been lost forever. But there in the crook of a branch rested a single feather, black but with a blue iridescence to it that brought to mind spells of magic and rebirth under the light of a full moon.

She let go of the tree, stood on her tiptoes, reached her arm up and let her fingertips find the feather — first the plasticky feel of its shaft, then the soft brush of its down, and finally the slick vanes. She closed her eyes and brought it against her cheek so as to imprint the memory of it on her skin. Why, throughout her life, had she not stooped down to pick up every feather she ever saw on the ground? Taken them home to frame, to display in boxes, to marvel at?

All those birds plucked for quills and feather boas, dreamcatchers and down pillows, what a cruel waste that had all been, when what she held in her hand was a wonder. Flight, freedom, and lightness, carried out of this world for all of time by one old crow.

"I see you standing there."

Marissa started at this voice breaking the silence she'd found herself enveloped in, and almost dropped the feather. Before looking up at him, she swiped at her cheek to rid herself of signs of the grief that had stabbed after all.

"I didn't see *you* standing there," she said with unnecessary sharpness in her voice, a sharpness brought on by one dreary date too many and a taken-for-granted crow.

"You had your eyes closed," said the man.

"Still don't appreciate being snuck up on," said Marissa, but her voice had softened now, because before her stood a man with dark hair that framed his face in feathered layers, his black eyes bright, but darting around as if he were shy of her, wary of unexpected sounds or movements. He appeared to be around her own age, and beautiful in that unfettered way of the wild.

"I walk these hills," said the man. "May I see it?"

He held out his hand for the feather, but Marissa hid it together with her hand inside her armpit.

"I've known her since she was a chick, you see?" said the man and let his hand fall. "Knew her parents too. I come here to look out for her as I told them I would."

"She's gone," said Marissa. "Along with all the other birds, maybe."

The man sighed, walked past Marissa, rested his back against the trunk of the tree and slid down into the winter-browned grass. His boots were creased and caked with mud, his jeans faded and dirt-splashed, and his fleece worn thin at the elbows.

"She said her time was nearing, that there was nothing left for her here, none of her own kind, no food for her to eat. It doesn't really help though, does it? To know that the worst has already happened."

"You speak crow?" said Marissa.

He nodded, looked up at her and hesitated before he said, "I think you might too, or at least *she* spoke to you, or you wouldn't be standing here by her tree holding her tail feather on the morning after she left us."

Marissa watched him for a moment before she sat down next to him, but not too close in case she should startle him.

"I'm Marissa," she said and handed him the feather. "She'd probably want you to have it."

"Kieran," he said and took the feather in his hand.

He turned it over, and then over once more, held it against his thigh and stroked the barbs until they were all smooth. A gentle glimmer appeared in his eyes, a soft turning upwards of his lips, a losing of himself inside the perfect shine of the feather.

"I've never seen you up here before," he said.

"I tend to stick to the paths," said Marissa.

"That would be why, then. I walk my own."

"I'm sorry," said Marissa. "About the crow. It only hit me, just now, that she might have been the last."

"It's the way of people," said Kieran. "Not to notice what's there until it's gone."

"Not with you though," said Marissa.

"Not with me," said Kieran. "I walk the hills.'

"You already said that," said Marissa.

"Pardon me," he said turning towards her, the glimmer in his eyes quietening to moonlight on the rippling surface of a lake as he smiled. "I'm not used to speaking to other folk."

Oh, how she wanted to believe in this seemingly gentle man, even if she'd just met him, and even if she was alone with him on a hill where she hardly met another soul these days. Even Albie from *GreenerGrass*, supposedly the dating app for nature lovers, had suggested a coffee at a local retail park for their first date. Clearly 'nature' had meant something different to every single one of her failed dates than it did to her. Something less messy and more contained perhaps. Sanitised, even. Something to be watched through glass and only approached if wearing the right equipment. Because as Albie had said, dirt didn't make for a good look on the socials.

But this Kieran was clearly no Albie.

"Hold out your hands," he said after a while.

He unzipped a pocket in his fleece and brought out a snail's shell wrapped inside a handkerchief. Two perfect brown lines followed the vortex of its white shell.

"This here's from a brown-lipped snail."

Marissa followed those two brown lines to the shell's centre with the tip of her finger. For some reason she felt like crying again, but how ridiculous would it be to cry over a snail she hadn't known existed until this moment?

"It's a pretty one for sure," said Kieran as if he'd sensed her mood. "I pick up all sorts, though mostly I'm one for the birds."

"One thing doesn't necessarily need to exclude another," whispered Marissa to that extraordinary shell once made by a snail.

"She liked to eat those," said Kieran. "But you can have it. Or borrow it, rather."

She looked up at him. He'd reaped a bunch of brown grass and was using it to wipe his hands clean with.

"Borrow it?" she said.

"I keep hold of the old girl's feather, and you keep hold of that shell. Then if you wanted to ... You could come around this evening, and we'll trade back."

She met his eyes. This time they did not dart, just held hers with what seemed to be open grace, and she thought of that fragile snail shell he'd carried in his pocket wrapped inside a handkerchief to keep it safe — *a thing you can learn and grow your love from, for all that is and still lives.*

Still, she was about to ask why she should trust someone she'd just met under a tree and who'd claimed the one feather left of the birds of this world that *she'd* found in the first place. But when she looked up to tell him so, she saw how the feather flowed in one continuous line from his index finger, how he held it gently to allow it to flow with the breeze, and knew that this was the way she'd always wished to be held.

Approaching on foot seemed to be the only way to reach Kieran's house, with a head torch to see her way forwards in the dark. It was her usual path up the hill at first, and it would've been easy to stumble if her feet hadn't known it so well, stepping over the roots they knew would suddenly leap out of the mud, and edging their way around muddy puddles like small lakes. Then came the turning into the unfamiliar that he'd taken such care to describe to her. The boulder on her left before the fork in the path, the yellow ribbon he'd tied to the dome weaved from living branches that she'd have to bow under and then a trail that seemed soft enough under foot to only ever be trodden by wild animals.

Marissa hadn't planned to go, because truly it would be a dumb thing for her to go alone to a stranger's house on a dark night. But whenever she'd made up her mind firmly to stay at home she'd remember the love on Kieran's face at the perfect shine of the feather, and how softly the snail's shell had rested in his hands before he'd handed it to her. So here she found herself now, on the footpath after all, being led by instinct.

She clasped the snail's shell in her pocket like a talisman, but only gently, because crushing it was unthinkable. The path ran now as if through a gulley, or as if along the bed of a deep stream, the banks rising high on either side, tall grass and thorny bushes shielding her from the world she felt she'd begun to leave behind as soon as she stepped off the path earlier that morning to seek out the fate of the old crow.

The hills had always been a comfort to her, so she wasn't afraid. What she actually felt was enchantment. Even more so when she turned a corner and the gulley opened up to a star-strewn sky and light spilling from the window of a thatched cottage that lay tucked in at the bottom of a hill, and nestling behind a thicket of young oaks.

She stood alone under the vast sky. Inside the house right now was her crow-man, and in a moment, if she dared, she would knock on his door. But before that she would drink this night in, to wrap whatever magic had weaved through her day around the sadness for the lost crow, a magic as precious as the stars in the sky, as soft as the smoke rising up through the chimney and as gentle as the night that had led her here.

"There you are," said Kieran, opening the door to her before she'd even knocked. "Step inside now and seat yourself down by the fire and I'll get you a brew."

Marissa hesitated for a moment, before she once more heeded some deeper and wiser mystery within her and stepped inside. She took off her boots, her coat, her head torch and sat down on the sofa in front of the fire as if it was something she'd done every day of her life.

"This is all the TV I have," he said and nodded to the hearth when he sat down next to her.

"There's no road to your house," said Marissa.

"Green-belted and off-grid," said Kieran.

"There must be more to it than that," said Marissa.

"I pay my taxes and follow the law," said Kieran "The two best tricks I know for staying invisible."

"Hmm," said Marissa.

They sat in silence, listening to the crackle of the fire, watching the flames dance, sipping their tea. And even though she didn't believe his story about greenbelts and taxes she thought how easy this man, this Kieran, in the sofa beside her, was to be with.

"You can tell me," she said after a while.

"I suppose," he said, "this house is built just beyond a sort of boundary. Or an edge, perhaps."

She turned towards him, "It's not subsiding, is it?"

"Oh no. That's happening everywhere *else* but here."

"I see," said Marissa. "Or actually, I don't see at all."

She rested back in the sofa, sitting just a tiny bit closer to him. The easy silence closed the gap between them further after Kieran had put another log on the fire. Marissa found herself waiting for him to reach out to her, but he kept his gentleness about him, his desire not to crush or destroy was there in his every movement. She was starting to feel sleepy, and hoped that he would at least let her stay over on the sofa.

"You can put your arm around me if you like," she mumbled.

"I would like to," he whispered into the quiet night. "Very much."

Marissa curled up against him. He smelled of fresh air and wet grass and sap and mud and snails and crows and wood smoke and dirt and precious stars, and although Marissa had only stepped in through the door that evening, she knew she never ever wanted to leave.

"I found a feather, and then I found you," said Marissa.

"The old girl had her ways," said Kieran and rested his chin on the top of her head. "All crows do."

"Did," said Marissa and felt the sadness from earlier try to peck its way through the weaves of smoke-and-star magic. "All crows *did*."

"Rest your heart now," he said as he placed a hand on her chest. A warmth spread through her to unbind, to unpeck, to undo, to un-Albie until all of her sat gathered whole beside him.

"Can we go to bed?" she said. "To sleep, or not. I don't mind which."

Inside the bedroom he shed his clothes and stood naked before her and started to peel hers off as if helping her to shed an extra layer of skin.

"Wait a moment," she said, staying his hands. "I have your shell."

She dug around inside her pocket, brought the shell out and placed it on the bedside table.

"That's a good place for it," he said. "At least for now."

Wrapped in the softness of the night and shielded by the dark, she could no longer tell her limbs from his as they both made themselves anew through the touch of the other. She woke to sunlight warming her face as morning fell in through the window and his eyes gazing down upon her.

"I'm glad you came," he said.

But she'd just seen beyond him to the shell she'd left on the table the night before. She wrapped a sheet around her nakedness and sat up.

"It's moving," she said, pointing. Because the shell that had been a dead thing inside her pocket had now sprouted a living snail, its feelers searching the air.

"I'll take it outside in a minute," said Kieran.

Marissa had no time to order her thoughts before there came a loud pecking on the window. She twisted round to meet the sideways glance of a crow.

"And there's herself with her feather, all shiny and made anew," said Kieran, placing his hand gently in the small of Marissa's back, before going over to open the window wide, and now she heard the songs of many birds, weaving through the morning, the humming of bees, the chirping of grasshoppers, a rustling in the thicket of young oaks. A hare?

"I don't understand," she said, wrapping the sheet tighter around her. "Last night it was cold winter."

"It was time to fold it up and stash it away for a while to give the critters a chance to thrive anew."

"If I ..." said Marissa. "If I wanted to go back again, would I be able to?"

"You could, if you wanted to," said Kieran. "Aside from me hoping you won't, I'm not sure what there would be left for you to go back to, though."

The crow hopped up on Kieran's forearm, from where it was eyeing the snail on the bedside table. Marissa quickly turned, tapped once on the shell to give the snail a moment to hide before picking it up and hiding it inside her hand.

"See there, old girl?" said Kieran and stroked the crow. "No breakfast in bed for you."

The crow pecked his hand once before taking off through the window and up into the blue skies. Kieran rubbed the back of his hand against his thigh.

"I walked the hills," he said. "Gathering egg shells and feathers and bones and droppings and tufts of fur and bird carcasses and seeds and snake skins and carapaces, and I brought them all here. Left them slumbering, ready for this new spring."

"You *walked* the hills?" said Marissa.

"The old girl was the last thing I had to collect," said Kieran. "I came for her just like I said I would and found you standing there under her tree clasping her feather."

Marissa dropped the sheet around her and came to stand next to him, meeting his bright eyes and inside them finally seeing herself as she'd always wanted to be seen, wild and free.

"You know," said Kieran and touched her cheek, "there never lived anyone wiser than her."

Marissa knew it was true. From her tree, the crow must have kept a lookout over them both, watched them walk their separate paths day after day, with Marissa searching for evidence of the living and Kieran collecting leftovers of the dead, but both with a wish to preserve. And then in her death the crow had brought *her*, Marissa, to Kieran, to this abundance and this, her forever home — because here were the birds, not only outside their bedroom window, but in every single flutter of her heart.

About the author

Lisa is a bilingual writer living on the south coast of England. In her native Swedish, Lisa is an award-winning children's author, while in her adopted English she's a writer of short fiction and novels. Her first novel, *The Shape of Guilt*, is a piece of literary fiction with streaks of magical realism published by époque press. She also works as a literary translator and a mentor to young writers. You can follow Lisa's writing on lisafransson.substack.com.

About the story

On the top of my road begin the Sussex Downs, an area of Outstanding Natural Beauty here in England. I walk these hills every chance I get. Sometimes in the mornings before I set to work, sometimes in the light summer evenings, always on the weekends. I'm by nature a gatherer, so it's not unusual for me to pick up a feather, or a snail's shell, or a stone, or a curiously shaped bit of wood. These treasures are gathered on the windowsill of my office and on my desk. Sometimes I will use them for crafts, and always they will inspire my writing. Kieran in "For All That Is and Still Lives" is, like me, a gatherer, only he's a gatherer with a plan for a more warm-hearted world.

A Bird Afraid of Feathers

B. Morris Allen

In the distant, dismal south, there's a flightless bird with no feathers. The ground is harsh, dry, barren, dusty. It's hot in the day, cold at night. Not much lives there. Aside from the bird.

The natives call it the bird-afraid-of-feathers. The natives don't live there either; there's nothing for them to eat and little to do. Still, they're the closest thing the region has to natives, and their name has stuck. For convenience, though, the bird is called the barebird elsewhere, when it's spoken of at all. In eastern salons and infusion halls, stiff gentlemen and languid ladies show each other photographs of the bird's nests from old magazines, and talk about how their great-great aunt was once part of an expedition to photograph them. They don't believe in the bird, though. It's just something to talk about, a fable to dream over when falling asleep and when sleeping late in the morning.

The bird is born naked and bumpy, skin straining to fluff the feathers it lacks; 'horripilated' is the technical term. It looks horrible enough. They're born as twins — one male, one female. Lucky parents will lay and raise three or four clutches of two. They have few predators. Nothing lives there, remember.

The birds are born bare and they die bare. But here's the thing — in between, they have the most beautiful feathers you've never seen. The male's feathers are iridescent, polychromatic; soft and long and elegant. They have abstract patterns that draw the eye into hypnotic swirls and eddies of color and magic and longing. Look at one and you'll forget to eat, to drink, to breathe, until you fall down exhausted and wondering what came over you.

The female's feathers are bland, monotonous beiges and browns that blend right into the landscape. You might not see a female if she were standing right next to you. It's even possible that the feathers are color-shifters, chameleonic. Or that they warp light around themselves. The feathers are hard to study because they're so hard to find. Once shed, you'd never see them again. The feathers are soft, fluffy, and invisible, like a rose petal made of finest spiderwebs.

Barebirds are protected by order of the Empress Jaleqon, or they would be if there were still an Empress, or an Empire. There hasn't been either for at least three centuries, but the birds are protected just as well by ignorance and isolation as they ever were by law. They nest in the high, stony peaks of the mountains, well above the tree line.

As the birds mature, their feathers start to grow in. Male and female, brother and sister, travel together away from the parents' nest. As the male's feathers grow longer and longer, he moves slower and slower and more awkwardly. Eventually, he stops, and his sister helps him build a nest of twigs if there are any and stones if there aren't. They usually get at least a couple of leagues from where they were born. Barebird territories are large, though it's mostly because of the scarcity of food.

When the nest is built, the female takes her leave. By now, the male's feathers are so long that he can barely walk. He spends the time he has left eating and gathering whatever seeds he can find, and stores them in a little nook of the nest. When he can barely move at all, he settles in the nest and starts plucking feathers.

It's a slow, calculated process. The natives say it's artistic. He sits in his nest for a day or two, getting the feel of it. Then he carefully, precisely, picks out a particular feather and plucks it out. It looks painful, and sometimes it's bloody, but the blood dries and the wound heals. The bird takes the feather and meticulously weaves it into whatever material his nest is made of. It always fits perfectly, and it looks stunning — a brilliant spot of color in a drab, harsh landscape.

The male keeps plucking and weaving until all his feathers are gone. It's hard to pluck the ones on his head and around his beak and neck, but he's patient, scratching and rubbing if he has to. Sometimes he uses part of the nest itself, as if it were designed for the purpose.

When he's done, the bird is as bare and ugly and horripilated as he was the day he hatched. But his nest! It's a jewel in the landscape, a spot of staggering beauty in a desolate vista. You can see a barebird nest for leagues. Maybe even his parents can see it if the time is right.

While the male is crafting his nest, his sister is traveling. She can't fly; her wings are too stubby, the muscles are wrong, and the feathers are too soft and floppy in any case. If anything, they slow her down even when she hops.

She creeps and crawls and occasionally races along open ground, trying to get as far away as she can. Barebirds don't mate if they're too closely related; they usually need at least three generations of separation to breed, which is tricky with such a sparse population.

Female barebirds have a trick, though, that lets them cross hostile territory — land so cruel that no seeds grow at all. There's a lot of it. It doesn't mean nothing lives there, though. There are at least three known species of arthropods there that eat lichen and algae. All three have the same curious habit — they form little pellets of foodstuff and mix it with their own feces into balls bigger than themselves. They store the pellets in wide tunnels and never eat or use them.

Until a female barebird comes along. When she comes across an arthropod nest or tower, she stops and does a little dance. It's thought that it's the vibrations the arthropods recognize, since two of the types are blind. When she's done her dance and the arthropods gather or peek out or form lines, depending on type, she pulls out one of her soft, fluffy feathers and lays it down. The arthropods come and climb all over it and, if it passes muster, haul it away to form the architecture for their egg trees, without which the eggs compact together and hatch poorly. When they've done that, they scurry over to their wide pellet tunnels and dig them open. The barebird eats the pellets — enough to sustain her for a day or more. If she's lucky, she'll find enough arthropods to make it across the terrain to somewhere more hospitable.

An unmated male barebird never leaves his nest. His whole world consists of the nest he hatched in, the few leagues of travel with his sister, and the nest he builds. They say you can see the journey in the patterns of his nest, if you try. They also say you can see the future, or the past, or the paths you didn't take. They say a lot of things.

The male sits in his nest, just waiting; waiting for some female who's not his sister or his mother to make the trek from some distant peak to the one bright spot in her landscape, find it pleasing, and come mate with him for life and raise some clutches of ugly babies.

If she doesn't come or doesn't find him or doesn't like his art, he doesn't leave. He eats the food he stashed away, and when it's gone he still waits, getting thinner and thinner and weaker until he dies. Most of them die.

An unmated female barebird can spot a male's nest from far away. She'll make her way toward it until she's a league or so away, then just sit and stare at it for a day or so. Most of the time, she'll turn away and keep searching. No one knows what she's looking for. The natives say it's art — that she's deciding whether his creative spirit is rich and innovative enough to merit fathering her children. The natives also say that they're descended from an Empire that used to span the continent, but they've yet to produce evidence.

What is known is that the female stares at the nest for a while, looking much like anyone else enthralled by a barebird feather. But after a while she wakes up and either goes toward the nest or goes away. It's not determined by how many feathers she has left. Females with virtually no feathers are just as likely to turn away from a rich nest as females with many feathers are to introduce themselves. It's a grueling trip for the females, and they often use up their feathers early. Most of them die.

If a male and a female do bond, they swap places. The males gather food for themselves and their new mates. Most nests are located quite near arthropod burrows. Male barebirds do a different dance than the females, more of a scratching, digging thing. While they're dancing, the arthropods form little phalanxes, and they seem to herd the males in one direction until the scratching dance breaks through the roof of a pellet tunnel. Then the arthropods withdraw and go about their lives. The male barebird gorges himself and then carries the rest of the pellets in his crop back to the nest for the female.

In the meantime, she's plucked out the rest of her feathers, if she has any, and threaded them into the nest, forming a soft, cushiony base and walls that will protect the eggs. When she's eaten the pellets her mate brings, they're both revived enough to seek out other food on their own — windblown seeds or fluffy lichen or fallen leaves or cactus spines. They spend their days scrounging and eating and getting their strength back until she lays two eggs. Then they alternate spending their days stretching their bareskinned bodies over the eggs while the other eats or brings food to set aside for the chicks.

They say seeing a barebird nest will change your life. The natives come to the region looking for artifacts of their ancestors and searching for the fabled treasure of Empress Jaleqon. But they seem happy enough with a glimpse of a nest. They never come closer than a league, in deference to the decree of an Empress only they believe in. Those who've seen a nest never come back for another look, but legend has it that they're happy in their lives, and that they have a knack for making choices that bring contentment.

Female barebirds in motion are almost impossible to see. And the male barebirds barely travel at all. But the nests exist, and the feathers come from somewhere. Though if you ask the natives, they'll say the nests aren't lined with feathers at all; they're lined with hope.

About the author

B. Morris Allen is a biochemist turned activist turned lawyer turned foreign aid consultant, and recently retired. He's been traveling since birth, and has lived on five of seven continents, but the best place he's found is the Oregon coast. When he can, he makes his home there. In between journeys, he works on his own speculative stories of love and disaster. He is the editor and publisher of Metaphorosis Publishing's magazine (2016-2024) and anthologies.

Find out more at www.BMorrisAllen.com and on Bluesky @BmorrisAllen.com.

About the story

Having found the cover art some years back, it wasn't until spring 2024 that I turned my attention to what to do with it. By then, it was already clear that in a year's time I'd either be celebrating hope or dearly in need of it, which determined the anthology's focus. I'm an idealist, but rather dour, and I ended up writing a story where hope succeeds despite the odds against it.

About hope

I tend to be pessimistic about the world and where it's going. But at my core is a tightly held belief that the world *can* be a wonderful fantastic place if we only learn to recognize its beauty and the lives it supports. Hope that we'll someday do so is what keeps me going and trying to contribute.

Inspired? You may also want to check out *Things With Feathers: Stories of Hope*, the 2021 anthology of speculative stories from Third Flatiron.

Copyright

Title information

HOPE: The Thing With Feathers

ISBN: 978-1-64076-009-7 (e-book)
ISBN: 978-1-64076-010-3 (paperback)
ISBN: 978-1-64076-011-0 (hardcover)

Library of Congress Control Number: 2025940951

Copyright

Plant Based Press is an imprint of
Metaphorosis Publishing
Neskowin, OR, USA

www.metaphorosis.com

"Metaphorosis" is a registered trademark.

Discounts available

Substantial discounts are available for educational institutions, including writing workshops. Discounts are also available for quantity purchases. For details, contact Metaphorosis at metaphorosis.com/about

Metaphorosis Publishing

Metaphorosis offers beautifully written science fiction and fantasy. Our imprints include:

Plant Based Press
Verdage
Vestige
Joyful Heave
Metaphorosis Magazine

Find out more at Books.Metaphorosis.com.

You can also find us:
@Metaphorosis.com on Bluesky

Plant Based Press

Vegan-friendly science fiction and fantasy, including anthologies of the year's best SFF stories, from 2016-2020.

Verdage

Science fiction and fantasy books for writers — full of great stories, often with an additional focus on the craft of speculative fiction writing.

Vestige

Novelettes, novellas, and novels by Metaphorosis authors.

The Nocturnals
Mariah Montoya

Night is Dangerous. Day is deadly.
Where day and night last thirty years, humans move constantly stay ahead of the night and cruel Nocturnals that call it home. But a boy is lost out there.

Science fiction and fantasy anthologies with innovative and unusual themes.

Museum Piece
an unusual collection

A gallery of the strange and outrageous

Step right up and enter a world of wonder and oddities! These museums are not your typical tourist traps. From the Museum of Lost Dreams to the Suicide Museum, each exhibit will take you on a journey you won't soon forget.

Metaphorosis

a magazine of speculative fiction

Metaphorosis magazine was active from 2016-2024. Stories and podcasts are still available at magazine.Metaphorosis.com, and you can find annual and best of compilations at books.Metaphorosis.com

www.ingramcontent.com/pod-product-compliance
Lightning Source LLC
Chambersburg PA
CBHW020417110726

47899CB00006B/2022